Fic GAB   SKTN

Gabriel, Eric.

Waterboys

Y0-BYD-571

WATERBOYS

WATERBOYS

A NOVEL

ERIC GABRIEL

Mercury House, Incorporated
San Francisco

This is a work of fiction. Names, characters, places, and incidents either are the product of the author's imagination or are used fictitiously. Any resemblance to actual events, locales, or persons, living or dead, is entirely coincidental.

Copyright © 1989 by Eric Gabriel

Quotations of lyrics from the following songs are by permission: SWINGING ON A STAR—words by Johnny Burke, music by James Van Heusen. Copyright © 1944 by Burke and Van Heusen, Inc., a division of Bourne Co. Copyright Renewed. International Copyright Secured. All Rights Reserved. Used by Permission of Bourne Co. "CALL ME IRRESPONSIBLE"—by Sammy Cahn and James Van Heusen. Copyright © 1962 and 1963 by Paramount Music Corporation.

Published in the United States by
Mercury House
San Francisco, California

Distributed to the trade by
Consortium Book Sales & Distribution, Inc.
St. Paul, Minnesota

All rights reserved, including, without limitation, the right of the publisher to sell directly to end users of this and other Mercury House books. No part of this book may be reproduced in any form or by any electronic or mechanical means, including information storage and retrieval systems, without permission in writing from the publisher, except by a reviewer who may quote brief passages in a review.

Mercury House and colophon are registered trademarks of
Mercury House, Incorporated

Manufactured in the United States of America

Library of Congress Cataloging-in-Publication Data

Gabriel, Eric.
    Waterboys : a novel / by Eric Gabriel.
        p.   cm.
    ISBN 0–916515–54–0 : $18.95
    I. Title.
PS3557.A2424W3   1989
813'.54—dc19
                                                            88–7849
                                                                CIP

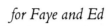

for Faye and Ed

Acknowledgments

I would like to thank the National Arts Club and the Goodman Fund of the City College of New York for their help in the completion of this work. To Jürgen John I am indebted for his technical assistance. I am grateful to the men of Running Water for providing me with a quiet space, to Malaga Baldi, my agent, for her belief in my work, and to Lisa Dunn and David Petersen for their support all through the lean years.

PART ONE

Mid-August

One

1

Matthew and Justin race alongside the late afternoon traffic of Eleventh Avenue, no more than a handspan between their shoulders. The dark fronts of the warehouses tumble past Matthew, the air slicks down his arms like a papercut and chugs down into his lungs. His head tilts back proudly. He leads with his chin, enjoying his speed. The concrete below springs him back into the air as soon as his sneakers touch down. From the corner of his eye he sees Justin straining to keep up. The cargo of Justin's belly shakes against the sluggish pump of his legs.

Good, Matthew thinks.

It had been Justin's idea to race down to the pier. He was always racing somewhere — to the corner, to the school, to the next johnny pump. Before Matthew even realized what was happening, Justin would be off, leaving Matthew to flounder after him. Today Matthew was ready. The two weeks he's just spent in the country have strengthened him and sharpened his senses. He banks around the corner and swims into the sunlight, exultant.

Something tugs at his back. His T-shirt knifes under his arms. It's Justin, grabbing from behind.

"Lay off!" Matthew shouts over his shoulder.

The shirt binds tighter. Justin closes in. His face funnels mean around the grit of his teeth. Matthew yanks free but stumbles off balance. His foot catches a crack in the sidewalk and he goes sprawling against a parked car, hip first. His arms fling up over the hood of the car as though it's a great beach ball. Justin sails by.

"Sonofabitch," Matthew mumbles, tasting the dirt of the car on his lips. Wings of pain beat inside his head. His breath, swift and rhythmic while running, now clogs in his throat. His throbbing hip feels ten times its normal size. Justin's face appears before him, bloated and ugly.

He peers down the block. Justin is nowhere to be seen. The neighborhood seems washed out, dirty as a pigeon. The old buildings look worn and squished together, as though there were too many to fit on the block. The street reminds Matthew of his own cramped apartment, full of Gramma's old dark furniture, his mother's things all around: dressers from secondhand shops needing to be fixed, paint-by-numbers kits, the colors dried and cracked in their little tubs, the portraits left eyeless (eyes were always the hardest part, she explained), piles of sheet music, empty beer bottles. Right after Gramma died his mother swore she'd throw out the old furniture and get new stuff. But she didn't. He knew she wouldn't. Everything would stay the way it was.

Matthew begins loping down the street. Each step stamps pain into his side. Down the block a truck edges out of a garage, looking like a snake shedding its skin. Midway it shudders to a halt. The driver tries to revive it. The engine flutters for a moment, then coughs and dies. Another brief rumble, then nothing.

A second man saunters out of the garage with a bottle in a paper bag, shakes his head. "Very sloppy, very sloppy," he says.

"Don't look at me. I didn't work on this baby."

"You can tell that to the big boy." He raises the bag in a toast, brings the bottle to his lips. His mouth opens pink and soft in the middle of his chin's blue stubble, his throat moves in muscular waves to swallow. His eyes are dark, his hair blue-black. Matthew thinks of Sal.

"The big boy can kiss my ass in Macy's window." The rest of what the driver says gets drowned out by another short-lived turn of the engine. "Shit," he says, vaulting down to the street.

"What's the matter, couldn't find the gearshift?" The man with the beer grins.

"Your mother does deep knee bends on a gearshift. Give me a slug of that."

The teenage guys in the neighborhood always seem to be ready to start a fight, Matthew thinks. Justin has begun to imitate them. The guy from the truck disappears into the garage; Matthew's eyes follow. Inside it's murky as a subway station, forbidding and enticing. Bare-chested men swim in the darkness, their arms smudged with grease. Their voices careen against the raw cement walls, they slap each other on backs as hard as sandbags. The blinding light of the welding torch leaves their faces lustrous and smooth as marble. They probe the underbellies of cars poised on hydraulic lifts, reminding Matthew of the picture of Atlas supporting the world, stamped on each volume of his encyclopedia. The blocks near the river are full of these cool, alluring caverns.

"Thirsty?"

The guy with the brown bag startles Matthew, whose face grows warm with embarrassment.

"Yeah."

"Beer'll stunt your growth," the man says. "How old are you?"

"Ten."

"Too young." The man winks and hands Matthew the bag.

Matthew lifts the bottle to his mouth, then drinks with pleasure, knowing that both men's lips have been there before his.

"That's enough. Hey, watch out, here comes the two-ton Hun."

A fat man in a baseball cap bounds out of the garage. His baggy pants jingle with keys. A frayed gauze bandage around one wrist trails behind him like a little flag. He heaves himself up into the cab, slams the door shut. He has no more luck starting the truck than the first man. He leans out of the cab. "Hey, Ernie, what the fuck you do with the engine?" The baseball cap falls into the gutter. Hatless, his head resembles an enormous, pale peach. "Shit," he mumbles, and goes down after it. His shirt rides up over a buttery ring of flesh as he leans over. Matthew laughs.

The man bowls an angry, crimson face at him. "Get your little ass the hell out of here before I break it." His gluey eyes look at Matthew from opposite sides of his face, giving him a dopey look.

"I think you should leave the kid alone," says the other man.

"Good thing I'm not paying you to think," he answers, then turns back to Matthew. "Aren't you one of Justin's—"

Matthew is already gone. He finds Justin leaning against a mailbox all the way down at the corner of Twelfth Avenue. The rush hour traffic of the West Side Highway rumbles above them.

"What took you so long?" asks Justin, smug.

"Your cruddy uncle was blocking the street with his truck. Why'd you trip me?"

"When?"

"Quit playing dumb."

"I didn't do nothin."

"Liar."

"Who you calling a liar?" His body tightens, ready to fight.

"Liar," Matthew repeats, then walks away.

"Hey, wait up." Justin scrambles after him. "Where ya goin?"

"Home."

"I thought we was goin to the pier?"

"You can."

"Don'tcha want to see what I got?"

"I don't care what you got." Matthew keeps walking.

"Wait." He grabs Matthew's sleeve.

"Lay off or I'll bust you!"

"How come you're so mad?"

"You knew I'd beat you running this time so you tripped me."

"I just wanted to show you what I got."

"Think I believe that?"

"But I really got something to show you, something neat."

Matthew puts out his hand. "Let's see it."

"Not here." Justin's eyes dart up and dawn the street.

"Why not?"

"Can't. Let's go to the pier."

"I don't want to go to the pier. It's now or never."

"Just to the beginning of the pier, then. Okay?" He scans the street again.

"What do you keep looking at?"

"Cmon."

Justin takes off. Matthew's about to follow when his eyes fall on the pier building across the street, set on precarious stilts in the river. Its metal-paneled walls give it a shacklike appearance. It looks placid and forgotten beside the traffic, the most run-down thing in this rundown neighborhood. The slightest push could send it crashing into the river. In the time he's been away more panels have fallen off, as though it's being taken apart to be worked on in one of the garages. He and Justin had discovered it together. It seemed like so long ago but it was only last spring. They had been real friends then.

Justin frowns at the other side of the street, pale in the highway's shadow. His baggy dungarees reach the sidewalk, his shirt's half in, half out. He looks angry and scared, as though he might even cry if he dared.

One step over the broken concrete sidewalk onto the pier's wooden planking Matthew stops. "Okay, where is it?"

Justin pulls out a black stump from his packet, about the size and thickness of a Pay Day bar. An instant later a flame of steel sparks into view as the knife snaps open.

"Holy," says Matthew. The blade is at least six inches long.

"Pretty neat," says Justin, examining it as a jeweler might a setting.

"Where'd you get it?"

Justin grins. "Secret."

"Your uncle?"

"No."

"Your mom?"

Justin sneers.

"Who then?"

"Give up?"

"Yeah," says Matthew, tired of Justin's game.

"Kevin."

Matthew glares at the blade with hatred, imagines Kevin's face reflected in it, lean and hard as the metal itself. "You got it from him?"

"Yeah."

"Is he your friend or something?" he shouts, giving Justin an angry shove. The knife leaves Justin's hand and skitters across the planking. Its plastic casing pops off. "Hey, look at your cheap knife!"

Justin leaps after it. "Look what you did!" He scoops up the knife with its missing part. "You busted it." He tries to force the plastic back into place but it snaps in two. "Oh, Jesus! You busted my knife!"

"Kevin's a creep!"

"Look!" Justin shakes the fistful of damage at him.

"It's just the outside part. You can use a little Duco cement —"

"You busted it!" He comes at Matthew with a mean swipe of the blade.

"Hey!" Matthew sidesteps the knife with a little skip. "Quit messing around with that thing," he says. Justin jabs at him again. Matthew is forced to break into a run.

"It's just a stupid knife," he shouts, looping back and forth across the pier. The river breezes whip against his face.

Justin pursues him toward the end of the pier, right to the edge of the water. Matthew sees the wooden rim coming near. He brakes, his toes crash into the rim, and his body wobbles like sheet metal. His arms swing out to keep his balance. The knife's right behind him.

Justin pulls the knife back with a laugh. "You coulda fallen in. I coulda made you."

"Asshole," says Matthew.

"You just wish you had a knife too."

"You can keep your dumb knife."

"I will. And I'll cut anyone who messes with me. My uncle did, and I cut him."

Matthew remembers the bandage. "You did that?"

"Yup. While you was away."

"Why?"

Justin's face darkens. He looks down at the planking. "He wanted to get me. But I got him instead. I got him good." He snaps the knife shut.

Matthew saunters back to the edge of the water and sits down, flustered from Justin's attack, and confused. The river is usually one of Matthew's favorite places, full of slippery mirrors. Now it appears dull and lifeless. The sun's glare hides the New Jersey side behind an orange film.

Justin sits down beside him. "You mad?"

Matthew thinks for a moment. He has reason to be He's warned Justin about Kevin. Justin knows that Matthew and Kevin are enemies. Now he realizes that Justin can't be depended on. No, Matthew tells him. He isn't mad.

Justin smiles. "What did you do up there in the country?" he asks.

"There were turtles, lots of turtles."

He tells Justin about the pond no one else ever came to, in the middle of the woods, ringed by bristly trees. The water was still and bottle green each morning, the banks shallow and seeded with black tadpoles, sleek as beads. Sal had said there were turtles too, but Matthew never saw any. Sal explained why: they heard Matthew coming and scattered. Their sense of hearing was so good that they could detect the slightest crack of a twig or a footstep from far away. Sal challenged Matthew to outwit them. "You gonna have to learn to go slow and graceful, like an animal." Each morning Matthew tried, placing his bare feet on the cold earth with the precision of a tightrope walker. One morning, he reached the pond and there they were, dozens of turtles, piled like biscuits on the rocks, their leathery legs flared out to dry, their shells gleaming like polished stone.

"Then what did you do?" Justin asked.

"I yelled 'Bonzai!' and watched them take off!"

Justin laughed. "How come this Sal guy knows so much about turtles?"

"He knows so much about everything."

"Your mom gonna marry him?"

Matthew's drawn to something floating in the river. He leans over. The water's dirty color resolves into layers of green and grey. A sour gas fills his nostrils. A fish bobs, weightless, on the surface and laps against the pilings, almost transparent. "Look at his eye, it's like cracked glass," says Matthew.

"The river stinks worse than a sewer. You wanna go get some candy?"

"Sure. Give me your knife, I can fix it." Matthew sees that Justin has forgotten about it. Justin stuffs everything into Matthew's hand, glad to be rid of it.

*

The inside of the candy store is brown and gloomy. Its walls climb cavelike up into darkness. Dust dulls the ancient display cases stacked with yellowed notebooks and bottles of Elmer's glue. A card of ballpoint pens with an out-of-date price hangs on the wall. Only the rows of candies and stacks of newspapers in the very front are fit for sale. Seated in a sagging armchair in the back, barely visible in the dingy light, an old man holds a newspaper. It sinks as they enter. The man peers over the edge. A ratty ski cap is pulled down to meet the bushy ridges of his brows. Justin's hand creeps up behind his back toward the candy bars.

The man rises. "Vat you doing?" he says in a grainy voice.

Justin's hand snaps back.

"You vant something, you buy it!"

"Whaddaya think I'm going to do?" says Justin, not moving from the counter. He winks at Matthew.

"I see vat you do." The man shuffles toward them. His baggy clothes drape his body, he wears house slippers.

"I just hafta make up my mind," Justin says, slipping a Forever Yours into his pocket.

"Hoodlum!" The old man points a quaking finger at him.

Justin backs off. The man's hand lurches after him but Justin escapes, laughing.

"*Ganef,*" the old man wheezes.

"Don't give me any of that Jew talk," says Justin. "Let's get outta here, Matty."

The finger keeps pointing at Justin. "Why do you bleed me?"

"Bleed?" Justin sounds scared.

The old man turns to Matthew. "You saw him, didn't you?"

"Leave my friend out of this!" says Justin.

Matthew hears the slush of the old man's breathing. Justin's knife gouges him in the leg. He can't meet the old man' s eyes.

"What's happened, *mein kind?* What has he done to you?" His hand grazes Matthew's, his skin smooth and waxy as an apple's. Its warmth repels Matthew, like the warmth of a bed somebody else has slept in.

"What do you mean?" he asks.

"He's crazy," Justin says. "Don't listen to him."

"You don't belong with someone like him," the old man says.

"Crazy Jew," Justin cries, desperate to break the man's spell over Matthew. "Cheap, crazy Jew!" Justin shouts, tearing the candy bar from his pocket. He throws it onto the floor. "You comin?"

Matthew stares at the squashed candy bar on the floor, unsalable now as the old notebooks. He senses the old man watching him. He goes to pick up the candy bar.

The old man stops him. "Let me do it. This is what I need to do to feel sorry for him."

"I'm splittin," Justin calls from outside.

"Go," the old man says. "He's waiting for you."

Matthew can't move.

"He's your friend, isn't he?"

Matthew has no answer, he runs out of the store, hating himself.

2

Matthew presses his bare back against the wall by his bed in search of a cool spot. When it grows warm, he scootches over to a new one. He'd love to sleep but after five minutes in bed the sheets are damp and clinging. The pain in his hip keeps waking him up. He thinks about where he was last night at this time: still in the country, asleep on the army cot in the bungalow's cool back room. The three of them—Matthew and his mother and Sal—were supposed to have stayed the whole month of August. Abruptly back in the city, he feels as though he's been flung from a moving car and left on the side of a road, suddenly still. The time left before school stretches out hot and empty before him.

He goes and sits on the windowsill. A slight breeze rises from the air shaft, carrying the smell of garbage that's been thrown down there. Somewhere in the next building, children cry, cranky from the heat. Their parents argue in the lighted windows behind the droning blur of fans. Televisions tuned to the same movie his mother is watching echo like loudspeakers within the shaft's narrow walls.

Matthew used to think a dinosaur rested beneath the mantle of garbage and would one day heave everything off its back with a King Kong roar. Now the darkness makes it seem bottomless. It reminds Matthew of a grave. Sal hadn't understood how he could think such a thing.

"The dead people I know would never wind up cramped between two apartment buildings," he said one morning, cutting up the chorizo for breakfast. "They need room to breathe."

"They can't breathe," said Matthew, "they're dead." Then realizing what he'd just heard, he said, "You know dead people?"

"Dead animals too," Sal said with a grin, stuffing a plug of the sausage into Matthew's mouth.

Last night he'd been with Sal at the pond.

Every night, an hour or so after supper, they rolled towels under their arms and took the path through the woods that crossed the state highway. They picked it up again behind the parking lot of the Blue Urn. Teenagers wore that stretch of the path wide and littered it with beer bottles. Light and jukebox music spilled through the trees. Then foliage sealed the path narrow and still; they were deep in the woods once more. Trees stooped over them like wise grandfathers, their branches sighing slightly. Matthew had come to know every inch of the path in daylight but at night it reclaimed all its secrets. Soon the woods parted. The night opened up and breathed. Frogs pulled invisibly under water with diamond-sharp splashes as they approached. The pond waited.

The first time they swam at night, Sal had surprised Matthew by pulling off all his clothes. Matthew'd never seen a man naked before. He went behind a tree to undress, peeking as Sal finally stepped out of the luminous band of his underwear, becoming a shadowy figure in the dark. Matthew kept his jockey shorts on, emerging gawky and pale, shivering from embarrassment. Sal fixed that; he'd heaved Matthew up with one arm and pulled off his underwear with the other.

Sal was always the first one in. His body parted the water with a shallow dive. A moment later his head emerged, smooth and glassy, epaulets of moonlight on his shoulders. Matthew entered the water on tiptoe, a clumsy skeleton. The air shaved his arms with chill. Iron rings of cold slipped up over his ankles, higher and higher. Then Sal disappeared. Moments later Matthew felt his legs clapped together from underneath, and he was thrust upward and shot into the water like a human cannonball. He paddled back up to the surface, giggling.

"Ready for the Circle Line?" Sal asked.

Matthew climbed onto his back. Sal pulled him through the water with broad, even strokes. His back muscles rolled against Matthew like turbines. "Kick," he instructed. They swam around the pond, then drifted for a bit. Sal kept them afloat with an easy stroke of his arms. Matthew rested his head against Sal's shoulder. The windy gasp of his breathing became calm. He felt Sal's heart beating thickly, as though lodged below the water, deep within the earth. Matthew wished he could stay like that forever.

It had been warmer than usual, that last night in the country. A nearly full moon hung in the sky, silvering the path through woods and floating a pearly disc of moonlight on the pond.

"Do we have to go back to the house right now?" asked Matthew after they'd climbed out of the water.

"We always go back right after. Otherwise your mom gets mad."

"Just a little longer."

"Something the matter? You been jumpy all night."

"Can we stay?"

"Just for a while. Then we'll have to go."

They sat down beneath a tree.

"How come she gets angry at you so easy?" Matthew asked.

"She gets angry at everybody easy. You know that."

"She and Gramma used to fight a lot, too."

"You always fight with people you like a lot."

"You and me don't fight."

"We did when you first met me. You remember?" He ran his hand through Matthew's hair. "You're still wet. Give me the towel." Sal rubbed Matthew's head briskly. "Masa head, masa head. Your head is just one big ball of masa. If my mama were here, she'd roll it out and make tortillas."

The water began to settle. The scattered drops of moonlight came together.

"You are precious to me, Matito," Sal said.

Matthew's heart stirred.

"I love you. I want to be your father. You want to be my son?"

Matthew nodded his head.

Sal edged nearer, banding him close with a thick arm across Matthew's shoulders.

Matthew sat up straighter. "You remember what you told me, the secret?" Matthew asked.

"Yeah."

"When are you going to tell her?"

"When the time is right, like I told you."

"How come it's a secret?"

"She might get scared if she knew."

"You said you'd tell her before you'd asked her to marry you, right?" His heart beat faster. He feared Sal could feel it.

Sal nodded.

"If you told her then you could get married right away, right?"

"I want to go slow. What's all this about—"

"If she already knew, then it wouldn't make a difference, right?" He was talking faster.

Matthew felt Sal stiffen.

"It wouldn't, right?"

Sal pulled away. "What do you mean, Matito?"

★

Matthew squirms on the windowsill. From where he sits he can make out his mother's reflection in the hallway mirror through the open door of his room. She sits in the dark living room on the couch, surrounded by packing cartons, her legs stretched out in front of her. She wears her old housedress, not the bright-colored shift Sal bought her to wear in the country. Her face is fixed to the screen. Her hand is the only part of her that moves, bringing the cigarette back and forth to her mouth in a mechanical arc. Her other hand holds an ice pack to one eye.

She moves. Zzzprisss. Another Rheingold. It's her fifth that night, at least. She had Matthew pick up a six-pack along with the take-out pizza for supper. She'd hardly said a word to him at the table, just pulled a slice from the pie and then left it half eaten.

The telephone rings. Matthew snaps alert, checks the mirror to see what his mother'll do. She doesn't move. Second ring. Third. Matthew's sure it's Sal. He's already called twice before. Each time she's hung up as soon as she knew who it was.

One more time, Matthew tells himself, then he'll make a run for it. It rings. He leaps into the hallway, grabs the receiver. "Hello, Sal?"

The light switches on, blinding him. His mother's bare feet slap across the linoleum toward him.

"Is that really you, Sal?"

"Get away from here!" she yells. The almond-shaped welt below her eye comes at him as she throws out a sunburned arm to grab the receiver.

"Goddammit, who is this?" she shouts into the receiver. A moment later, "Drop dead!"

"Don't—" Matthew says.

It's already slammed down. "Go back to bed, you."

"Why can't I talk to him?"

"I said go back to bed." Her eye twitches. Someone bangs up on the pipe.

"Go to hell," she shouts at the floor. She hits the light shut. "Don't give me any shit tonight, Matty, I'm warning you," she says, heading back to the living room.

Matthew retreats but only as far as the door. When she's on the sofa, he creeps back. He dials Sal's number, keeping on eye on the mirror the whole time. It rings five times without an answer. He trudges back to the sill, sidestepping the boxes near his bed.

Sal had sounded frightened, Matthew thinks. He tries to keep the sound of Sal's voice alive in his head, as though losing it might mean that Sal would drift away forever. He glances at the mirror. His mother sits like a statue enveloped by cigarette smoke. He doesn't know whether to hate her or feel sorry for her. Fewer lights are on in the air shaft. It's quieter, as though all the noise had been used up.

★

"Did you tell her?" Sal had asked.

Matthew hadn't answered.

"Why did you tell her? I told you not to . . ."

Matthew had run back barefoot through the woods. Branches slapped at him, stones tore at the soles of his feet. Good, he thought, I deserve it. He threw open the screen door coming into the bungalow and dove face down into his bed. His mother followed, clasping him from behind. "Baby doll," she murmured. "What happened?"

He wouldn't answer and pulled away from her. Finally she left. He pulled the thin blanket over him and lay trembling on his cot.

Much later, he heard the screen door slam.

"Hey Jo-Jo," Sal bellowed. He sounded drunk. Matthew pulled his thin blanket tighter around him.

"Keep it down, for Chrissakes. Matty's asleep," his mother said in a brittle voice.

"Matito," Sal shouted. He gave a wicked laugh.

Matthew grasped the blanket in his fist. He heard the sound of the high-riser being rolled out in the other room.

"What do you think you're doing?" his mother said.

Sal didn't answer.

"You're not sleeping here tonight."

"Why not?"

"I don't want no thugs around here."

"You calling me a thug?"

"You're goddam right I am."

Sal mumbled something in Spanish.

"Hey, where are you going?" Marjorie demanded.

"I got to talk to Matito."

"The hell you do."

There was a scuffle of feet near his door.

"Let me through!"

"Get away!"

"Matito!" Sal bellowed.

Matthew pulled to a corner of the bed, beginning to cry.

"Why you do it, Matito? Why?"

"Get the hell outta here, you — "

A punch thudded her silent. A moment later the screen door slapped shut again. Matthew ran in and found his mother on the floor. A blurry redness shadowed one eye. Sal was gone.

They packed during the night and drove back to the city the next morning in the car Sal had rented. Marjorie did seventy most of the time. She kept looking into the rearview mirror as if she expected Sal to be following.

★

Matthew slides off the sill, too tired to stay awake. On the way to bed he trips over a carton.

"What happened?" his mother cries out.

"I'm okay," mumbles Matthew, rubbing the toe he's stubbed, hoping she won't come in.

He falls into bed, closes his eyes. From the other room he hears his mother crying.

Two

Matthew's halfway up the block, heading nowhere in particular. His eyes ache from the glare of the morning sun. He's tired from the restless sleep of the night before and in a bad mood from not knowing what to do today. He wishes he were back in the country.

"Matthew."

The voice is as smooth as ball bearings. Matthew recognizes it immediately. He turns to see a tall black man approaching, wearing a dark suit, complete with bow tie and Panama hat. The man comes to a halt as though having chosen where to stand.

"Welcome home," Mr. Sloane says, extending a hand. He smiles and his cheeks pull into tiny marbles.

"Hi, Mr. Sloane," says Matthew.

"When did you return?"

"Yesterday."

"We didn't expect you until after September."

The "we" warms Matthew.

Mr. Sloane gives him a sidelong glance. "How come you're back so early? Did something happen?"

Matthew shuffles in place. "We just left," he says, hearing his own voice betray him.

"Well, you certainly picked the hottest time of the summer to return. I thought it was supposed to get cooler in August. It must be as hot as that first day of mine in New York, which I don't think I'll ever forget."

"If you're so hot, how come you're wearing a suit?" Matthew says with a trace of nastiness.

"I always wear a suit, Matthew. You know that." He pauses. "Are you sure everything's all right?"

Matthew nods.

"If you don't mind my saying so, it seems otherwise. What have you on your morning's agenda?"

He could talk like a school principal sometimes, Matthew thinks, already annoyed at Mr. Sloane for having wormed more out of him than he'd wanted to reveal. "Nothing, I guess."

"Then won't you come along with me? Today is a red-letter day."

Matthew follows, regretting having snapped at him. Mr. Sloane moves weightlessly, economically, hardly creasing his suit as he walks. His arms swing at his sides, straight as plumb lines. His head is a slow-moving beacon, surveying everything around him. The little flowers at the ends of his shoelaces dance on the polished floor of his shoes.

"How are the others?" asks Matthew.

"Fine, fine. They'll all be glad to see you."

"Are we going to the house?"

"Not yet. I want to see Mr. Glaubach first."

They stop before the boarded-up windows of the piano repair store. Mr. Sloane opens the door with a key. Inside, it's dim. The air is sweet with varnish and wood glue. The front of the store is a thicket of soundboards and piano cabinets. Actions are stacked, skeletal and silent, against a wall. Nearby, rows of spinets line up like pews. Mr. Sloane and Matthew make their way down a narrow aisle toward the back.

Mr. Glaubach works in a brightly lit clearing, kneeling before a great studio upright. Its bottom is half exposed; it looks like a proud cat poised on its haunches, submitting to a veterinary examination.

"Ach," he says, pulling himself up when he sees them. Mr. Sloane removes his hat.

"Nice to see you again, Mr. Sloane. You bring the little boy." Mr. Glaubach offers Matthew a large, fleshy hand that always squeezes Matthew's too tightly. His gold-rimmed glasses and soft face make him look like a doctor. Matthew forgives Mr.

Glaubach for calling him a little boy since foreigners always talk funny.

"She looks fine," says Mr. Sloane, running his hand over the top of the piano. Dense waves of satin swim in the gleaming wood.

"Almost finished," Mr. Glaubach says.

"That's the one you're going to move into the house, Mr. Sloane?" asks Matthew.

"That and no other."

"Look at zis," Mr. Glaubach says, lifting the lid. A golden glow lights up Mr. Sloane's face.

"What did you do to the harp to make it so shiny?" Mr. Sloane asks, peering inside.

"I clean it good. And look what I find," he says. "You see zat date on ze top.

"Where?" Matthew says, standing on tiptoe.

"Above zat hole."

"1892," Mr. Sloane reads.

"Yesss. And you see zat number?"

They nod.

"You know what zat means?"

"That the piano is seventy-two years old," says Mr. Sloane.

"Ze harp, anyway. But not only zat. It means it comes from ze old factory in Hamburg, Germany, where I am once working. It is ordered special because all ze ozer Steinway pianos in America, zey made here. But zere is somesing else." He pauses for full effect. "Do you know what is in 1892 happening in Hamburg?"

Mr. Sloane and Matthew shake their heads.

"Ze cholera plague. It is very bad. Tousand people die. Zey have terrible pain in ze stomach." He grasps his belly and grimaces at Matthew until he laughs. Mr. Sloane lowers the lid somberly. "But I fix zis piano's stomach so it doesn't die." He winks at Matthew.

Matthew smiles. Mr. Glaubach and his corny jokes, he thinks. What a pair, the two of them: Vanilla and Chocolate, Humpty-Dumpty and Daddy Longlegs. He starts to wander through the store, remembering Mr. Sloane's story of how they met.

It was just after the Second World War. Mr. Sloane had left Asheville, North Carolina, headed for New York, with no more than a change of clothing in a cardboard suitcase, some money, and a title deed.

The deed was the reason for the journey, a document written on paper become brittle and yellow, penned in the fancifully flourished script of the last century. Folds separated the text into four stiff planes that couldn't be completely exposed without cracking the paper. Matthew'd seen it once. Mr. Glaubach kept it in his safe. Mr. Sloane had sheathed it in an oak-tag bankbook envelope from the account he'd closed to pay his bus fare, and entrusted it to his shirt pocket for the duration of the trip north. (He recalled the wartime story of a Zippo lighter deflecting an enemy's bullet from a soldier's heart. The deed, he was sure, would serve him no less.) It left the pocket only once during the long bus ride, at the halfway point, just outside of Washington, D.C. He eased it from its envelope and unfolded it just enough to see the magical address in New York where he was headed. Outside his window, the Capitol Building was coming into view. He replaced the envelope in his pocket, proud of what he was determined to do.

And with no help from the government of the people, by the people, and for the people, he said, addressing the birthday cake dome.

The bus deposited him at dusk on a Friday evening of a sweltering August. The crowds and traffic of Forty-second Street streamed past in a jagged neon blur. The victory delirium of the year before seemed to have been revived, as if it were to be an annual event. Even the Negroes in this town were like no others he'd seen, all finely dressed and vaguely suspicious-looking. They didn't seem to notice him. He was especially wary of the police, who might easily ask him to produce the draft card he didn't have. (He was no Marcus Garvey, but he'd had no desire to fight in some white man's war, especially when most of the white men didn't even speak his language.)

He reached a corner and checked the street signs. He'd heard that the city was laid out in a grid and assumed he'd be able to find his way. According to his calculations, the house on West Fifty-second Street was close enough to be reached on foot. But he was tired and soon lost his way. The lights of the marquees along Eighth Avenue seemed to flicker on and off in time to the painful throb in his head. His feet soon began to ache as though they carried suitcases of their own. He wound up going in circles, unable to quit the inferno of Times Square. In desperation he switched directions, turned a corner, and set off anew. The street numbers began going up, and it seemed he was getting his bearings at last. At last the sign for Fifty-second Street came into view below the earring-shaped street lamp. Then he noticed to his horror that the W. on the sign had become an E., which it wasn't supposed to be. He set his suitcase down between his legs, mopped his forehead with his handkerchief, and reached for the deed, which he hoped would give him the strength to continue.

"You lost?" A white man startled him.

"Yes," Mr. Sloane said. "As a matter of fact I am. I want to find my house."

The man pointed to the piece of paper. "You need a map for zat?"

"That's not a map," said Mr. Sloane with some injury.

The man apologized, his accent becoming more pronounced in his nervousness.

"That's all right," Mr. Sloane said, replacing the letter in his pocket. "Maybe you can help me find it. It's on West Fifty-second Street."

"West Fifty-second Street? Zis is East Fifty-second Street."

"I know."

"We take bus."

Mr. Sloane thought of the crowds around the terminal. "No, no. I want to walk."

"Zen I go with you. I live around zere."

"Are all the white people in New York as friendly as you are?"

"I no white. I German." He held out his hand. "Ernst Glaubach."

"Timothy Sloane."

As they walked crosstown Mr. Glaubach told his story. He was a piano builder who'd learned his trade at the Steinweg works in Hamburg. It was just after the war, the first one. Inflation. No work. He had a cousin who lived on Eighty-second Street ("East Eighty-second Street," he explained with a grin), who sent him money to come over to America. He arrived with a pocketful of useless Weimar reichmarks and an address. He got work tuning pianos. After Germany, it amazed him that the people could afford piano tuners. He got himself a shop of his own. He met an American girl, he became an American.

Then came the crash. The Nazis started. Adolf was on the front page of the *Stadt Zeitung* every day, a hero. There were rallies in Yorkville. Times got bad. People stopped bringing in their Chickerings to be refelted, especially by someone named Glaubach.

"But I no believe all zat 'Deutschland über alles' crap. When Joe Louis fight Max Schmeling I stand in front of radio and say, 'Kill him! Kill zat Schmeling!' You know Joe Louis? He ze Brown Bomber."

"Boxing should be outlawed," Mr. Sloane said. He was too tired to concentrate on the friendly man's chatter. The city seemed to be spinning around him. The wide streets they crossed were like the fiery spokes of a wheel that had no center. East Fifty-second Street was quiet, but it exploded into light and music when it became West Fifty-second Street.

"Zen Roosevelt come on in ze middle of George Burns and Gracie Allen," Mr. Glaubach continued. "We make war. Next morning someone srow a brick in ze shop window. I pick it up and look at it. 'What are you doing here?' I say to it. Ze people who srow it, zey sink I am like ze Germans in Deutschland. Not so. I married to American, I American too. So what? I put boards in front of ze shop. It is not fair. No one srow bricks in windows of ze Steinway factory in Long Island City. It is German too, but zey are not called Steinweg anymore. Maybe I should have changed my name too. Maybe Gladbag. You like zat? Herr Gladbag!" he laughed.

"Do you still have your piano shop?"

"Yes. You want to buy piano?" he laughed.

"No. But perhaps play one."

"Come. I let you." They stopped before a boarded-up storefront. "What number on West Fifty-second Street is your house?"

"Six hundred twenty-two."

"Zat is maybe between Eleven and Twelve Avenue. Not far. We stop in my shop for a drink, you play, and zen you go home, yes?"

Mr. Glaubach led him to the back and gave him a chair. The moment he sat down Mr. Sloane felt himself falling asleep.

"You tired. Maybe you go home now?"

Mr. Sloane rubbed his eyes. "Well, actually, I don't have a home. At least not yet."

"But you say —"

"It's a long story."

Mr. Glaubach put up his hand. "No problem." He rose and pulled back a curtain to reveal two beds, a bureau, and the rudiments of a kitchen. "You stay here."

"What about your wife?" Mr. Sloane said. "Where will she sleep?"

Mr. Glaubach appeared not to have heard. Mr. Sloane was too tired to ask again.

★

They worked out an arrangement. Mr. Sloane could stay there as long as he needed to get settled in return for helping Mr. Glaubach. He swept up around the shop, helped move the heavy piano actions. Mr. Sloane remembered the music he'd heard along Fifty-second Street that first night and went there to see about finding work. He got some nights in some supper clubs and dance halls, but not much. Jazz was what everyone wanted to hear those days, and what Mr. Sloane played was ragtime. Mr. Glaubach loved to listen to it. After the supper he cooked for them, he poured out two glasses of schnapps, and Mr. Sloane played.

One night he returned from a gig at a basement joint in the Village and found Mr. Glaubach slumped over the exposed guts of a massive upright. His face was red, he was sweating and mumbling to himself in a drunken slur while his fists pounded a baroque confusion on the strings.

"Evie," he murmured.

Mr. Sloane noticed a photograph in a frame whose glass was broken. He picked it up. A youthful Mr. Glaubach stood in a stiff-looking suit beside a handsome young woman in a wide-brimmed bonnet. Mr. Sloane helped his friend into bed.

The next day Mr. Glaubach apologized for his behavior. "Zat piano. I was building it for my wife when she die."

"Then you must finish it," Mr. Sloane said.

★

Deep within the labyrinth of actions, Matthew hears Mr. Sloane start to play and snakes his way toward the piano. Mr. Sloane sits straight as a dowel. The silver kinks in his hair glisten. His fingers graze the keys lightly or ring them like drum taps. A graceful melody in the right hand leaps through the latticed music of the left.

"Zat's ragtime!" says Mr. Glaubach when the music's over. "You play it gut."

"Thank you," says Mr. Sloane. "And thank you for rebuilding such a wonderful instrument for me."

"My Evie would be happy to know zat you play it."

"Why do you always play ragtime?" Matthew asks.

"Ragtime, child, is the sound of a sad heart dancing just fast enough to forget but slow enough to keep on going. That's why I play it."

The word "child" nestles around Matthew. "Are you really going to move this piano into the house?" he asks.

"And why not?"

The sharpness of Mr. Sloane's voice tells Matthew he's asked the wrong question. He should have known better than to say anything against Mr. Sloane's house project. He tries to smooth over the error. "The floors. Maybe they're not strong enough . . ."

"We'll make them strong, Matthew, you mark my words," says Mr. Sloane. "The floor and the walls and the roof and everything in between."

★

Two steps out of Mr. Glaubach's shop, Matthew sees a white streak coming at him. He blinks away the dark of the store to decipher it. It's a kid, arms poking winglike through his short sleeves, shirttail flying up in the back, coming his way. Their eyes meet for a moment. The kid's face is milk-white except for the prominent blue of a vein on one side of his forehead. He looks scared. His lips part as though he might speak but he doesn't stop. Matthew follows. Three blocks later the kid slips into an alleyway. Matthew keeps after him. The alley goes a long way, then cuts a corner and gets narrow. Suddenly there's a row of garbage cans, a dead end . . .

The kid's disappeared. Matthew turns, confused and winded.

"I'm over here."

The kid huddles in a doorway. In his clean white shirt he looks like a dab of plaster flung against the dirty metal door.

"Jesus, you can run fast," says Matthew, gulping bucketfuls of air.

"Did you see him?" the kid asks.

"Who?"

"My father."

"Huh?"

"He was chasing me."

"I didn't see anybody." He looks around. "I never knew there was an alley on this block."

The kid folds over, relieved.

"Your father was chasing you?"

The kid nods.

"Why? What'd you do?"

"I didn't do anything. He wanted me to go to the shul with him but I didn't want to. I hate going there. I'm never going back there again." He speaks in a high voice like Mickey Mouse.

"But there isn't any school yet. It's still vacation."

"Not school. Shul. He goes every Saturday and says I have to go, too."

"But today's Saturday, there's no school on — "

The kid's lips purse. "I already told you. Shul, not school. Don't you know what a shul is? It's where you go and pray."

"You mean church?"

"Church is for the goyim." He looks Matthew over. "You're not Jewish?"

"Nope."

The kid hesitates, then continues, as if having decided to ignore what he's just heard. "I don't care what my father says. I'm not going to that place. It's hot and the air smells like spit. My father goes so he can talk to God. My mother says he talks to God so much he doesn't know what to say to anyone else."

"Does he really talk to God?"

"He thinks he does. He talks to himself, that's for sure. Today was a close call. He almost caught up with me when I tripped going down the stairs. He was faster than usual. But I was still faster!" he sings, shaking a tiny fist in the air.

The kid reminds Matthew of a rubber-band motor that keeps getting twisted. He waits for something to snap.

"But I'm used to running," the kid continues. "I've done it before. If I wasn't so smart and didn't want to waste my intelligence, I could become a marathon runner in the Olympics."

Matthew looks around. "It's cooler here than in the street, at least," says Matthew.

"I know a better place. Do you want to come?"

The next thing Matthew knows they're off and running again, this time toward Eighth Avenue. They join a flank of people descending into the subway, duck under the orange arms of the turnstile just as a train pulls in, and slip between the closing doors. The train lurches forward and they reach for the pole, exchanging wicked grins. Matthew's dizzy. Warm ozone air wafts around him. The lights give a cold, yellow glow. The train rocks and sighs, nearly empty.

"When do we get off?" Matthew says.

"Next stop. We have to change trains." He leads them across the platform at Forty-second Street.

"You know the trains good," Matthew says.

"I used to ride them to school every day. Here comes ours. Let's ride in the front."

They trundle through car after car like the many rooms of a strange house, past sleepy passengers who don't seem to notice the trail of slamming doors they leave behind. They reach the first car and press against the front window.

"What's your name? I'm Matthew."

"I'm Asa."

"Is that a real name?"

"It's a Jewish name. You don't know anything, do you?"

Creep, Matthew thinks. No wonder his father wants to beat him. Yet he's dazzled by the strange Asa. Matthew's never been on the subway alone and would never have managed sneaking on. Still, there was the time his grandmother took him to the Bronx Zoo. It was Matthew who got them on the right train after she almost had them going to Astoria.

A tiny point of light pierces the darkness, enlarging like the shutter of a lens as they approach, until the train breaks into daylight and pulls up over streets lined with small houses. Farther on, the train lowers toward the ground. It runs past the racetrack and the airport and then shoots out over the water. Above them, the sky arches gaseous and pearl-white, freed at last from the city.

"Where are we?" Matthew asks, wide-eyed.

"Jamaica Bay. Let's ride outside." Asa scampers through the empty car. He pulls open the door, and the car fills with the train's clacking. Asa slips out onto the narrow platforms of the adjacent cars, grips the bars mounted beside each window, secures a foothold on the headlights, and hangs like a billowy sail between them. "Look at all those birds!" he says.

"You sure that's okay?" Matthew says, standing with one foot on each platform, more and more terrified with each rise and dip.

"Look, there they are," says Asa, pointing to the sky.

"Don't let go . . ."

Asa's arm reaches up as if trying to touch them. His head arches back. His shirt flaps loudly in the breeze as though the wind wants to loosen him from the mast of the subway car. Matthew glances up at the narrow strip of sky between the two cars. White gulls circle and cross in a sprawling script that threatens to knot around him and and carry him aloft. He's relieved when pudgy fingers of shore begin to loop close to the track. The marshes thicken, land slips beneath them. The train slows.

"We get off here," Asa says. "Get ready to run."

Matthew doesn't bother to ask why. Just before they reach the turnstiles Asa darts under and makes a run for it.

"Here they make you pay to get out," Asa explains outside the station. They walk past rows of tiny white houses set behind a dense ridge of shrubbery. A solitary car passes them.

"Did you see all those birds from the train?" Asa says.

"Sort of," he says, not wanting to admit that he was too chicken to climb up as Asa had.

"Is this still the city?" Matthew asks.

Asa smiles. "It's Birdland."

The street ends in a clump of bushes. They plunge through the foliage until they reach a narrow path bordered by tall grass. The birds sound clearly in the desertlike silence.

"There are so many," says Asa, looking up to the sky.

"Why are they here?"

"Because it's safe. They know no one will come after them."

A greyish bird ruffles out of a nearby tree. Its wings whistle to pull it aloft.

"Cormorant," Asa says, savoring each syllable of the bird's name.

Matthew follows its flight until the sky swallows it. A little farther down the path a sharp sound slices through the air. A tiny white-headed bird appears from out of the bushes, hops from branch to branch just above them, investigating, then disappears.

"What was that?"

"Sandpiper, which is also known as a sandrunner. Quick, look over there."

The moment Matthew turns his head he hears the sound again. "Hey, I saw that!" Matthew shouts.

Asa grins. "What?"

Matthew reaches inside Asa's shirt, pulls out something dangling around Asa's neck that's flat and made of metal. Another bird wings by. "What's this?"

"Bird whistle, what else? Bet you can't make a sound with it."

Matthew leans over and puts it to his lips but only a Bronx cheer comes out.

"Hah," says Asa. "Listen to this." He makes a series of short, whooping sounds with it. The sky remains empty.

"You're not so hot, it was just luck before . . ."

Asa puts a finger to his lips to signal silence. Moments later something flutters just above his head.

"See, they think I'm one of them!"

"How do you do that?" Matthew asks, watching the bird retreat.

"I'll show you sometime. Let's go down to the beach first."

The path leads through dunes rustling with tall, airy phragmites to the shore. Far away, on the other side of the water, the buildings of Manhattan poke through a bluish cloud.

"How'd you find this place?" Matthew asks.

"One day after school I didn't feel like going home so I stayed on the train to see where it would go. I didn't come home until it was dark. My mother and father were both crying. I'd seen my mother cry before, but never my father. His eyes were red like strawberries. He even kissed me. He wanted me to say where I'd been, but I wouldn't. I knew I'd found a good hiding place."

"You think he's still looking for you?"

"No. He's probably sitting at the kitchen table reading. That's what he always does on Saturday afternoons. I feel bad for him. All he does is go to work and read the paper. Sometimes he plays the violin. He knows we live in a cruddy apartment and don't have a car. We're the only Jews who live in the building. None of my aunts or uncles come to visit; they say we live in a slum. We have to go visit them. We take the subway to Penn Station, then get on the Long Island Railroad."

Matthew takes off his shirt and rolls it into a pillow. Asa sets his down like a beach towel and stretches out. His ribs gleam in the sun and his ribcage protrudes from his chest like a pair of gills. A tiny disc of shadow marks his sternum.

Matthew's never seen anyone so skinny. "How many ribs do you have?" he asks.

"Same number as you."

"You sure?"

"Of course." Asa sits up. "Twenty-four." He counts down one side of his ribcage, then up the other. "See?"

Matthew does the same. "Twenty-three, twenty-four, twenty—"

"Stop!"

"What about these two things?"

"They aren't ribs, they're clavicles."

"They're what?"

"Clavicles." He shakes his head. "Collarbones, what else?"

"Oh yeah?"

Asa nods.

"Well, what's this thing then?" he asks, pointing to his upper arm.

"Do you mean the muscle or the bone?"

"Just tell me what it is!"

"The muscle is, naturally, the biceps and the bone, the humerus."

"This?" He touches below the knee.

"Tibia."

"And this? The muscle, I mean." He pats the back of his upper arm.

"Triceps."

Matthew smiles, enjoying the game but barely able to control his stupefaction at Asa's knowledge. "This?" he asks in a tiny voice, afraid that Asa will know it, too.

"Scapula, but you can call it the shoulder blade."

"You're not making all this up, are you?"

"Why should I?"

"How do you know this stuff?"

"I read encyclopedias."

"Nobody reads encyclopedias."

"I do. I'd do it all the time if I could, but I have to go to school. The school I used to go to was far away and I had to take the train, so I brought a volume of the encyclopedia to read. Now I won't be able to since my new school's near my house."

"Which school?"

"P.S. 73."

Matthew's startled. "What class?" He hopes it won't be his, so he won't have to contend with someone like Asa. But Asa is one grade behind him.

"Where was your old school?"

"Brooklyn. It was a Jewish school. I told my father I wasn't going there anymore. In that school all the teachers are like my father. If they catch you doing anything wrong you get hit. Nobody fools around."

"Hey, Asa," Matthew says, feeling restless. He springs up. "Make a muscle. Let's see your, um, what did you call this one again?" He makes a fist and curls his arm.

"Biceps."

"Yeah, let's see your biceps."

"Why?"

"Cause I want to see."

Asa bends his arm, barely producing a bulge.

"Mine's bigger than yours," Matthew says.

"Jews have more brains than muscles," Asa says drily.

Matthew gives an exasperated sigh. "I'm going swimming," he announces. "You coming?"

"No."

"Why not?"

"I don't want to. I don't like swimming."

"Come on."

Asa shakes his head.

"Why don't you like swimming? It's so hot," Matthew says.

"I don't care. I don't like to swim. Besides, I don't know how."

Matthew smiles. "I'll teach you." He grabs Asa's arm.

"Leave me alone!"

Matthew yanks at the bottom of his pants. "Strip tease! Strip tease!"

"Leave me alone," Asa screams, holding onto the top of his pants.

Matthew steps back, a little frightened. He takes off his pants, throws them down. He's about to pull off his jockeys too when he notices Asa sneaking a look. He leaves them on and storms down to the water.

★

They return to Birdland almost every day. Matthew waits for Asa on his front steps, and they head for the subway, their pockets stuffed with whatever they can smuggle from home. Each day they find a new corner to explore, discover paths twisting between dense flanks of rhododendron, peer into tidal pools seeded with spinning, streaming creatures Asa gives scientific-sounding names to. Matthew teaches Asa how to tumble and do somersaults. ("You look like a Jewish starfish, Asa," Matthew says.) They construct pyramids, canals, and towers — Asa calls them pylons — in the sand. They both grow brown, Asa from the waist up, since he won't remove his pants no matter how hot it is, Matthew almost all over. (Marjorie asks him, "Where do you go off to every day, Florida?") Matthew learns not to bother Asa about swimming.

Always, not far away, circling overhead or marking the limits of the sky with slow-moving specks, are the birds, more than Matthew ever believed could exist. He and Asa hide stock still in the bushes, Asa whistles, and the birds swoop low enough for the boys to hear the whoosh of their wings and to see their speckled bellies. Matthew is thrilled by their nearness. He begins to understand why Asa comes here; Asa, too, is a bird, running as though one day he might take off, flying through the subway's tunnels and over its bridges, unstoppable except by his father, who would shoot him down if he could.

Asa's changed since they've met. He doesn't snap off answers to Matthew's questions as he used to. "In the beginning I thought you were Mr. Machine," Matthew confides to Asa.

One day Asa stubs his toe on a rock. He begins crying uncontrollably and Matthew holds him, a bony package in his arms. Asa's head is so round and his summer crew cut makes it look like a fuzzy ball. Matthew yearns to stroke it. He does. Asa smiles at him.

"How's the toe?" Matthew asks.

"Better."

They return to the city, their feet caked with sand in their socks. The air of the subway feels almost too thick to breathe. They fall into a doze and get jostled awake by the crowds pushing in at Broadway–Nassau Street. As usual, Matthew walks Asa home. They'll see each other tomorrow, Matthew knows, but each homeward trek brings the school term closer, when they won't be able to go to Birdland as often. Matthew watches Asa disappearing into the hallway of his building, imagines him entering the strange, fearful world of his father.

★

"How come you make such a big deal about being Jewish?" Matthew asks Asa one day on the beach. There are plenty of Jewish kids in his school but the only way Matthew knows they are is because they have names like Greenberg and Schwartz and they take off school for the Jewish holidays.

"We're different," Asa says.

"How?"

"Jews don't swear, they promise. They don't believe in Jesus and never eat bacon but always rye bread. Albert Einstein was Jewish, Harry Houdini was Jewish, and the guy that started the Breakstone cottage cheese factory was Jewish, too."

"What else?"

Asa thinks. "Everybody hates us."

"Why?"

"Because we're Jewish, of course. Why else?"

"Do Jews all think they're better than everyone else?"

"I didn't say better. I said different."

"Big deal," says Matthew, getting impatient. "You think you're different from me just because of that? We're both boys."

"It's not so simple," says Asa softly.

Matthew takes a fistful of sand and lets it trickle back out. "My mother said Franklin Roosevelt was Jewish."

"He wasn't."

"How do you know?"

"Roosevelt isn't a Jewish name."

"Houdini isn't either. It sounds Italian."

"In the first place," Asa says, ticking the point off with his fingers, "he changed it. And in the second place, a person can be Italian and Jewish."

"Oh, that's right. My grandmother said Roosevelt wasn't really his name either, it was really Rosenberg, but he changed it so that more people would vote for him. Rosenberg's a Jewish name, isn't it?" Matthew says, pleased at what he knows.

Asa frowns.

"Come to think of it, my father was Jewish, too."

Asa's eyes widen. "Your father was Jewish?"

"Yeah."

"You never told me that."

"Well, he doesn't live with us anymore."

Asa's speechless.

"He went away. I don't remember him, it was right after I was born. My grandmother used to say that of all the Jews running around why couldn't my mother have found a rich business-man to marry instead of a good-for-nothing piano player."

"Who's your mom married to now?"

"No one. She has a boyfriend. Well, she used to. Hey, if my father was Jewish does that mean I'm Jewish too?"

Asa shakes his head sternly. "Absolutely not."

"Why not?"

"Your mother has to be Jewish."

"I think you're just saying that because you want to keep on thinking that you're better than I am."

"No, it's the rule."

"My mother says it was on account of my grandmother that my father went away. My grandmother didn't like him. She said if my mother hadn't gotten mixed up with the guy, she wouldn't have gotten into trouble."

"What kind of trouble."

Matthew beams. "Me. My mother says I look like him. She gave me his picture."

Matthew brings it along the next day. "Look at this," he says, taking out the crinkled snapshot.

"Yup," Asa says, after a quick glance. "He's Jewish."

"How can you tell?"

"He looks sad. All Jewish people look that way. Both my mother and my father do, even when they smile."

Matthew remembers the candy store man. "How come?"

"It's a trick to get God to feel sorry for them."

"You don't look that way."

"That's because I'm still young. When I get older, I bet I will. But I hope I don't look like my father. You should see him." Asa pulls down his lower lip, crosses his eyes, and looks up at the sky. "Oi, oi," he says. "That's how my father looks."

"What if someone who isn't Jewish looks sad? Will God feel sorry for him?"

Asa shakes his head firmly. "Nope, it only works for Jews." He smiles with satisfaction.

That night, stuffing his father's picture back into his dresser drawer, Matthew comes across Justin's knife and the broken pieces he'd promised to fix. It looks mean and threatening beside the friendly tumble of his balled-up crew socks. He's hardly seen Justin since that first day back in the city. Any time he spots him with Kevin around the neighborhood Matthew makes a U-turn. He shoves the knife way in the back.

Later, Matthew switches off the light and gets into bed. He lies there for a long time, his eyes open. He hears his mother rummaging in the refrigerator for another can of beer. Sal hasn't called again since that first night. Matthew can't sleep. He gets up, slips off his pajamas, gets back into bed naked. A breeze pulls against his chest and the front of his legs. His fingers take inventory of his ribs. Matthew hears Asa's voice. Asa's tiny fingers explore the taut skin over Matthew's stomach and the twin cords of muscle buried underneath. He imagines them lying side by side on the sand. Their pants are off, their legs touch, then they scootch together. Asa touches Matthew's face, his chest. They press tighter. Matthew feels a tickle between his legs. It feels so good. His hands move faster and faster.

Marjorie punches open the can, and it explodes onto the living room floor. "Oh shit," she says.

*

The last day in Birdland before school starts Matthew sneaks up to where Asa lies asleep on his shirt. His hands are cupped around the jellyfish he's planning on scaring Asa with. He stops. One of Asa's pants legs is pushed up almost to the knee. Crimson welts marble the pale, exposed skin. Matthew creeps closer, unsure of whether they're really bruises or the shadow of the pants.

Asa sits up, startled, sees Matthew looking, pushes the pants leg back down.

"What was that?" Matthew asks.

Asa looks at him. Then he stands up and takes off his pants. Both legs are covered with bruises, gleaming terribly. "That's what my father does to me when I run away. Or even when I don't."

Matthew sets the jellyfish down.

"I'll show you something else." He pulls out a memo pad from his back pocket and hands it to Matthew. Most of the pages are full. The handwriting is so perfect it could have been printed. Matthew hardly understands what the words mean.

"Every time he beats me I write it down. I learned all about the different parts of the body so I could describe what he does to me accurately. I have five more books like that, all filled up. I haven't missed one single beating."

"Why do you do it?"

His eyes assume a terrible sparkle. "I'm going to take him to court and use the books as evidence to have him sent away."

"Doesn't your mother do anything?"

"She locks herself in the bathroom and cries."

"How come he hits you?"

"Because he's insane. Afterwards he tells me he's sorry and kisses me and asks me to kiss him It'll be just like that tonight."

"What? You think he'll do it tonight?"

"He might."

"You could stay at my house. He wouldn't be able to find you there. My mother wouldn't let him in."

"He'd just wait until I came back. Besides, he doesn't hit me so much since it's hot. And the big Jewish holidays are coming up in September, so he doesn't want to sin too much before then. I also have to be home because he likes me to turn the music for him in case he plays the violin after supper."

Matthew looks down at the pants. "Is that why you didn't want to go in swimming the whole time?"

Asa looks down. "Sort of."

"Come on!"

They race to the shore and splash in. Matthew crouches down. "Let me take you on the Circle Line. Grab my shoulders."

Asa feels boxy and nearly weightless but his fingers grip like clamps.

"Not so hard. You're hurting my clavicles," says Matthew, laughing. "Ready?"

"I think so," says Asa in a shaky voice.

"Bonzai!" Matthew kicks off and starts stroking furiously but soon they flounder. "You gotta kick too!" he shouts through mouthfuls of water. He hears Asa gasping as his body struggles against Matthew's. They push against the tide until it flings them back to the shore and they spill apart.

On the way back from the subway they come across a convoy of black men hauling something on a dolly, heading up Eleventh

Avenue. It looks like a throne being carried in a royal procession. Mr. Sloane walks briskly beside them, barking commands.

"What's going on?" Asa asks.

"Holy," Matthew says, barely making out Mr. Glaubach's piano beneath the thick cloth wrapped around it. He's about to wave when he notices two kids, one fat, the other blond-haired and mean-looking, crouched behind a parked car, surveying the black men's progress.

"Let's beat it," Matthew says.

Three

1

Halfway up the stairs Matthew knows his mother's at it again. The hallway is thick with peculiar aromas that deepen with each step. He seeks relief at an open window in the stairwell.

After Gramma died, his mother took over the cooking and it was franks and beans almost every night. Then Sal came and starting making them pernil, sweet with fat, served on a bed of yellow rice scented with achiote, yuca mashed up smooth as cream and flavored with chopped pimiento, and wonderful satiny flans. Without meaning to, he set up a rivalry. On the off nights when Marjorie cooked they ate what she'd concocted from a Julia Child recipe or something torn from the *Ladies' Home Journal*. The results were often nearly inedible: Hamburger Aspic (it sounded like ass-pick to Matthew), Ham in Mint Chocolate Sauce, something with peanut butter, tripe, and radish, his least favorite vegetable, and the worst, Candied Veal ("How come it's so orange, Mom?"). Since returning to the city they eat that way every night. It makes Matthew miss Sal even more.

He pushes through the front door into a sticky cloud coming from the kitchen. The clang of a spoon beats out a haphazard rhythm to Marjorie's singing along with the radio.

> *Or would you like to swing on a star,*
> *Carry moonbeams home in a jar*

The spoon clatters to the floor.

40

"Jesus, Mary, and Joseph!"

Matthew tiptoes to his room.

"That you, Matty?"

He doesn't answer.

"Matty? If you're there and you don't answer me I'll—"

"Yeah?"

"Don't 'yeah' me. Come here."

"I don't feel like cooking."

"Matthew Douglas!"

The kitchen windows are wide open. The table's cluttered with utensils, dishes, and empty boxes of Jell-O. His mother's face rises like an oracle's over a great bowl of steaming red liquid. The heat leaves her light brown hair frizzy as cotton candy. She stands barefoot in her housedress whose floral pattern has been washed out to a pinkish shadow. Before her a heap of chopped fruit — ugh, it's prunes — waits on a chopping board. Jell-O again, he thinks. They have it often. Marjorie read that it's nonfattening and good for her fingernails. She gets it free, because she's a secretary for a company that sells it.

"Why do you have to make that stuff when it's so hot?" Matthew says.

"Stop giving me advice and help me pour this into the custard dishes."

"Use a ladle."

"I'll be here all night then. Come on, we could have had it finished by now. Grab a pot holder."

Together they heave the bowl. Resinous waves break across the surface of the gelatin. A hot tongue of fluid lances his wrist.

"Shit!" he says.

"Watch your lip."

From under the table comes a scratching. A grey, furry thumb-shaped head appears near the wall.

"Get him," Marjorie cries, grabbing the bowl and running with it like a quarterback. She corners the mouse, he darts away but she catches him in a shower of gelatin. He squeals, falls in gummy shock, twitching pitifully. Matthew's mouth drops open.

"Your old mother ain't so bad, is she, Matty?" Marjorie says. "Okay, now get ready for supper. Tonight I made something really special."

★

Matthew stares down at the clump of spaghetti on his plate. A suspicious purplish sauce spills over it.

"Eat. It'll get cold," Marjorie says.

Matthew tries a forkful. He frowns "How come it tastes sweet?"

"Sweet and sour," she corrects. "It's Oriental."

"Spaghetti isn't Oriental, it's Italian."

"That's what you think. Spaghetti originally comes from China. Marco Polo brought it to Italy. And if you don't believe me, ask Julia Child."

He spears something with his fork. "What's this?"

"Just eat, for godsakes."

"It's a piece of prune. You put prunes into the spaghetti sauce!"

"That's the sweet part. And anyway, there was no more Jell-O left and I didn't want to waste them."

"I'm not eating any prunes," Matthew says, pushing back in his chair.

"Fine."

He watches her eat. "What did you do with the mouse?" he says after a while.

"I threw it out."

"Where?"

"In the garbage, where else?"

"Was it dead?"

"Yes."

"What did it look like?"

"It looked dead. And if you don't mind, I'd rather not talk about it while I'm eating."

"Sal always said that death was part of life."

"That's very nice, Matty."

"He said there really wasn't that much difference between the two."

Marjorie twirls her fork in the spaghetti.

"Can we sleep on the roof tonight?"

"We'll see."

That's her way of not saying no right away. "Why not? It's so hot."

"I said we'll see."

Silence.

"You don't play with that Justin kid anymore, do you?" she asks.

"No."

"What about that other kid, the little one. Is he in your class?"

"No."

"He looks like a real egghead."

She'll talk about anything except what's important, he thinks. "When's Sal coming back?"

She sucks a noodle into her mouth.

"Mom, answer me!"

"Let me eat my supper in peace."

"You never answer me when I ask about him."

"Sure I do. You just don't like what I say."

"What did you say?"

"I said no. No, he's not coming back. No. I don't want him to."

"Why not?"

She sets down her fork. "Because I don't like people who give me black eyes. Or have you forgotten about that?"

"He didn't mean to."

"You mean it was an accident? You mean he really meant to give me flowers but he punched me out instead, is that it?"

Matthew idly rakes out a piece of prune with his fork. "If I hadn'ta told you about what he did, the whole thing wouldn'ta happened, right?"

She stops for a moment. "Maybe. But sooner or later something had to happen. I'm lucky he didn't do anything worse that night than hit me. With men like Sal you can never tell."

"Sal wouldn't do that—"

"Please, Matty. I don't want to talk about it."

"Don't you miss him?"

"Yes, I do."

"Don't you want to get married again?"

Marjorie laughs. "Again? I wasn't even married the first time. You know that, Matty." She pauses. "You want a daddy, don't you?"

Matthew shrugs. "Maybe."

"I'd love for you to have one but it isn't so easy."

"Why don't you talk to him when he calls?"

"I have nothing to say to him."

"Give him another chance."

"I don't think I can."

"Then at least let me talk to him."

"Don't you understand? I don't want to have anything more to do with him."

"I don't believe you!"

"What makes you so sure he wants to speak to you?"

"He does! I know he does!"

"So call him yourself if you want to talk to him."

Matthew pushes back in his seat, crosses his arms over his chest.

"Quit the sulking act and finish what's on your plate."

"The stuff tastes yucky."

"Suit yourself."

"You cook this way just to prove that you can cook as good as Sal did."

"That's enough."

"Sal can cook ten times better than you. A hundred times—"

Her fork slams down on the table and she gets up. "You can get started on the dishes right now, Big Mouth." She takes a can of beer into the living room with her.

A moment later Matthew hears the radio switched on. She sings:

Call me irresponsible
Call me unreliable

The sauce on his spaghetti has hardened and dulled. He'd like to dump it onto the floor. In the four weeks they've been home she's mentioned Sal only when he has. Once Matthew went over to the Woolworth's where Sal worked but they told him Sal didn't work there anymore.

"Get a move on in there!" Marjorie shouts.

He's probably blown his chance to sleep on the roof, he thinks, getting up. He tries another forkful of the noodles. Cold, they're not so bad, he concedes, except for the purple color. He scrapes them into the garbage, puts the plate in the sink along with some Joy, plugs the stopper in, and turns on the hot water. While it runs he fixes himself a peanut butter and jelly sandwich and peeks into the living room.

Marjorie's on the couch with her singer scrapbook on her lap, drinking her beer. She turns over the black pages very slowly, but hardly looks at what's pasted onto them; her eyes are off somewhere else. She goes through the book like that almost every night. Matthew's looked through it. There a clipping of Earl Wilson's column where she's mentioned ("Marjorie Mason" — her singer name — "the little girl with the big voice . . ."), a publicity shot of her looking like a boy in short hair, pencil-thin eyebrows, a long, shiny dress, and two hanging balls for earrings; the menu from the Hotel Pierre where she once sang before a convention of accountants. There's also a photograph of Matthew's father. He sits at a piano, a tall man in a white shirt, sleeves rolled up to show bony arms, his spidery fingers poised on the keys, smiling at the person taking the picture. Matthew knows him only from this and a few other pictures. He's tried to will the figure into motion, to lift him off the stool and give him speech. But his father stays where he is, smiling silently, just about to begin playing a song Matthew can't hear.

His mother sings

Yes I'm irresponsible
Guess I'm unreliable
And it's undeniably true

Her arms sweep up over her head, her eyes close, and one shoulder creeps up to meet her jaw, she looks like she might cry.

> *I'm irresponsibly mad*
> *About you.*

Matthew hears water dripping in the kitchen. "Holy!" he says, running back in.

"Matthew? What's going on?"

"Nothing," he says, battling a billowing cloud of suds back into the sink. He prays she won't come in and make a stink. He pulls out the stopper and the water sucks down the drain. Another song comes on the radio and soon she's singing again. There's an envelope stuck into a corner of the small shelf above the sink. Matthew spots Sal's name and address on it. Matthew's already reaching for it when he hears Marjorie coming toward the kitchen.

"What the hell happened here?"

"Nothing," he says. "I'll mop it up." He grins. "The floor was dirty anyhow." He points to the red gelatin stain.

She shakes her head as she takes another beer from the refrigerator.

"You really want to sleep on the roof?" she asks, sounding tired.

He thinks of the letter. How is he going to read it on the roof? But he says, "Sure."

★

Matthew leans over the edge of the roof. The chilly, tarred rim presses into his belly through his pajamas. Heat hangs in the dark, muffling the neighborhood quiet, except for the tinny hiss of his mother's transistor radio. The river hardly moves. His street glows blue under the new street lights they've just put up. He maps out what's below: to his left the moving line of headlights on the highway like a connect-the-dots, Mr.

Glaubach's piano store to the right, the wet-looking glow of Forty-second Street behind him, the park up ahead, and, just before it, Mr. Sloane's house: the borders of a dirty, gleaming neighborhood, his own.

"Only your grandmother would pick out such an armpit to live in," Marjorie used to say. She swore they'd move somewhere else. There was talk of them getting an apartment in the projects up along Amsterdam Avenue. Gramma didn't want to because she said only low-class people lived in the projects. Sal spoke of them leaving the city for good and moving to the country, but that seemed out of the question now. The city had torn down a bunch of buildings across from the projects for the new music hall; maybe theirs would be next. Then they'd have to move. But where would they go? He knows every sidewalk crack in the neighborhood. He likes his building with its mysterious air shaft, the hallways that always smell of cabbage, and, most of all, his river.

"Don't stand so close," Marjorie calls out from her cot. Her cold-creamed face glistens in the flicker of a citronella candle burning in their corner. Her hair is combed back smoothly, still damp from the shower. Shadows hollow her cheeks. She's serene and elegant in her long white bathrobe.

"Yeah, yeah," Matthew says, pulling back.

"Go to sleep. You have school tomorrow," she says.

"Just a little longer."

The letter cuts against Matthew's middle under his pajamas. He surveys the roof. Candlelit encampments of his neighbors dot the lemon-scented darkness. Two old women have set up a small card table; they look like gypsies telling each other's fortune. The man from downstairs who bangs up on the pipes is snoring thickly in a far corner. Old people, he thinks, all of them old, like Gramma was, like the building is. Was that why his mother used to joke that they'd carry her out of here in a box? His eyes jump to his mother. Her eyes have closed. She lies still and white in the light of the candle. He panics for a moment until he sees her chest move. She looks softer, nicer than when she's awake, but her upper lip still curls no matter what, as though she's just about to say something smart-assed.

The inside of the air shaft glows with light from a top-floor window. He edges toward it, his belly puffed out to keep the letter from falling. He waits until he's on the far side. His mother sleeps. He extracts the paper, dips it into the light.

> *Hey, Jojo. I hope you not going to rip this up when you see it come from me. When I call up you dont give me no chance to explain. You know I got a temper. Sometime I lose it. Sometime you say things and I get so mad*

The letter looks as though it had taken a long time to write. Matthew imagines Sal sitting down, staring at the chilly white paper, afraid to ruin it with his pen. Matthew races through the rest of it, fearing that any second Marjorie'll sneak up behind him and pull the letter away as she grabbed the receiver when Sal called. From somewhere he hears the siren of a fire engine. On nights like these something in the city was always going up in flames. From the air shaft comes the sound of arguing. A door slams. He prays for the light to stay on.

> *I love you, I love Matito too*

Matthew hears Sal speaking, accent thickening his speech, as though each word carried its Spanish translation along. Matthew stares at the words until they look upside down and backwards. A hot column of shame works up his throat. He's explained to himself a thousand times why he disobeyed Sal and told his secret to his mother: Sal was going to tell her anyway. Matthew thought the sooner she knew the sooner they would get married. He figured, if she heard it from him instead of Sal, it might not be that bad. It's no use; the heat in his throat remains and sends up a sickly aftertaste of the prune spaghetti sauce.

The sound of the siren shifts as a breeze juggles it first closer, then farther away. The man who was snoring sits up in his bed and peers over the edge of the roof. The siren heads uptown.

I want to come back Jojo

The ladies have stopped playing cards and have gone to the edge of the roof. Matthew thinks he can smell smoke. Fire engines seem to be coming from all directions, then pulling together up Tenth Avenue.

Mr. Sloane's house, the piano . . .

Matthew runs to join his neighbors at the edge. The letter falls into the air shaft with playful swipes. Matthew lunges over to get it.

"Matty!"

He feels himself hooked around his chest and pulled backwards. Marjorie clutches him, warm and pulsing and smelling of soap.

"My baby," she says.

Matthew sinks into her embrace. The sirens grow louder until they are the distorted melody of a piano being eaten by flame.

2

"Class 5–1, stop here!" Miss Macarof holds up her hand. The double lines buckle to a halt in a chain reaction up the stairs. Kids tumble forward through the dimly lit stairwell. Two girls giggle as their schoolbooks fall from their hands and cascade over the shoulders of the girl in front of them. The boys amplify each push into a shove. Matthew grabs onto the bannister to keep from ramming into the next kid.

Shit, he thinks. Just the thing to end the most boring week of his life. It's hot. All day, the street noise through the school's open windows has carried his attention outside. The lingering smell of the freshly painted walls has given him headaches. He's thought of Birdland, of Asa. He's waited a week for Friday. Then it comes, and he's waited the whole day for school to be over. Finally the bell rings, they march to the stairway, Matthew's about to start counting the 104 steps to the ground floor, and then this. He lowers himself onto the metal step, into a forest of knee socks and pants, and throws his books onto his lap.

A toe digs into his back. "Quit it," he says. His voice flings into the chasm of silence like a party streamer and gets answered by chorus of falsetto imitations. From the corner of his eye Matthew sees Gary Lisnack grinning like the idiot he is. Matthew knows that the moment he tells Gary to keep his stupid foot to himself Gary'll just say, "Who me?" Matthew doesn't move. A moment later he gets the toe again.

"Hey, quit that—"

The pierce of whistle cuts him short. Everyone's quiet, thinking the same thing: that was no teacher's whistle. Muffled sounds of chaos begin to filter up from the lower floors. Someone says, "It's a fight!" Dispatches from the front quickly follow: The new kid, the little one. Socked in the face. He's crying. Bleeding. Teacher didn't do nothing!

Matthew knows he's heard that whistle before. He reaches for his books as if in a trance, and slowly, as if preparing himself for what's to follow, he rises. Then he flies down the stairs.

"Hey, look what Matthew's doing," shouts Gary Lisnack.

Matthew pushes through the clusters of kids, using his books to clear a path. Miss Macarof steps aside in terror, then yells, waving the Demerit Book at him. Matthew hardly hears her above the echo of the whistle. Asa's face swims before him like a photograph coming to life in developer's bath. Matthew plunges past class after class until he's on the ground floor. A confusion of kids and teachers trample the looseleaf pages littering the floor. Matthew spots a cluster of people in a corner. He pushes through; Asa lies stretched out on the floor, his eyes half-closed, his head resting on his briefcase, blood . . .

"Asa!"

Strong hands pull him away. "That way out," a man teacher says, motioning toward the exit.

"He's my friend!"

"Out!"

A moment later two men in white uniforms appear. They load

Asa onto a stretcher. Matthew catches a final glimpse of him, small and jiggly, as they carry him out of the building.

"Justin swiped some money from him," a sixth grader explains to Matthew when he asks. "Then the little guy tried to get it back." Wonder mixes with derision in his voice. "And just for a quarter."

"School's over." The man teacher comes over to them. "Everybody leave the building."

Matthew thinks fast. "I'm getting his stuff," he says, picking up Asa's pencil case. A quarter, he thinks. Enough for a cheeseburger with hotdog relish at Meyer's Luncheonette, the forbidden treat that Asa ate every Friday after school. Asa would emerge from the school building, proudly displaying to Matthew the coin he'd use to defy his parents. Meyer's was just far enough from his house so that he could finish the cheeseburger before he got home. Matthew picks up the empty briefcase. Asa's inscribed his name and address in pen on the rough leather inside.

He'd dropped the quarter, Matthew thinks. He imagines the hollow clink on the steps and Justin grabbing. Asa hadn't met Justin yet. Maybe if he had, he wouldn't have messed with him, a chubby boy angry at getting left back. But Matthew knew that wouldn't have stopped Asa if he thought he was right. He was willing to endure his father's beating to prove his own innocence, wasn't he?

Matthew remembers Asa's description of his teacher, a young woman, her first time teaching. Asa said she didn't know what she was doing. "She wears a hundred bracelets that make a racket the whole day," he said. "They'd never let someone like her teach at the Jewish school. They didn't let any women teach. When I told her I wanted to be an ornithologist when I grew up, she thought I meant an eye doctor."

He'd blown the whistle to call attention to the theft, but when the teacher looked up Justin slipped back up the stairs out of sight, the sixth grader explained. Asa told her where Justin was, and she ordered Justin down. When he didn't come, Asa blew his whistle again. The teacher forgot about Justin and told Asa to stop. Justin made a run for it; Asa stuck out his foot and tripped him. Justin pulled himself up, enraged, threw Asa a punch that sent his head crashing into the wall. He tore away Asa's briefcase and threw everything out and fled.

Matthew hears those bracelets rattling as he assembles Asa's things: textbooks neatly covered with brown paper cut from a bag, lying open to the dirty floor; loose leaf pages lettered with the same meticulous hand as the memo pads, now torn and blackened with footprints. He leaves the school and walks to Asa's house. He knocks on the door, almost hoping no one will answer it, neither Asa's father nor his mother, who bakes him the dry poppyseed cookies Asa used to bring along to Birdland. He looks at the door, the same metal painted to look like wood as the others on the floor. He imagines Asa standing before it, knowing the beating that awaits him inside.

Matthew puts the briefcase by the door and leaves.

*

That evening Nathan Schandau, Asa's father, sits alone in the living room. The house is quiet, except for Asa's crying. He cries less often now than when they first brought him home from the Roosevelt Hospital emergency room. Each time, Mrs. Schandau soothes him with a kiss and wrings out a fresh compress for his head. Then, for a while, Asa lies in his bed, quiet. But the silence that follows brings Mr. Schandau no peace, it rings and grows taut, as if pulled by the next outburst to come. It seems the skies will never darken, the day will push into night, as it had when God commanded the sun to stand still over Joshua and the Gibeonites. Before Mr. Schandau, a violin rests on a chair. He yearns to rosin the bow lithe and glossy, to press the fragile wood shell to his chin and play. But he is forbidden to disturb the sanctity of Sabbath with any music other than that of the human voice.

Asa cries out.

His father bolts from his chair, then he remembers. Whenever he's gone to his son's bedside, Asa has screamed for him to leave.

He's begged for Asa to relent, but the boy's eyes have only widened beneath the ridge of bandage around his head any time Mr. Schandau's lingered in the doorway. He walks only as far as the kitchen, where the Sabbath candles flicker and leave a cold gleam on the rims of the three unused dinner plates around them. He waits for Asa's cry to subside, for the sound of his wife plunging the cloth into the basin of ice water; then he returns to the living room and takes his seat before the violin once again. His hands clamp together, needing something to do.

The proscription against making music was part of the commandment against working, he reflects. But how much work did it take to lift a violin and bow? No more than it took to draw a pencil or a brush against a sheet of paper or to knit. They were all prohibited. It wasn't the actual physical labor that came into question, then, but creation itself, the bringing into being of what wasn't there before. It was as if God didn't want any human creation drawing attention away from His, which the Sabbath was there to sanctify. Belief required a deference of the human will to the Divine. The Most Holy, Blessed be He, had thought out 613 different ways of deference, the 613 commandments. And because Nathan Schandau believed, he was willing to defer. Still, the commandment not to work on the Sabbath was the most difficult. It didn't seem fair. One could read, one could pray; one was permitted to work with one's mind, it seemed, but not with one's hands. The world was divided into those who did one kind of work better than the other. Why should one be given preference?

He knew to which group he belonged. It had taken him a long time to accept it, but he had. His hands. They were among the few things he understood and liked about himself. They'd always belonged to a freer dominion than the rest of him, outlying provinces able to escape a harsh capital. As a child fanning his fingers, he'd been mystified by the smooth working of their muscles and tendons, in motion like a factory behind the window of his skin. He was poor in sports and only average in school, but his hands performed small wonders for him alone with scissors and glue and balsa wood. He'd even taught them to knit.

When he came of age his father brought him tefillin to put on. At first he'd resisted. The stiff black straps felt unnatural wrapped around his fingers and the sight of his hands so bound was frightening. When he was first brought to the synagogue to join the minyan, his head went dull from the long Sabbath service. He understood the prayers, but they seemed to be the language of strangers. He glanced at his finger holding down the thin page of the siddur and imagined it lost and helpless in the maze of Hebrew script around it. Then he was filled with a longing for which he had no name. But in time he learned the prayers so well he hardly even had to look in the siddur, and the straps of his tefillin grew soft, oiled with his own sweat. He no longer resisted either.

The progress of Nathan Schandau's hands meant more to him than the changing landscape of his face or body; their grace and innocence seemed to mirror what was hidden and floundering in his soul. As they lengthened and lost their childish stubbiness, they developed character and an identity all their own, even while he himself retreated further into his own melancholy. With them he filled the pages of journals and underlined the passages of novels whose style he hoped one day to master. They served him uncritically, always faithful, never questioning, never mocking him, as Nathan's father had, when he asked if Nathan really hoped to make a living "scribbling poetry on the backs of envelopes."

Nathan might have rebelled. But when it came time to go to City College, he didn't sign up for literature courses or violin instruction but went for a business degree instead. One night, returning home from school on the train, the car screeched to a stop and the lights went out. Nathan looked down. His hands were bathed in the yellow glow of a solitary bulb on the tunnel wall. They rested on his accounting books as if on an altar, looking like a woodcut, their veins thrown into relief and the valleys between them etched in darkness. He held them up. They were handsome and full of promise. Then the lights came on and tore away their beauty. The other passengers caught him with his palms before his face, posed like a piece of sentimental sculpture. The train jolted forward, throwing his books from his lap. He scrambled after them and, crouched on the dirty floor, he realized that his father's choices had become his own. He wouldn't have wanted to change them anymore, even if he could.

When Nathan married, his hands explored the milky flesh of his wife's body. He was more curious than desirous; his curiosity was soon sated. He lost interest even while his hands pursued, like blind moles tunneling irrationally toward what they needed. He marvelled at their industry, how they coaxed the rest of him into performing, like matchmakers, bringing him and his wife together over and over again.

Soon Asa was born. He was a delicate, pale infant who always seemed on the verge of slipping into lifelessness. As if to assert his will to live, he began to talk sooner than Nathan had dreamed possible. He began reading soon after. The supper table rang with the daily discoveries Asa culled from the encyclopedia: about insects, trains, and sewer pipes, how the map of New-foundland looked like a rabbit and Georgia, like a fat man's belly. He spoke in a high-pitched, tensile voice with an exacting slowness, molding his lips to fit the vocabulary of science and history. His speech shone with the joy of knowing. And when he wasn't lecturing, he asked questions. Grace Schandau chuckled at her own ignorance but her husband grumbled at every answer he couldn't provide. Asa was testing him, he was sure.

"Eat now, talk later," she would chide little Asa, sensing Nathan's growing impatience.

Asa would fall silent for a mouthful or two but a new explosion of talk was never long in coming. Only the warning rap of his father's hand against the table quieted him.

Rather than rejoicing in his remarkable son, Nathan Schandau felt plagued by him. Every date or name Asa memorized and recited reminded Nathan of the empty pages left in his journal after he'd stopped writing, of the novels he'd pushed aside, of the high school melancholy that might have led to fruitful solitude but had simply hardened into bitterness. Hadn't he been as full of wonder at the world as Asa was until it was crushed out of him? Hadn't he dreamed his way through books until his own father had stopped paying for his violin lessons?

In the evening when Nathan Schandau played his violin, the single joy his hands still brought him, his wife perched Asa on the sofa after his bath, looking fresh as a blossom in his pajamas. His round eyes never left his father for a moment. He followed the motion of the bow meeting the strings until he fell into a sleep from which he hardly woke as his mother carried him to bed. Yet the boy's attention frightened Mr. Schandau instead of flattering him. He imagined Asa silently teaching himself to play the instrument, preparing for the day when he'd interrupt and ask to be given the violin. He'd take it in his hands and begin playing it effortlessly. Mr Schandau thought of forbidding Asa to listen, then a sickening feeling struck him: he was jealous of his son, of a child not even old enough to enter school. He felt like Saul, jealous of the vigorous David, who had wanted nothing other than to serve him and love him.

Following the commandment, he began teaching Asa Hebrew. The Passover came when Asa was ready to recite the Four Questions. Just before the seder was to begin Mr. Schandau looked around the table. The kitchen was fragrant and gleaming. The tablecloth was old, but linen. In the middle stood the silver cup of Elijah, shining on its matching dish, his grandfather's. Asa sat beside his mother, wearing a grown-up's yarmulka that covered his ears. Mr. Schandau felt a rare lightness in his chest to see it all, but the pleasure proved fragile and easily shattered by a screech of brakes from the street, reminding him of the kind of neighborhood they lived in. He began to notice the spots where his wife had scrubbed the walls so hard that the paint had rubbed off. She and Asa seemed huddled together, far away from him.

"*Ma nishtana halayla hazeh mekol halaylos?*" Asa began in a ringing voice. "Why is this night different from all other nights?"

His mother watched him in a trance.

"*Vayawreynu osanu ha-mitzrayim.* And the Egyptians ill-treated us and oppressed us," recited his father. "*Kameh shene'emur—*"

"*Shene'emar,*" corrected Asa.

He looked up. His son faced him, eyes wide, finger poised at the mispronounced word. There was a windy silence, as though a precipice had opened between them. *"Shene'emar,"* the father repeated, lowering his eyes to the book.

The service proceeded. Asa corrected him once more, his terse voice snapping at the heels of the mistake, sharpened by the seven-year-old's joy in being right. The wine in the silver cup of Elijah trembled slightly. Once again Mr. Schandau reread the word.

"Vayomru hachartumim el par'oh, etzbah elohim hi," he continued. "The soothsayers said to Pharoah the plague is the finger of God. *V'al hayam mah hu omer, vayarey yisroel —"*

"Vayar yisroel. The last vowel is silent."

"Asa," said his mother, putting her arm around him.

"He said it wrong. If he says it wrong then God won't understand him."

"He'll understand, he'll understand. Now be quiet."

"It's all right," said Mr. Schandau in a voice damming impatience. "The boy knows."

His voice began to quaver, stumbling more and more over the ancient text. Asa excised each mistake neatly. The seder dragged on. Each line seemed like a string pulled back and ready to snap. Anxiously Mrs. Schandau cleared away the various ceremonial foods: the boiled potatoes and saltwater, representing the slave rations of the Hebrews under Pharoah and the tears they shed; the chopped nuts and apples, representing the mortar they used to build his pyramids; the horseradish, symbolizing the harshness of their plight. Each brought them closer to the meal itself, which she hoped might dispel the tension. But there were still pages to get through.

"Had God from Egypt led us out and brought not all their hordes to rout . . ."

Asa and his mother answered: *Dayyenu,* it would have been sufficient.

"Had He brought judgment on their hordes but had not unmasked their priesthood's frauds . . ."

"Dayyenu."

He raced through line after line of the song that enumerated God's generosity to the Children of Israel. Slow down, his wife thought. Slow down or else you'll make another mistake.

Halfway through Asa shouted, "Now I want to read some."

"No," his father said.

"Why not?"

"I'm hungry and I want to finish."

"Let me read!"

"Asa," warned his mother.

"Why can he read and not me?"

"Had He but made the seawall stand but had not led us onto dry land . . ."

"I can read it better than he can!"

"Had He their oldest sons laid low and not made Egypt gifts bestow . . ."

Asa pounded his hand on the table. Elijah's wine rippled like a small sea threatened by a storm. "I want to read some too!"

"It's getting late, Asa. We're all hungry."

"Elu nosan lanu es hatorah v'lo hichnimanu —"

"Hichnisanu," screamed Asa. "It's wrong —"

"L'eretz yisroel —"

"Say it right." He turned to his mother. "Tell him he has to say it right before he can go on."

"Be quiet," she pleaded.

Asa blurted out the passage. *"Elu hichnisanu l'eretz yisroel v'chol banah lanu es beit hab'chirah —"*

"Dayyenu!" shrieked his father. His voice broke as his hand struck Asa's face. The yarmulka slipped from Asa's skull. He toppled back in his chair. The table shook, throwing over the cup of wine in the center. A bright sea of crimson spread across the white linen. Mr. Schandau's hand pulled back, as though it had been pitched into fire. Mrs. Schandau carried Asa screaming away from the table.

That night, for the first of many times, she brought her husband his linen and told him to make his bed on the sofa, since she would not sleep in the same bed with him. He struggled to pull the sheets smooth with one hand; the other still burned.

★

Nathan Schandau can no longer bear the silence between his son's screams. He rises from his chair, and reaches for the violin. His fingertips graze the wood's gentle curves but when his hand tries to grip, the familiar sickle-shaped pain cripples his joints and leaves his hand useless. It has happened time and time again since that Passover night. A mocking grin comes to his face. God has punished him with a wisdom befitting His divinity, in the most appropriate way, Nathan Schandau thinks; through his hands. It is a punishment without mercy, without end. Anytime Asa has rebelled, Mr. Schandau has struck him, forcing Asa to acknowledge the power of his hands. But Asa's skin returns the pain amply and leaves Mr. Schandau's hand senseless. What is more, he is sure Asa understands the diabolical cycle God has chained his father to: Asa taunts him with pedantry, defies him, and mocks him, inviting the wrath of the hands, knowing they will in turn be punished. Mr. Schandau has even seen Asa watching him when he sits in the living room afterward, weeping and bent over, his hands pressed into a stinging clump in his lap.

The pile of linen his wife has set out for him glows faintly in the dark. A trace of daylight leaves everything in the living room looking like stone. He rises and spreads a sheet over the sofa as he has done every night for the past two years. The last trace of daylight leaves the sky, huddling the violin into darkness.

3

Matthew shivers in the cavelike chill below the stairs of his building. He got up early, not even eating or changing out of his pajamas, to retrieve Sal's letter. But he can't pry open the little air shaft window behind the stairs. His bare knees are sore from

kneeling on them, his fingers blackened with soot. He tries once
more. It's the kind that swings in at the middle. He positions his
blackened fingers on the window frame, lifts himself up for extra
leverage, counts to three, then pushes. No way. The window
doesn't budge, there's too much crud. He falls forward, his face
presses against the wire-veined opaque glass.

"Shit," he mumbles.

The front door to the building opens. Someone's coming. He
squeezes himself into the tight angle the stairs make with the
floor, hears the plod of feet and the creak of a shopping cart
trailing behind. Then he hears nothing.

Cmon, he thinks, get moving.

The crank of mailbox keys, the whistle of a hinge, a slam. The
cart starts its ascent, crashing upward step by step, a heavy bar of
breath in between. Soon it's directly overhead. It makes Matthew
think of the guy carrying the sun in a chariot across the sky.
Apollo carrying the sun back from the A & P, got to get it home
before it burns up the bag. He laughs. The shopping cart freezes
in midair. Matthew holds his breath.

Justin's knife, he thinks. To dig the crud away. He has to wait
until the coast is clear. Cmon.

As soon as he can, he springs up the stairs to the apartment,
gets there out of breath and sweating, slips into his room.

"If that's the March of Dimes we already gave."

Matthew freezes.

"Matthew, is that you?"

"Maybe," he says, continuing into the bathroom to wash the
incriminating dirt from his hands. When he walks into the
kitchen he finds her at the table, writing on a yellow legal pad, a
pile of sheet music before her. She's fresh and alert, wearing a
pair of Levis, sneakers, and an oversized football jersey with "23"
on the back. (He'd once asked her what the number stood for.
"My waistline, what else?")

"What are you doing up so early?" He can barely hide the
irritation in his voice.

"First you can tell me what you were doing under the
staircase."

"Who said I was there?"

"Mrs. Jessup from down the hall."

"Nosybody." So that's who it was.

"Well, what were you doing there, throwing a pajama party?"

"I was looking for something."

She gives him a you-can-do-better-than-that look. "Well, did you find what you were looking for?"

"Sorta."

"Anyway, I got some good news. Guess what your mother is going to start doing again?" She holds up the sheet music for "Blue Moon."

"You're going to be a singer again?"

"You got it."

"You said you were too old for that."

"That's what your grandmother said. Once upon a time I believed her. Not anymore."

"You're really going to do it?"

"Why not? The way I figure it, the only difference between me and Patti Page is that when she sings she gets paid for it and when I do that creep from downstairs bangs on the pipes. I already got something up my sleeve."

What if someone throws garbage on top of it? he thinks. It'll be lost—and what's worse, then she'll know he took it.

"I spoke to a piano player, a guy I used to know in the old days. He told me about this club that has a talent night where people come and sing, but I said to him, 'Listen, I've already been through that. I'm trying to making a comeback, for godsakes.' But he says it's a nice place, not just a pass-the-hat operation and besides, he knows the guys that run the place. He even said he'd help me get my voice back in shape. How's that sound?"

"You're not going to quit your job, are you?"

"You think I want to stay a lousy secretary for the rest of my life? Jesus, you sound like my mother. What's the matter, you worried that your mom isn't good enough to make a living as a singer and support you in the style to which you have become accustomed? Listen to this." She goes into the living room, shuffles through a pile of forty-fives, sticks one on the changer, and returns. A repeating scratch comes through the speaker, then Doris Day singing *"Que Sera."* Marjorie sings loud enough to mask the voice on the record. She works her way around the kitchen table, holds the pencil as though it were a mike. She looks directly at Matthew; he squirms until she looks somewhere else. Her arms rise up at the end. She tries to hold the last note but her voice breaks and Doris finishes the song alone.

"Well, what do you think? It's not so bad, is it?"

"When are you going to do it then?"

She glances at the pad. "A week and a half from now. It's not much time but I can swing it. But that means you have to be nice to me and help around the house and not give your mother a hard time so she won't be nervous."

"I don't give you a hard time."

"You do when you carry on about Sal."

★

Matthew works the knife into the grime around the window frame. A line of dirt collects on the tile floor. When he's all the way around he tries the window again. There's a hesitant creak, then suddenly a full scraping whoosh as the bottom part swings up. Warm air seeps in. There's barely enough space in the lower part for him to crawl through. Why do they put in such small windows anyway, he thinks.

He tumbles into the air shaft. The air is still, dense with junglelike heat. His sneakers sink into the damp topsoil. A bag of fresh garbage spills over in the corner. Bright green shoots loop out of a mound of potatoes. The letter isn't anywhere. With his foot he pushes at the bag of garbage. Its contents spill out like a horn of plenty. A thousand shiny cockroaches break away and burrow invisibly. A kick unearths bottles full of rust-colored water and soggy magazines as soft as foam. Still no letter. He crouches down to begin digging.

The muck feels like a layer of meatloaf as he plunges his hand into it. Close to the ground, the smell becomes sharp and foul. Soon he's sweating and exhausted from the heat. He touches something hard. Glass? His fingers pull away, then inch back, curious. He unearths something encased in a muddy mound of coffee grounds: the skeleton of a tiny bird. He blows away as much of the grounds as he can, transfers it to his clean hand to get a better look at it. The bones are the color of old teeth, the beak is frozen open, and the ribs are like the handles of tiny coffee cups. It resembles a little, crushed machine. He holds it up against the sky. The bones shape the blue like the leading of a stained glass window.

He searches for something to wrap it up in. Strange the way something that belongs in the air winds up stuck deep down, he thinks. If Sal were here he'd probably say something like "The universe has no up and down, only what is." Matthew finds a paper cup, slips the bird in it, and sets it aside. His hands are slimy with guck. He's dug through every inch of the ground until it looks as though it's been ploughed.

Someone is looking down at him, no more than a silhouette against the bright sunlight.

"Why don't you go play in the playground?" says Mrs. Jessup.

"It's a free country. I can play where I like."

She disappears. A moment later she empties a bucketful of water on him.

"Hey—" He swallows his yell, realizing that his mother could stick her head out of the window any second. He grabs a piece of cardboard to hold over his head, in case she comes back, and continues looking. Then he notices it, right underneath.

Hey Jojo. I hope you not going to rip this up when you see . . .

He stuffs it into his pocket and scootches back through the window, taking the paper cup with him.

Out on the street, the sun broils directly overhead, forcing Matthew to search for shade. He sits down on the stoop of the building across the way in case his mother or creepy Mrs. Jessup should walk out. First he takes out the bird and sets it on the ground. Then he unfolds the letter.

Hey, Jojo. I hope you not going to rip this up when you see it come from me.

A shadow falls over the page.

"Whatcha reading?" says Justin.

Matthew sticks the letter in his pocket. "Nothing."

Justin looks puzzled. "I saw you reading something."

"Now you see it, now you don't."

"What's the matter with you?"

"Don't play dumb. You punched out my best friend. Get lost."

"Your best . . ." Justin shakes his head. "He ain't your best friend!"

"Why'd you do it?"

"He tripped me."

"You stole his money."

"How do you know?"

"You creep!"

Justin sees Matthew's tight-lipped frown, shakes his head. He spies the skeleton, springs down and grabs it.

"Gimme that!"

"Show me what you was reading first."

Matthew thinks for a moment and says, "If you touch anything that's dead you get poisoned." He watches the sneer on Justin's face slide away.

"Take your lousy skeleton," Justin says, throwing it onto the ground where it clatters to pieces on the pavement.

"You sonafabitch!"

"There they are!"

A knot of kids run toward them up the block. Before Matthew and Justin can escape, they're surrounded.

A tall boy pulls Justin by the collar of his T-shirt, keeps him in place by stepping on his toes. "I thought you said he wasn't your friend no more."

"He's the one who got his Spic friend to fight for him because he was too chicken to fight his own battles, right, Kevin?" says a little kid.

"I don't need you to tell me that," Kevin answers him with a sneer. He turns to Justin. "You know what you are, Fat Boy? A traitor. And you know what us Bloodhounds do to traitors?"

Matthew makes a run for it. A broad-shouldered kid yanks him back. "We ain't finished with you yet."

Matthew shoots his elbow into the kid's soft stomach. He gasps, and Matthew pushes free.

"First one who gets too close gets this," he says, snapping out the knife.

"Where'd you get that?" Kevin says. He turns to Justin, tightening the hold on him. "You gave it to him, didn't you?"

"Yes," Justin wheezes.

"Get off him," Matthew says, directing with the edge of the knife.

Kevin flings Justin away. Justin scampers behind Matthew.

"You don't scare me," Kevin says. "I can get all the blades I want."

"No he can't, Matty," says Justin. "He told me it's the only one he got so I'd better not lose it."

The little kid sneaks around the back, kicks the knife from Matthew's hand. It slides under a car. Justin snatches it up and runs.

"You're dead, man!" Kevin shouts, bounding after Justin, taking the rest of the kids along with him.

Matthew's left alone on the empty street. On any other Saturday he'd be off with Asa on the way to Birdland by now, but he knows Asa can't leave the house. He thinks about going over to see how he is but remembers that Saturday's some kind of a special Jewish day. He sees the skeleton, kicks it down the street.

He decides to visit Mr. Sloane and the others at the house. He feels a little bad because he hasn't visited the house since he's been back in the city. He goes the long way, down to the river, along Twelfth Avenue.

There's a faint breeze along Twelfth Avenue but he loses it as he turns up Fifty-second Street. When the house comes into view he staggers to a halt. The house stands, stripped and brittle-looking. The windows on the upper story are framed in black, like the eyes of gypsies. The walls gleam with shiny black carbon scales. Matthew blinks from the glare, the sweat stings around his eyes. It is almost as if the sun itself had set the house aflame. He pushes through what's left of the gate and stamps through the rubble of the yard, tumbling and tripping on the way, hardly knowing where he goes. He peers in through the ragged mouth burned into the wall. Inside is a confusion of charred wood and fallen plaster, lit by sunlight through the walls. From out behind the back of the house he hears men talking.

"Mr. Sloane!" he cries, running toward them

PART TWO

The Winter Before

Four

1

Several days after Gramma died it snowed so hard they closed the schools. Marjorie had gotten Matthew up at the usual time. He'd just begun pulling on the long underwear he hated when she came back into his room. She was still in her nightgown, but her face was already made up for work, looking to Matthew like the Simmons Beautyrest lady.

"You can climb right back into the sack, Kiddo." she said. "I just heard it on the radio. But your old mother has to go in."

Matthew ran to the living room window to see the neighborhood iced like gingerbread. He ate in a hurry and went outside. The snow was still airy and fresh but for the thin trail people had blazed on their way to the subway. A yellow blur of sun burned coldly through the thick clouds. The snow left the neighborhood snug as a village whose streets were lined with parked cars turned into igloos. The front of his own house looked pretty, trimmed with white. He walked in the middle of the empty street, hearing nothing but the crunch of his boots. The dense, cold air stuck inside his nostrils as he breathed and chilled his lips.

At the viaduct he stopped and leaned over. The wind churned the snow to a dry powder and howled as though a ghostly locomotive were passing. Wind slipped under his jacket and into his pockets as a warning, in case he should lean too far over and trespass the wilderness below. Gramma went to a place like that, he thought. He imagined her being suspended from a crane like a wrecking ball, lowered slowly. They had brought her all the way to Queens to bury her. They could have done it down there, he thought. The trackbed was wide enough, she'd have fit into it easy, there was plenty of snow to cover her.

Marjorie had asked Matthew if he wanted to go to the burial. He thought of the flowery stain of blood Gramma often coughed up into the kitchen sink and imagined the snow in the cemetery speckled with it. He shook his head no.

★

"Eggs, scouring powder, mayonnaise . . ." Gramma mumbled, bending over in her chair to tie her shoes. Her dress shifted with a hiss and its checked pattern was pulled smooth across her broad back. "Eggs, scouring powder, mayonnaise, tinfoil, tomato sauce . . . what else do we need?" Her thick fingers worked the laces of her boxlike shoes.

"Bacon," said Matthew, without looking up from the page of homework before him.

She fit her foot into the second shoe and began again. "Eggs, scouring powder, mayonnaise, bacon . . ."

"Why don't you just write everything down?"

"If you're so worried about the shopping, you should get off your duff and go to the store yourself."

"Mom says I have to finish my schoolwork." He grinned.

"Then do it and leave me in peace."

She pulled on her frizzy, tentlike coat with its three large buttons and trundled the shopping cart out the door, repeating to herself what she had to buy. The cart went rattling down the hall and against the stair rail to the syncopation of her coughing. He heard her several flights down, like the man on the street who played a drum rigged up with several other instruments.

There goes our Lady of the Soft-Boiled Eggs, he thought, using his own name for her, which came from what she always ate for breakfast. He had to look away when she smeared her slice of toast with the yellow slime that she cracked out of the shell. It was especially bad on Sunday mornings when she woke Matthew up early to go to mass with her. On one side of the table

Gramma sat sucking at her eggs. Heaped on the other side were his mother's things from the night before — pocketbook, perfume-scented scarf, empty cigarette package, lipstick. Anytime Matthew complained about having to go to church, Gramma threw a scornful glance at that collection, as if no other explanation were necessary. The real reason, Matthew knew, was that she needed help getting back into her seat after kneeling.

He'd sit on the hard pew swallowing yawns, his itchy, wool suit pants sandpapering by turns his behind and his knees. Everything in the church seemed too large, built for a race of giants. The cross with Jesus on it in the front was a huge version of what his mother wore around her neck. The windows were too high up for anyone to open or look out of and the colored glass tinged the sparse winter light with gloom. The drafty church reminded him of a Pennsylvania Station that was strangely quiet, as though something terrible had just happened. During the warm weather it was comfortably cool, but winters his nose and ears were capped with chill. The drone of the prayers saddened him except when the priest's voice came over the PA system, reminding him of the Miss America guy. Matthew liked one other thing: the flickering garden of candles. After the service, Gramma always lit two: one for her husband and one for John F. Kennedy.

Churchgoing transformed her. The dark dresses she wore lessened her bulk and lent her dignity, white gloves hid the gristly veins of her hands, pearl clip-ons covered the unsightly hang of her earlobes, and she gave her doughy face shape by applying powder to it. When the journey to the church was completed, when she had settled into her seat and caught her breath, Gramma's face softened, grateful to be there at last. (She used to say to Matthew that the six blocks they walked to the church stood for the six days of the week in between masses.) She'd sit with her black missal held open, her eyes fixed to the pages filled with sturdy print, her thumbs pressed to the margins like curtain stays, as though the book were a stage and each prayer a play that enthralled her.

When the time came, she gave Matthew one hand while she grasped the pew in front of her with the other. As he lowered her, she shuddered and hardly dared to breathe. A horrible putty of sweat cemented his palm to hers. He imagined himself clutched by someone drowning who might pull him down. Finally, her knees came to rest. Getting her back up meant plunging into that frightening sea with her once more.

One Sunday morning in the middle of the winter when there wasn't any heat, Matthew curled himself up in his blanket and refused to get out of bed.

"You'd better, unless you want me telling your mother what you do with yourself each night," she said, laughing wickedly. "Don't think I don't know."

He peeled away the covers and stepped into the icy room. If you don't watch out I'll drop you one of these days, he wanted with all his heart to say. But he didn't.

*

"I heard what you two were up to last night, Marjorie," said Gramma, circling the table with the pot of soup she was ladling out.

"Oh? Well then, why don't you tell us?" Marjorie said, opening a bottle of beer. "I know you're dying to. I'm sure Matthew would love to hear about it."

"I ought to slap your face for that."

"Why did you bring up the subject then?"

"Do you expect me not to say anything?"

"Spit it out, goddammit!" Marjorie glared at her mother. Gramma's lips pulled into her mouth as she emptied a ladleful of soup into Matthew's bowl.

He never knew how he was supposed to behave during these eruptions—whether to pretend he heard nothing or to act as though he understood, since it seemed the two of them were performing for his benefit.

Marjorie broke the silence. "Don't you think I'm a little old for this routine?"

"Not as long as you're under my roof."

"Your name might still be on the lease, Mother dear, but who pays the rent? And besides, do you expect me to play nun, like you?" She winked at Matthew.

Gramma shook her head. "Haven't you learned your lesson by now, Marjorie?" She nodded in Matthew's direction. "Maybe this time you'll have twins."

"I'll name them both after you, I promise. Let's see some of that soup. I'm hungry. I worked seven hours today. I'm not in the mood for a sermon."

"If you have to carry on, at least have the decency not to do it here."

"What's all this about carrying on? I bring a man home, drink a beer or two with him —"

"In your bedroom."

"Where then? Matty sleeps in the living room, and the kitchen has no door."

"I heard every word the two of you said."

"You heard, Mother, because you listened. You eavesdropped."

Marjorie's eyes darted over to Matthew. He could tell she was embarrassed. It had to do with being married or not; more, he didn't understand.

Later Marjorie called Matthew into her room. The room was thick with clutter. It felt like being in the tent of an Arabian princess. Clothes cascaded out of drawers, were draped over the back of a chair, and bulged out of her closet. The air was scented with a dozen different perfumes and cosmetics that crowded the mirrored top of her dresser. He jumped onto her unmade bed.

"It's about time you knew a couple of things," she announced, pulling out a Whitman's Sampler box from the guts of a closet shelf. She sat down beside him, rummaged through a spongy thickness of snapshots, selecting one of them, square and crinkly edged. "That's your father, Matthew."

Matthew studied it.

"You have his brown eyes, his mouth. Your nose is hers," she said, motioning toward the kitchen. "But your beautiful wavy hair, that's mine, of course."

"How come his hair has that big flip in the front?"

"It's called a pompadour. It was the style then."

"Where is he now?"

"In the city, doing good for himself. I see his name in the papers once in a while, playing with some band."

"What's his name?"

She told him. "But everybody called him TJ because he always drank Tom and Jerrys."

"Do you miss him?"

"I miss having a husband." She squeezed Matthew's hand. "But TJ really wasn't my husband."

"You mean he's not my father?"

"Oh, he's your father, all right. He's just not my husband." Matthew looked puzzled. "We weren't married. That's what your grandmother was making a stink over tonight." She paused. "Do you know what I'm getting at?"

He shook his head no.

She sighed. "At times like this I wish I was your father instead of your mother." She looked at him, thought for a moment, and shook her head. "No. I don't have the strength to get into that whole thing tonight. Anyway, it can wait. Remind me about it the next time Gramma starts in with her Whore of Babylon number."

"That guy in your bathrobe who was here last night, are you going to marry him?"

Marjorie reddened. "You been spying on your mother too? Oh hell, I don't know. You think I should?"

Matthew looked at the picture as if comparing fathers.

"If I had my way, I wouldn't get mixed up with no man," she said. "But unfortunately, it's not that simple, at least not for me."

"Gramma didn't like him," Matthew says, pointing to the picture. "She told me."

"There's a lot of things she doesn't like, much more than what she does like. That's why she goes to church so much, because there they tell you what you shouldn't like. There are a whole bunch of people just like her running around telling other people what they should do, what they shouldn't do. But no matter what, I'm still your mother, Matty, and I still love you, you understand?" She held him close. "You don't think I'm bad, do you?"

Matthew shook his head.

She began to cry. "Come and give the mother what loves you a kiss," she said, offering him a damp cheek.

"Mom," Matthew asked, "is it true that Gramma can't read?"

"Shhh!" Marjorie grinned like a schoolgirl with a choice piece of gossip. "Did I tell you that?"

"I figured it out."

"Well, don't ever mention it to her. She's very sensitive about it. TJ used to kid her about it, which is why she didn't like him. Hey, listen." From Gramma's room came a clacking of her rosary beads. "The cultured pearls," she winked. "She's praying for my soul again."

★

Gramma's coughing started getting bad as soon as the cold weather set in. Matthew returned from school each day to find her gripping the edge of the kitchen sink, her great shoulders rolled forward like a sumo wrestler's, her face plum-red from coughing up rubbery phlegm. He'd help her to the sofa. She'd ask Matthew to get the rosary beads for her. She'd sit there, exhausted and staring, until suppertime, the rosary clutched in her hand. At night another round began. The fluid in her lungs puddled; her heaving danced the bed off the floor. Her fists sent savage blows to her chest as she tried to breathe.

"Marjorie," she'd gasp.

Matthew would hear his mother running into Gramma's room. There'd be the chug of the spray, the slap of Marjorie's hands against Gramma's back, and her gurgling complaint. Then quiet. Next morning he'd find her propped up in bed, peacefully combing her hair with her prized rhinestone-trimmed comb. She pulled the silver strands from its teeth one by one, as if reckoning up what her last attack had cost her.

"How come she never has her attacks during mass?" Matthew asked his mother.

Marjorie smiled. "Because she doesn't want to mess up her dress."

The cold weather showed no sign of letting up, and they were getting snow right up until the beginning of March. Each week Gramma's cough tore deeper and deeper into her.

"The next time you're in church, stick in a prayer for your poor Gramma," Marjorie said to Matthew just before tucking him in one night.

"What should I say?"

She thought for a moment. "Ask God to put her out of her misery."

One night, when Matthew woke up to the coughing, his mother got up but she didn't go into Gramma's room. He heard her dialing a number in the hall.

"Marjorie," Gramma groaned, barely more than a whisper. Matthew heard his mother giving their address over the phone, then she waited in the hall. Only when Gramma was silent did she go into her room. Matthew crept in after and found his mother standing there, leaning against the door, staring at Gramma, who lay still. The ambulance men arrived in their dirty white uniforms. Marjorie bundled Gramma up and kissed her forehead. The men shifted her to a stretcher with a frightening jerk of the sheet, and moments later she was moving down the hallway. Matthew ran out after them. The hallway rang as they barked instructions back and forth. From the top of the stairs it looked as though they were maneuvering a large white sofa. It was the last he saw of her.

2

"Wake up, Justin."

He opened his eyes. His mother's pale face was framed by her hair, so dark and startling, pulled back, smooth and shiny as a helmet. She kissed his forehead: her nursing uniform left a stern reminder of bleach in his nostrils, mixed with the perfume of her hand cream. The nursing pin, its snake curled around a stick, gleamed just below her collar. He imagined that the stick must have tickled, since the snake's tongue was always curled out.

"Remember, Uncle Frank's coming tonight," she told him, returning to the kitchen. The squeak of her thick-soled nursing shoes followed her to the kitchen.

Justin climbed out of bed after her. "Why does he always have to come?"

"It's only once a month. Go wash up and eat your breakfast."

"He smells funny."

"Don't talk about him like that. He's your uncle, Justy. We're the only family he has now. Besides, you used to like him a lot."

"That was before."

She almost said, "Before what?" but stopped herself. She knew: before what happened to Ralph.

When Justin returned, his breakfast was waiting for him on the table and the shades had been pulled up, filling the room with bright winter sunlight.

"Why does Uncle Frank always squeeze me so hard?" Justin said between spoonfuls of cereal.

"It's his way of saying that he likes you."

She rose, spilled what was left of her coffee into the sink. She took a sandwich that was wrapped in tinfoil out of the refrigerator, put it into her pocketbook along with an orange, then went for her coat. Her rubbers were on; she was ready to go. "Mrs. Cleary will be up in a few minutes."

"Don't go," he whispered into the folds of the coat, too embarrassed to say it out loud.

After the door closed he looked around, wondering what to do until Mrs. Cleary came. Both their beds had already been made, his mother's, wider, his opposite it, both covered with wavy lines of short blue grass. The screen she set up between their beds at night had been put away; their house was one big room again. He liked it that way. The first time he'd been in the apartment, he'd been puzzled. He had wandered around the single large room, looking for a door that would lead to all the others. There were no ceilings high above decorated with cake icing, no spongy carpeting. Where was his room? he'd asked his mother.

"Here," she'd said.

And hers?

Her answer had been the same.

Justin crouched low, planted his palms on the floor, bent his head down. It had taken him a while to get used to doing headstands on a bare floor. He cranked himself up with a few bounces, flung his stockinged feet up into the air and began counting.

"Four, five . . ."

His legs began to sway as if they were dizzy from the height.

"Six . . ."

He strained them back the other way. It was the longest he'd kept them up this morning. He counted faster.

"Seven, eight, nine —"

He wanted to keep his legs up until eleven, which was his age. But they buckled, Justin's waist swiveled, and he tumbled down again, pleasantly dizzy. His nose pressed to the wooden floor, cold and smelling of wax. He heard Mrs. Cleary speaking on the telephone, one floor below. He flipped over and felt like a crab lolling comfortably on the bottom of the sea. It was good lying on the floor like that. The ceiling looked so fluffy and white. Mrs. Cleary said he'd catch cold that way but his mother told him that you caught cold if someone sneezed in your face. Floors couldn't sneeze, he reasoned, so Mrs. Cleary had to be wrong.

In the old apartment there was carpeting on almost all the floors. There were large doors, with knobs made of glass. Justin would lie on the carpet just outside the door to his parents' room and listen to them. Daddy spoke louder. His voice seemed to slip around what his mother said. She never sounded happy. But no matter what they said to each other, when they sat down at the table they smiled at each other and at him. But not Uncle Frank. He lived in the apartment, too. But Justin hardly saw him. His door was always closed. He didn't eat with them. He kept his room bolted shut with a hasp and a lock. Justin never knew when he was home. He'd surprise Justin by suddenly leaving his room, wearing only socks and boxer shorts, to go and forage in the refrigerator.

Justin had never seen what the inside of his uncle's room looked like. One time when the door was left open Justin snuck in. The air was humid and soiled, the floor cluttered with clothing and empty potato chip bags. The bed was unmade and the sheets grey from not being changed. He turned to leave. Frank stood in the doorway. "You come in here again I'll wring your neck, you little brat," he said. As Justin slunk out of the room Frank gave him a shove that set him sprawling down the corridor.

Then Daddy began going away all the time. He stayed away longer and longer each time. After he left his mother would go into her room, close the door, and not come out for a long time. He didn't know what she did, but sometimes he heard her crying. Sometime after that Uncle Frank began being nice to Justin. He gave Justin candy and took him for piggyback rides around the apartment. Each room was a different place. Justin's bedroom was the moon. The kitchen was a place Justin named Zimbozamba. The hall was Fifth Avenue.

Justin put his ear to the floor. Mrs. Cleary was still talking. Cleary drink a beery, he sang to himself. He walked over to the wardrobe. It stood near the door, the only piece of furniture left from the old apartment, which dwarfed the new one. Its two wooden columns flanked a pair of mirrored doors and were topped by a Greek pediment. It might have been the portal to a small palace. It rested on four wooden spheres, which were echoed in the brass door pulls.

Justin polished one of them with his shirt and watched his fat-cheeked reflection slide across it. He remembered returning from a weekend with relatives just after his father had gone away for good. He found the apartment nearly empty. Sunlight streamed in through the windows where drapes had hung. The bare wooden floors gleamed, stripped of their carpets. Uncle Frank's voice boomed through the empty rooms, directing workmen as they carried off the remaining furniture. The wardrobe stood stranded in the middle of everything.

"Uncle Frank," Justin cried, running to him. "What's going on?"

"I'm too busy right now to talk."

"Tell me what's going on!" Justin demanded.

"I'm getting rid of what we don't need anymore," he said coldly, not looking at him. Justin tried to push the wardrobe back to its original place but it didn't budge, and his shoes slid against the slippery floor.

Now he opened its doors with a key he took from his pocket. Jackets and coats spread before him, silent and patient, waiting for him like shy friends. Hats sat on a shelf above, a row of pumpernickels. Camphor needled his nostrils along with the oily aroma of cedar. He stroked the shoulders of the clothing tenderly.

"Daddy," he whispered.

He imagined himself to be in an elevator crowded with grown-up people, safe in betweeen hips and pocketbooks. He selected a blazer, pulled it out from the closet and sank his arms into its sleeves. He wrapped it about him. Its bottom hem reached the floor. The watery silk lining slid against his flannel shirt and its shoulders sat upon his, stiff as meringue. He danced around the room, the blazer rode up and down like his clumsy partner. He pulled it off, grabbed another. He spun around in it and watched it float open like a skirt around him. Then another, and another. The pile of discarded clothing grew. Then, he made a running leap into the heap and sledded across the room on it. He got up and began putting everything back. When all the clothing was in the closet again, he climbed in after and closed the door tightly.

He squatted down, resting his head between two jackets in the dark, and nestled his feet in the cool of his father's giant shoes. He closed his eyes. He began to feel long, soft breezes against his face. Soon, Justin knew, Daddy would appear. Some days it happened right away. Today it was taking longer. He clutched the sleeves of the jacket. His heart paddled with excitement but with fear as well. Was Daddy angry with him? he wondered. Was he riding in a plane, going somewhere far away, the way he used to, when he left the house carrying his big suitcase and his little suitcase? Maybe that was why he hadn't come yet: because he was too far away. Or else maybe Daddy wouldn't come at all, maybe he was . . . Justin clutched the sleeve tighter. Maybe he — no. No! He'll come. Yes, he would. The camphor began to make him feel light-headed. His eyes began to burn so he shut them tighter.

A wide band of beach filtered into view. Blue-grey water lapped its edge. The sun sent lightning-shaped bolts across the water. It was the biggest beach in the world and it was empty except for Justin, but soon Daddy would be there with him. Justin scanned the horizon, looking for Daddy's red-and-white striped trunks that reminded Justin of candy canes. He clutched the jackets tighter. Suddenly a figure at the far end of the sand appeared. Was it Daddy? Yes, yes! And he was waving.

Hey, Justy! Hey! Daddy called.

Justin began running. The sand was hot, he was barefoot. It wouldn't be long until Justin reached the shoreline. But no matter how fast Justin ran, he couldn't get any nearer. Come on, Justy, come to Daddy! Justin's legs began to weaken, he was out of breath.

Justy! Justy! The waves began cresting over Daddy, the red and white stripes disappeared in the angry water.

"Daddy, Daddy, wait!"

The darkness broke, the doors pulled open. Mrs. Cleary's nose thrust in at him through the clothing.

"You just wait until I tell your mother that you've been in there again," she said. "Now get out."

★

Frank's elbows were planted on either side of his plate during the whole meal, as if he were afraid someone would pull him away from his food. He gripped a piece of chicken with both fists and stripped away the meat. Each swallow made his eyes bulge. It was mostly because of Frank's eyes that Justin tried not to look at him; their dark middles stuck to the opposite ends of his face, giving him a wild, stupid look.

"There's no doubt in my mind," he said, speech thickened by a mouthful of food. "One of those creeps in the garage is stealing from me. At first I thought I was crazy. Every time I went through my receipts at the end of the month something didn't jibe. Those creeps. I give 'em jobs and what do they do? Bite the hand that feeds them. It ain't right. I built that garage up from nothing. Before they worked for me most of them didn't know the difference between a fan belt and a rear axle. Some of them still don't. I don't know why I keep 'em on."

Justin peeked across the table at him. He hadn't seen his uncle for a long time after moving out of the old apartment. Then Frank began eating supper with them. He made Justin uneasy. Anytime Justin looked, Frank would be smiling at him. Justin avoided his glance. His uncle seemed different now than he used to be. He'd gotten fat, spoke in a growling voice, and darkened his corner of the room. He made the apartment feel damp. The way he grabbed everything—his food, his glass, the salt—made Justin fear that one day his uncle might lunge over the table after him, too, as he had the time Justin'd snuck into Frank's room.

Frank had come an hour before, the way he always did the first Saturday of the month. When the bell rang, Justin snuck behind the wardrobe and watched. Carlotta met Frank at the door. He was red in the face and sweating in his coat and tie. He carried a boxed bakery cake and flowers. She let him kiss her cheek. When his lips touched, her eyes shut as though she were having a splinter removed. She took the cake and the flowers. A moment later she was back at the stove.

"Where's the kid?"

"Justin's watching television."

Justin shrank deeper into his hiding place.

"I don't see him."

Frank clung near the door, conscious of the space he took up in the kitchen area but not knowing where else to go. He offered to help Carlotta but, as usual, she refused, saying that she was almost finished. He asked if he'd come too early and she said he hadn't.

"You sure you want me to eat with you?"

"You ask me that every time."

"Well, do you?"

"Of course, Frank," she said, peeking into the rotisserie.

"Are you sure? It was a while ago when you first asked me. Maybe you changed your mind."

"No."

She bustled through the rest of her work as she spoke, setting the table, checking what was on the stove, and then sponging off the counter. She moved around the tiny kitchen smoothly, her shoes making little taps against the floor tiles. Frank looked on, helpless.

"Justy! Supper!"

Justin made a beeline for his seat.

"There he is! Hey, Champ," said Frank.

Justin mumbled hello without lifting his eyes from the floor.

★

"Am I such a terrible person?" Frank was saying. He looked at Carlotta and waited for her to answer.

"No, Frank. You're not."

"So what have I done to those guys to make them want to steal from me?"

"It's just the way they are. You shouldn't take it personally."

It was the most she'd said to him the whole evening. Frank smiled, grateful. He was always forced to invent conversation, which usually turned into a monologue about his garage, about which Carlotta and Justin knew nothing.

Frank paused. "Maybe I'm just too soft with them. You know, the last thing I want to do is boss people around."

Carlotta shook her head sympathetically.

"Maybe I need someone who could help out around the garage so I'd be able to keep an eye on the other guys."

"Maybe," said Carlotta.

Frank paused. "What I was thinking was that maybe the kid could come around and help out."

Justin's head shot up from his plate.

Carlotta stopped eating for a moment, then continued as though she hadn't heard.

"You know. After school." He smiled nervously, worried by her silence.

"No," she said evenly.

Frank's expression shifted instantly. "Why not?"

"I said no."

"Why the hell not?"

"Keep your voice down."

"Maybe the kid wants to."

"Justin," she said, emphasizing his name, "is busy enough with school." She went to cut a piece of meat but her fork scraped against the plate.

"I'm only talking about a couple of hours a week. After school."

"I don't want my son to become a grease monkey."

Frank glared at her.

"I'm sorry, I didn't mean to say that."

"The hell you didn't. I know that's what you think I am."

"I said I'm sorry."

"I want to know why you don't want Justin working in my garage. He ain't a baby, even though you treat him like one. Look at the way you two live . . ."

"I like the way we live. And so does Justin."

"Don't you think he's too old to be sleeping in the same room with his mother?"

"And you want to make a man out of him, is that it?"

"A kid like Justin needs more than just a mother. He needs a father too."

"He has a father!"

"Where? In the cemetery?"

The walls were stretching, Justin thought. His uncle would say just a little more and soon they'd explode.

Carlotta's voice chilled. "Why are you doing this, Frank?"

"I just wanted — "

"Tell me why you're doing this."

"What am I doing?"

"The same thing you did before that caused all the trouble — forcing yourself into where you don't belong."

"I thought you said wanted me to come for supper."

"For supper, yes. But not to influence my son."

"What am I, a criminal? I'm not going to have him running numbers for me."

"Don't act innocent," she snapped. "Your garage isn't the Cub Scouts."

Frank shook his head slowly. "When are you going to stop trying to blame me, Carlotta?"

"I'm not blaming you. I just want to live my life and raise my son in peace." Her voice grew unsteady.

"When are you going to stop blaming yourself?"

She looked down. "Maybe it is a mistake for you to come here. But I didn't want you to feel left alone."

"Keep your pity," he said, getting up. "I don't need it." He turned to Justin. "Remember, Champ. Anytime you want to, come to see your Uncle Frank." He clapped Justin on the shoulder. Justin watched him leave. The door closed just a little too loudly.

Carlotta sprang up in an instant. "Look what your uncle brought," she said, pulling a knife through the cord around the bakery box.

★

Carlotta lay awake, staring at the screen that separated her bed from Justin's. She heard him shifting under the covers, restless, unable to sleep. It's been like that often during the past few weeks. What's on his mind? she wondered, sure that she already knew. But she was afraid to ask. Damn Frank, she thought. Damn him and his stinking garage.

Justin hadn't been a good sleeper for quite some time. It seemed to have begun around the time Ralph started staying away longer and longer.

"Where's Daddy?" Justin would ask, waking up crying in the middle of the night.

"He's working," Carlotta had said, repeating what Ralph himself had told Carlotta when she'd asked. She had believed him at
first: telephone calls for him from far-flung clients seemed to
confirm his story in the beginning, as did the good money he
brought home. But what about the trips that were supposed to
last one week and stretched into two or three? She soon gave up
looking at the postmarks of his letters and simply fished out the
checks he sent. She drifted up the long hallway of the apartment
like the last guest left in a hotel at the end of the season.

"When will he be back?" Justin asked.

"Soon," she always said. "Soon," Carlotta repeated to herself
when she found herself missing him. The word became a kind
of magic formula that might restore her marriage. She wanted it
to be restored, since she couldn't imagine living any other way.
Ralph had made marriage to him seem so inevitable. He'd had to
work to convince her of that. She'd met him just when she'd
accepted her solitude, a twenty-five-year-old woman from a
small town in upstate New York grown sure and serious from
caring for sick people. (He'd been her patient; he'd been quite ill.
Was that why she clung to the belief that he would always need
her?) She'd formed all the habits of those who live alone: rising
early, eating at home, remembering other people's birthdays.
Ralph took one look at the old-fashioned locket she wore around
her neck, heard how she said "quite" instead of "very," and with
his salesman's instinct set the tone of his pitch accordingly. He
was tall and slender, and he moved with a grace that was almost
feminine and reassuring to her. He slipped notes into her mailbox addressed to "The Convent" or "Sunnybrook Farm," nicknamed her Joan after the saint who must have been her French
forebear, according to him, and appeared one night with a
birthday present that turned out to be a hair shirt discovered in a
costume shop. She'd evaded him until he was able to do what
every successful salesman must: convince the buyer she can't live
without his merchandise.

Just when he'd brought Carlotta out of her solitude and taught
her to fear it, telling her it made her somber, he began staying
away. It was almost as if he'd decided to test her to see whether

she'd learned his lesson. She had. She no longer wanted to be alone. More than the late-night phone calls from strange women who hung up when they heard her voice, more than the fear of having lost her attractiveness or of having driven Ralph away, it was the loneliness that pained her, a loneliness she'd once accepted and let ripen into solitude but was no longer able to endure. It made her despise him.

She'd felt less isolated in the two rooms she lived in before her marriage. Her apartment was on the second floor; her windows faced the front, never far from the sounds of the fights in Dirty Nellie's down below. Married, and with Ralph away, she imagined herself shut up in a used castle. Ralph's mother, Rose, had lived in the apartment for twenty years, cluttering it with fern stands and uncomfortable chairs, before retiring to Arizona. The rooms bore an uncomfortable patina of quiet, too leaden with age and habit to ever seem fresh on even the sunniest of days. The great maple bed they slept in with its altarlike headboard had belonged to Ralph's parents. (Carlotta had insisted on a new mattress.) Frank still lived there; he'd refused to move out when Ralph asked him to and brooded in his room, refusing to speak to Carlotta for almost a year. Carlotta felt like an intruder. Ralph promised they would move as soon as they found something else.

Still needing him when he wasn't there, Carlotta reconstructed him in her mind. With the care of an anthropologist, she reassembled him each night before she got into the great empty bed: the wiry tickle of his mustache against her upper lip, his papery thin ears that glowed red when he stood in front of a light, his smooth, thin limbs and knobby joints like a wooden soldier's — an imaginery frame on which to hang her most tangible recollection of him: his beloved clothing. She sent everything in the wardrobe to the cleaners regularly, kept his shoes gleaming, inserted collar stays in his shirts, and had his hats cleaned by a milliner.

After Ralph had drowned two years ago, Justin began calling "Daddy" in the middle of the night. His screams rang through the cavernous Upper West Side apartment. She'd run to him, past Frank's room, past the forgotten dining room and the kitchen, each room like another scene in the movie of her married life. She pulled Justin out of his sweating nightmares, his eyes still fixed in terror at what had just been revealed to him in sleep. She'd bundle him up and carry him back down the echoing corridor to her bedroom as though rewinding the film. Beside her, he was able to sleep. She remained awake, looking down at his face, which was empty of color and soft as tissue. She prayed that the fragile peace of his breathing would not be broken. His suffering, she knew, was the strain of trying to remember. She could help him. Yet she didn't. He was too young to understand, she told herself. She would tell him, yes, but when he was older.

One night when his screaming wouldn't stop she flung herself out of bed, hardly knowing what she was about to do, sick with confusion, enraged at Ralph for dying, for leaving her alone with Justin to face it. She threw open the door of the wardrobe.

"Here," she said, standing breathlessly before it. "Here's Daddy! Look!" She guided his hands over Ralph's suits, letting him pet them as though they were a pony at the Bronx Zoo. She let Justin clump around in the huge shoes, gave him silk ties to play lasso with.

It became their bedtime game. She let him pick out something to wear, she put on a record, and the two of them danced. When the music was over she whisked him up into the air and carried him off to bed. Then he'd sleep through the night. It was a good game, she thought. Justin seemed never to tire of it and there was enough clothing for a different costume each night. To Carlotta's relief, Justin stopped asking where Daddy was. Well, she'd reasoned, now he knew: Daddy was in Mommy's room, in the big wardrobe.

But Carlotta knew she had to get them out of that apartment.

"How come Daddy isn't going to live here too?" Justin had asked, tucked into his bed for the first time after they had moved.

It wasn't the question of a child who didn't understand, she thought, her throat tightening. He knew, and was giving her the chance to come clean about what had really happened to Ralph. She had yearned to. Wasn't that why she'd moved into a small apartment, too small for them to have secrets from one another? And yet, at that moment, looking down at him sunk into his pillow, safe in the new apartment, which seemed like a perfect, controllable world, and far from all that had happened in the old one, she couldn't bring the words to her lips that might shatter it.

"Daddy is still away," she said.

Her throat clamped tighter. She had never lied, and the ease with which she could now do it astounded her.

"What's he doing?" was his reply.

"Working."

"When's he coming back?"

"Soon."

One day, as she was collecting Justin's dirty clothing for a wash, something clinked out of a pants pocket onto the floor: the wardrobe's tiny brass key. Carlotta stared at it. She imagined a panel on the wall suddenly shifting to reveal a hidden vault, which contained Justin's recollection of his father's death. He'd been living with two strains of memory, she realized, what he knew to be true, and what she'd tried to make him believe. Or what she'd tried to make him forget about for as long as she could. One had nothing to do with the other. He was living in two different worlds. This morning had been the third time Mrs. Cleary had found Justin in the wardrobe. He'd yelled at her and told her to get out of the house. The poor woman had to stay with him for the rest of the time with Justin scowling at her. Lately he seemed to be moody and disagreeable for no reason. This morning, as he put his arms around her, she'd had the feeling he'd wanted to tell her something.

She'd been careful to leave the key among his things, lest she awaken his suspicion.

Carlotta listened. Justin had fallen asleep at last. She turned over in her bed. She might sleep as well if she could shake the rumble of Frank's voice from her head. She thought of Justin in his bed, her child. She remembered the weight of his head against her this morning. Tell him, she told herself. Tell him or he'll learn to hate you, she thought. But she didn't dare say when she would.

Five

1

The green pitted face of the soldier peered down at Matthew through blank eyes as he walked into the park. The snows had washed away the bird doody; the metal looked dark and cold beneath in the afternoon's overcast sky. For the thousandth time he read the inscription on the base:

> From Flanders Fields
>   If ye break faith
> with us who die
> We shall not sleep,
>   though poppies grow
> In Flanders fields.

It never made sense; something was missing. And Flanders sounded like something to throw up. Some kids said the devil lived beneath the statue; if you walked too heavily on the sidewalk he'd get mad. Matthew didn't really believe that but he kept on tiptoe just in case, until he was well behind the statue's back. He noticed something going on at the other end of the park near the bleachers and broke into a run. The softball field was soggy after the snow.

Kids were clustered on either side of the entranceway through the tall fence behind the field. Between them hung something on a string that they batted back and forth. Matthew spotted some blue uniforms of the Sacred Heart School; Catholic school kids could be mean. He went only close enough to see what was going on: the gashed pulp of a squirrel hung by its neck. Its tail dangled limp and sopped with blood. A crimson trail had formed on the concrete below.

"Lemme at him," said a blond-haired kid. He pushed someone else out of his way and speared the animal with his stick. Its side tore open and a shiny mash of guts slouched out, hitting the ground with a gurgly slap. The kids cheered. The withered remains of the squirrel hung like the drape of a puppet.

"Look at his stomach," someone said, standing before the steaming entrails.

"It ain't his stomach, it's the heart," said the blond-haired kid, plunging his stick into what still throbbed faintly, then holding it aloft. Another kid tried to poke down the rest of the squirrel.

"Beat it," said the blond-haired kid, brandishing his loaded stick. "It's mine!"

"It was me who caught the squirrel," the other protested.

The stick was aimed, the heart flew off into the kid's face, leaving a red splotch. The boy's hands flew up in horror. The others laughed until he fled. The blond-haired kid accepted their praise. Then they fell silent, not knowing what to do next. The blond kid spotted Matthew.

"Whatcha lookin at?"

"Let's get him!" said a short kid.

Matthew hardly had time to think before they were running after him. He scrambled up the wooden planks of the bleachers, wondering what he was going to do when he reached the top. They were coming at him from all directions.

"Get back, all of you!" A megaphonelike voice boomed up from the field.

"It's the nigger!" a kid shouted. Their feet paddled against the planks as they ran away. The blood-stained stick whizzed past Matthew and hit the wall, then disappeared through planks.

"We don't gotta listen to no nigger!" another shouted over his shoulder, still running.

Matthew saw a tall Negro man heading his way up the bleachers. "What were you doing with those hoodlums?" he demanded. He wore an old-fashioned overcoat with a muffler, and he spoke in a precise, clipped voice.

"I wasn't doing anything," said Matthew, watching to see if the kids were coming back.

"Then why were they chasing you?"

"Who are you, anyway?"

"Answer my question and I'll answer yours." His words snapped like sheets.

"I don't know, they just came after me."

"They must have had a reason." He was very skinny and very tall.

"I didn't do nothing," Matthew said, bewildered.

The man winced. "Anything. You didn't do anything."

"Yeah, that's right!"

"Do you like seeing squirrels get tortured?"

"How come you were watching?"

"I watch everything that goes on this neighborhood."

"If you were really watching you would've known I wasn't doing anything."

The man smiled. "Well put. And as a matter of fact, I was watching and therefore I know that you were indeed doing nothing. Forgive me, but I was giving you a hard time on purpose to try to trip you up. If I were you I would keep away from Kevin and his cronies."

"How do you know that kid's name?"

"I've already told you. I keep my eyes open."

"You still haven't told me who you are."

"You may call me Mr. Sloane." He extended a hand. "What's your name?"

Matthew regarded the slender hand and its border of white cuff with suspicion; he'd heard about cops going around without uniforms. But, he reasoned, he hadn't done anything wrong. And something in the man's manner made it impossible to refuse shaking hands with him. Afterward he realized it was the first time he'd shaken the hand of a Negro.

"Those kids were scared of you," Matthew said.

"They have reason to be. I've caught them doing things they didn't want to be caught at. Because of me, that Kevin — he's their ringleader — has a JD card. He knows I mean business. I feel sorry for him. His parents beat the daylights out of him all the time, even when they're sober. Do you see what happened to that squirrel?" He pointed to the squirrel skin. "That's how Kevin feels the world treats him. The saddest people in the world are the most dangerous." He shook his head. "First squirrel this season, but there'll be more."

"Are you a cop?"

Mr. Sloane smiled. "No."

"How'd he get a JD card?"

"Arson. Do you know what that is? Playing with matches. Because of him, a Chinese laundry went up in flames. It's a wonder the poor people working there weren't burned as well."

"Why'd he do it?"

"So people would pay attention to him. So one person would throw him into a police car and another would ask him what his name was and another would talk to him and try to find out what was troubling him, which is probably more than his parents have talked to him in a whole year."

"Don't you hate him for calling you ni — " Matthew hesitated.

"Nigger. In the South the word 'niggra' is often used. The answer to your question is no. It hurts me to hear it, but if I hated him I would do something bad to him that would get in the way of other things."

They left the park. Halfway down the street, Mr. Sloane stopped. "What do you see here?" he asked.

They stood before a rickety fence constructed of bedsprings and chicken wire lashed together. Behind it rose a two-story heap of warped wooden boards and corrugated aluminum panels and tar paper. Two shopping carts from the A & P had been chained to it as well. It seemed as if the cold wind blowing up from the river would topple it if it didn't have a neighboring building to lean against.

Matthew shrugged.

"This is my house."

"You live here?"

"No, not yet. But I will." He pushed open the gate. The entire fence rippled and swayed. He motioned for Matthew to proceed. A cat darted across the opening and disappeared.

"May I invite you in for a little tour?"

"I don't know," Matthew said.

"A wise response. Never talk to strangers. Or if they've engaged you in conversation, don't let them take you to any run-down shack they claim to be their future home. Very prudent of you." He extended his hand. "I certainly hope we meet again." He turned to go.

Matthew looked disappointed. "Mr. Sloane?"

He smiled. "Yes?"

"Are you sure you're not a cop?"

"I would never be. Why?"

"Then how come Kevin got a JD card because of you?"

"Policemen aren't the only people who have a right to determine right and wrong. They might think they are, but they aren't. I made a citizen's arrest."

"But why? It wasn't your Chinese laundry."

"It wasn't my squirrel either. But that makes no difference to the squirrel." He winked at Matthew.

Matthew looked away shyly. "Can I still see your house?"

Mr. Sloane led them down a narrow alleyway clogged with garbage like the bottom of the air shaft. They came to an ancient porch. "Be careful on the steps," he said, motioning to the gaps where the wood was missing. "The cold weather has certainly taken its toll." He produced a key from his pocket and, amazingly, there was a lock on the door that it fit.

"If there weren't boards nailed to the windows, you'd see what's been done here," Mr. Sloane explained, opening the door.

A bit of bluish light spilled into the room, giving only a hint of its limits, but otherwise it was dark. The smell reminded Matthew of the cabinet under the kitchen sink. He took a step forward, tripped, and fell against a wall. There was a cracking sound like a short laugh; then the wall caved in. A geyser of dust rose up. Matthew tumbled into the middle of it.

"Don't worry about it," said Mr. Sloane. "I was planning on tearing that wall down anyway to enlarge the dining room."

What dining room? Matthew thought, coughing as he picked himself up. This place is an indoor junkyard. "You're not really going to live here, are you?"

"And why not?" Mr. Sloane sounded insulted. He stood in the doorway, a stately silhouette.

Matthew was coughing too much to answer.

Back on the street, Matthew asked Mr. Sloane why he had bought a house like that.

"I didn't buy it. It was a present."

"From who?"

"It's a long story. When do you have to be heading home?"

"Five."

Mr. Sloane explained as they walked to Mr. Glaubach's piano store.

The house had been willed to Mr. Sloane's great-grandfather, a North Carolina slave, by the eccentric abolitionist son of a New York banker shortly after the end of the Civil War. It had been a livery stable for the banker's prized Andalusians. He rode them along the river as far up as Spuyten Duyvil until the construction of loading docks and terminals for the Pennsylvania Railroad spoiled the pleasant riverside. That had forced him to give up his riding until Central Park was laid out. He found a new stable near the park on West Eighty-ninth Street and left the Clinton stable empty. When he died, his son assumed title to all the banker's holdings. His father had sustained certain notorious Alabama planters during the war by extending them credit on easy terms. His son used the forgotten piece of property to avenge his father's unscrupulous dealings. He chose a recipient at random from a plantation's old slave roster; Nathaniel Sloane appealed to the son as the kind of name an upstanding, dignified freedman ought to have.

Nathaniel Sloane received the notice of his inheritance by mail at the same plantation where he'd worked as a slave, fulfilling the same duties after the war as before, while the same Samuel Winslow owned the land. The notice arrived on his seventy-first birthday, the first piece of mail he'd ever received, which proved beyond the shadow of a doubt, he boasted to the others, that he was no longer a slave.

"If you so free, let's see you read it," they'd said.

He couldn't — the war hadn't altered his illiteracy, either — so he surrendered it to Winslow's daughter. When he understood what the letter was about, Sloane exclaimed that he'd never heard of anything so funny. These white people certainly did have some peculiar notions, didn't they? He knew better than to journey for days and days on the Federal Road, which was especially dangerous right then, to take possession of a stable in the middle of New York City. But even if he was fool enough to want to go, how was he supposed to get there? The banker's generous son hadn't mentioned paying for the stage.

Everyone joked about it; "livin in Sloane's Stable" became local parlance for a pipe dream. The document was slipped into the family Bible, which made its way to the hands of the first Sloane to complete high school.

It was what Mr. Sloane showed to the policeman who tried to boot him out of the property just as he'd booted out all the bums he'd found there.

"What's that, the Declaration of Independence?" the cop asked, looking at the brittle document Mr. Sloane held before him, just out of his reach.

"This verifies my claim to the property."

"Go take your business to the Bowery," said the cop.

Thus began Mr. Sloane's fight with the City of New York, waged with city clerks, the Eighteenth Police Precinct, and the Department of Sanitation, who refused to haul away his rubble. He scoured the records of the Department of Buildings, the Municipal Archives, the Office of Real Estate, and the Housing Department, searching for evidence that might further substantiate his claim. The young woman at Legal Aid was sympathetic; the NAACP was impressed. But when neither offered more than a smile and a handful of brochures, he began spending nights teaching himself property law at the New York Law School Library and drafting form after form, which he dropped off at various municipal offices downtown. In the end, the City of New York refused to honor the claim on the basis of a document that could hardly be read and in any case hadn't been notarized.

It didn't keep him away from the house. He returned with a shovel and a cart to haul away the rubble. The neighborhood cops got to know him, and soon they were at least listening to his story before ejecting him.

Mr. Sloane, who had by then acclimatized to life in New York, hit upon a plan. "I've seen lots of things going on in the park over there much worse than someone cleaning out an old house," he said to Patrolman Garlick, whom he'd gotten to know.

"What sort of things?" Garlick asked.

"Drug business, for instance."

"How do you know?"

"I have eyes, same as you."

The cop looked at him, unsure whether he'd been insulted. Finally, he made Mr. Sloane an offer. There was a whole new ballgame starting these days, he said: hard stuff. It used to be kept among the colored, no offence, but now it was getting around everywhere because of the Mob. The cops would leave Mr. Sloane alone in return for tipping them off whenever he saw something. They'd even let him salvage from the houses being torn down around in the Sixties between Broadway and Amsterdam. Was it a deal?

As far as Mr. Sloane was concerned, black folk had no business doing business with the police. But here was a chance to do what he needed to do. Drugs seemed truly evil, at least the people who sold them were. And as soon as he got the city to recognize his claim he could let go of his end of the deal. He agreed.

"Is the house really yours yet?" Matthew asked.

"No. But it will be."

They reached the piano store. "I trust I'll see you around the neighborhood again. Remember, keep away from that Kevin."

Matthew said he would. "I can help you with the house," he said.

Mr. Sloane smiled. "Perhaps. Perhaps," he repeated, opening the door with another key and slipping out of sight.

2

Ovid stood by the battered pot set into a cinderblock fireplace. Thick fingers of steam rose up and faded into the chilly air that blew up from the trackbed. His doughy brown hand pulled a ladle back and forth through a bubbling jelly of soup. His heavy, round head hovered above like a protective moon. He leaned over and breathed in.

"If that don't smell good," he said, shaking his head. His eyes lifted. "And just look at that sun going down, look like fire up in heaven. It make a man believe, it really do. And I believe this year we gonna finish what we doin here —"

"You think you're cooking soup for the Salvation Army?" Skip said from his milk crate near the fire. The long coat he wore hung around him like a blanket. The corners of his eyes slid downward wearily toward his haggard cheeks. He wrapped the coat tighter around him and pulled his porkpie hat lower on his head. "You musta stirred that soup back into water by now."

"I do what I know to do," Ovid answered in a slow, thick voice.

Skip threw his cigarette into the fire. "Shit, it's cold."

"That butt ain't going to make the fire no hotter."

"Why don't you throw some more wood on?"

"I would if you get some, Skip."

Skip pulled out a flask from his pocket and took a furtive swig.

"Sure hope Mr. Sloane don't catch you doin that here."

"You quit telling me what I can and can't —"

There was a rustling in the brown mesh of branches around them. Skip shuttled the flask out of sight. A tiny man appeared carrying a bundle of scrap wood that he threw down beside the fire, moving on short legs with an insect's agitation. The rubber boots he wore reached past his knees. His left jacket sleeve hung empty; he stuffed it into a pocket with his one hand and then brushed himself off.

"I am one hungry man," he said, his speech honed by a West Indian accent.

"Soup woulda been done already, Ancil, if Skip had gotten some wood earlier," said Ovid.

"Goddam," said Skip, storming over to the edge of the clearing.

"Go easy on him, Ovid," Ancil whispered. "You know he has a temper."

"I ain't his mama lookin after him."

"I know. But he just lost another job."

"And I know why, too." He lifted an imaginary bottle to his lips.

"Where is Ephesus?"

"In the cave, resting."

"And Mr. Sloane?"

"He down in City Hall fillin out some papers." Ovid fed some of the wood into the fire.

"Hope he gets back soon. What do you have for us tonight?"

Ovid beamed. "Surprise."

Ancil looked worried. "What kind of surprise?" He stepped closer to the pot.

"You'll like it," Ovid said hurriedly.

Ancil peered in. "What's that lumpy stuff floating around?"

Ovid moved to block his view. "Just some fat, that's all."

"Ain't you done with that soup?" Skip said, staggering back.

"What's biting your ass, Skip?" said Ancil.

"What's biting my ass is that I'm sick and tired of being treated like a child round here."

"You act like one sometimes, I swear you do." The empty sleeve pulled out of his pocket again. He put it back in.

"Tell the truth. Don't you feel like a fool, carrying on like a Campfire Girl here?"

"No, Skip, I don't. But I know you do. That's because you still don't understand what we're doing here. We've all tried to explain it to you. Trouble is, you don't listen."

"Yeah I know. We all one big happy Negro family that Massa Sloane done brought across the Red Sea into the land of plenty, amen."

"Why can't you be grateful for what you got?" said Ovid.

"Quit carrying on like Shirley Temple. You ain't got the right kind of hair."

"Ovid's right," said Ancil. "And by the way, I never hear you complaining when it's time to eat."

"You call that slop that Ovid makes food?"

"You don't gotta eat it," said Ovid.

"Go back to your pot, Chef Boyardee. I was talking to Ancil here."

"But you was talking *bout me*. You always talking bout me. You always talking bout somebody. But you sure don't like it when somebody talk bout you."

Ancil scurried between them. "You got work to do, now don't you?" he said, winking to Ovid in warning.

Ovid glared past him toward Skip. "I really don't know why you here at all."

"I know why. I'm here cause I'm a clown. All niggers is clowns."

"Speak for yourself," said Ancil.

"Excuse me. We's all clowns but Ancil's a genuine Spice Island fool."

"And you is nothing but an ungrateful nappy-headed Niggra with a mouth as big as Kingston."

"If we wasn't all fools then nobody'd have to come along and drag our asses out the gutter, where they was taking up residence, as you well know. And if we wasn't fools then they wouldn't have fallen down there in the first place." He took out the flask, lifted it in a toast and took a long swig. "Lord if that ain't the best thing since central heating."

"My ass wasn't in no gutter," said Ancil. "It wasn't my fault that I lost my arm in a paper-cutting machine."

"That ain't the point. You is all fools because you all think you doing the right thing, you all think you is being good boys, and if you keep being good boys one fine day Uncle Remus gonna move you into that fire trap and everything'll be happy ever after. Every night Chef Boyardee'll cook up some of his slop and then afterwards you'll all gather round the pi-anna while Uncle Remus plays you some of his famous ragtime music designed to warm the Negro heart. Ancil can do a little cakewalk across the floor and Ephesus'll read from the Bible. I can just picture it. A nice big happy nigger family . . ."

"I don't know about you, Skip, but this is the only family I got," said Ancil.

"You know, it wouldn't be so bad if Sloane was doing this to get something out of it. But the dude really believe he gonna finish it. Well I don't. Know why? Because I'm a fool and fools don't understand the kind of fancy words he uses like 'inheritance' and 'birthright' and — what's the real good one he pulls out sometimes — oh yeah — negritude. Negritude. It sounds almost too good for black folk. A word like that you could name a hair-straightener after. Make a bundle of money, too. Then maybe Uncle Remus could pay off someone to get the water turned on in the house. Course, there'd have to be pipes first."

"Ephesus is working on the plumbing," said Ovid.

"Well that's fine, that's really fine. Indoor plumbing. And I was just getting used to the privy we got over yonder."

"I swear he got no business being here," Ovid whispered to Ancil softly. "He here only cause Mr. Sloane too good to throw him out."

"Trouble with all of you," Skip went on, "is that you all so damn happy with whatever scraps get thrown to you. You all so used to getting nothing that you don't even know to ask for something better."

"Ain't nobody throw no scraps to me," said Ovid.

"Oh no? What do you call what Uncle Remus grubs from the thirty-day pile at the dry cleaner's for you to wear? Don't get me wrong, I ain't complaining. This coat I got on musta cost a hundred dollars new. Too bad it's three sizes too big for me." He fanned it out around him.

"We don't have to ask for nothing better. We takin it."

"You mean freezing your proud black asses off while he building that house of cards?"

"It's going to be our house someday," Ancil said.

"When?" asked Skip. "How long has it been already?"

"Been a while."

"Give me a number."

Ancil shrugged.

"See? It's been so long you don't even remember. But I do. Seven years. We been living here like jungle bunnies for seven years."

"Things take time."

"Time? Time? I don't know about you, Coconut, but I ain't getting any younger. How much time you planning to wait until Uncle Remus can scrounge up enough wood to put a floor down? You might as well ask Jesus to hop on down from the clouds and buy you a drink."

"Back part's just about done," said Ovid.

"What about the front part? What about the middle part? Uncle Remus—"

"Why do you keep on calling him that?" asked Ancil.

"Take a look at him sometime. His getup's from thirty years ago, those big old ties of his, those pants. He look like he graduated from Tuskeegee Institute, Class of 1932. And the way he talk. He sound like Mother Goose."

"The way a person talk don't mean much," said Ovid.

"When a nigger don't sound like a nigger it do. The man is living in a dream world, Ancil. You better face facts."

"Maybe he is. But it makes more sense to me than what goes on out there." He pointed up toward the street. "What was I doing with my one arm before Mr. Sloane came along? I was handing out notices for fortune-tellers."

"What are you doing now? Scavenging wood like you Davy Crockett."

"Yes, but at least I'm doing it for me. What happened when I tried to sue the printing press over what happened to my arm? They turned it around and said it was my own fault. I knew sure as hell that the damn machine needed to be repaired, but the boss man wouldn't fix it because that cost money and he wasn't going to be spending his money on some black midget. We'll finish this house, and we'll live in it."

"Those who help will," said Ovid.

"Don't none of you start telling me I don't do my share. If it wasn't for me there wouldn't be no roof on that house. Everyone here knows what kind of a fucked-up back I got but I went up there and roofed that mother, and nobody here best be forgetting that."

"I don't think you'd let us," said Ancil.

"That nice little white boy Mr. Sloane found help us out too, but he don't make such a fuss like you." said Ovid.

"The nice little white boy," said Skip, imitating Ovid. "Maybe he should come and integrate our dormitory?" His voice shifted. "Why doesn't Sloane find himself some nice colored boy to help out if he so big on negritude?"

"If I was you I wouldn't be talking about messing round with white folk," said Ovid.

"Skip is diluting the race, isn't he?" said Ancil with a grin.

"No wonder you are always cold, Skip," Ancil said, winking at Ovid. "You have wasted your vitality on that shanty Irish tramp."

Skip's eyes narrowed. "What are you two fools talking about?"

"Don't make like you don't know. We saw you with that woman."

"More than once," said Ovid.

"Mr. Sloane said she's the mother of that Kevin kid."

"Speaking of women, you both can talk more than any woman I ever known," said Skip. He turned around and went to rub his hands before the fire. It was dark by now. He pulled out a packet of cigarettes but it was empty. He tossed it into the fire. "Damn," he said. "Damn all of this."

Ovid looked over. "You just hungry, Skip. You need something in your belly and you'll feel better."

Skip's mouth twisted into a snarl. "Ain't it just like a nigger. If somebody gave you big shoes and a warm place to shit you'd be happy, now wouldn't you?"

The ladle banged against the side of the pot. "I'm tired of you talking to me like that," cried Ovid, shaking the ladle at Skip. "I know I ain't smart but I ain't ashamed." His voice rose to a cry. "But you. You never quit talking bout that bad back of yours. You act like the whole world done you a bad turn by making you fall off that roof. But it wasn't nobody's fault but your own. If you wasn't so drunk it wouldn'ta happened."

"You best shut up, Chef."

Ancil ran up beside Ovid but Ovid pushed him away. "Skip, you ain't no one to be tellin me to nothin."

"Go back to your soup."

"Get away from here," said Ovid, waving the ladle. Skip kicked the pot so that it toppled on its frame of cinderblocks. Ancil reached out and grabbed the handle with his bare hand.

"It's hot!" shouted Ovid.

Ancil set the pot back in place, then turned to Skip. "Take a walk," he said.

Skip pushed out of the clearing. They heard branches cracking behind him. Ovid threw his arms around Ancil and cried. His head drooped over the small man like the heavy crown of a sunflower. Ancil struggled to stuff his sleeve back into his pocket. "Now, now. It's all right. He's gone."

"But he be back!"

"I thought you weren't going to let him get to you anymore."

"Why he have to be that way?" Ovid wailed. "I was just tryin to be nice."

"Skip doesn't trust anyone being nice to him. That's why he doesn't trust Mr. Sloane. Well, a part of him does, otherwise he wouldn't be here. But the hard side of him don't."

Ovid returned to his stirring. Ancil stood beside him, staring into the darkness beyond the clearing. "I understand the way Skip feels. Seven years is a long time. He was right. This past winter was so cold I thought my blood would freeze from sleeping in that cave. You remember the first time Mr. Sloane brought that white boy round, what's his name?"

"Matthew."

"Yes. Do you remember what he said? He asked how come we lived here. He didn't mean it in a bad way but he couldn't understand why a bunch of grown men should be living in a cave on the side of a hill near the railroad tracks." His nose wrinkled. "Ovid, what did you put in that soup that smells so —"

"Secret, like I told you."

"I don't want any secrets. I've had enough excitement today."

"I make this soup just like my mama used to."

"I'm sure you do. Now let me have that ladle, Ovid."

Ovid held it behind his back.

"Ovid . . ."

"Why don't you just close your eyes, and I'll let you taste it," he said.

Ancil snapped his fingers. Ovid surrendered the spoon. Ancil plunged it in, then brought its content close to his eyes. "What is that?" he said, pointing to a brownish sediment settling to the bottom of the ladle.

"Spice."

Ancil flung the soup back into the pot. "You did it again, didn't you?"

"I only used a little."

Ancil waved the spoon at him. Ovid retreated to the other side of the pot.

"What did we tell you?" Ancil said.

"But dirt is good for you. It make a man strong, dirt do."

Ancil was putting down the spoon and reaching for the pot.

"What you fixin to do?" cried Ovid.

"Grab the other end," Ancil ordered.

Ovid stepped back, tearful. "I been cooking all afternoon."

"Take the handle."

"It's hot!"

Ancil took out a glove from his pocket that he threw to Ovid. Together they heaved the pot off the fire and flung its contents into the trees. A glistening brown sheet of fluid flew over the branches. A piercing howl answered. A moment later Skip burst into the clearing.

"You all trying to cook me alive? Can't I take a shit in peace?"

Ancil smiled at Skip. "Might soften you up some."

"Take more than a pot of soup to do that," said Ovid.

"What smells so good?" someone said. They all turned. Mr. Sloane had just entered the clearing.

Six

1

Marjorie flung her cigarette to the sidewalk and stamped it out. "Wait here, Matty," she said. "I'll be right out."

Before Matthew could say anything she'd slipped through the revolving doors of Woolworth's. Matthew watched her bright blue scarf disappearing down an aisle. He was mad. She might be in there an hour. The Bulova clock outside the jeweler's said three o'clock. The shoe store would be closed by the time they got there. Should he go in after her? If he nagged too much she might say that he'd blown his chance for the sneakers. It would just be an excuse; she could always find reasons for not spending money.

He'd spent the whole morning convincing her he needed a new pair of sneakers. There were holes in the bottoms of the ones he had, he argued. It was already March, the warm weather was coming. And he wanted Keds, high-tops, not the low ones, which were cheaper but not as good. She'd finally agreed. He'd been ready to go right after breakfast. Then he heard his mother in the shower. He banged on the bathroom door in protest.

"Hold your horses," she shouted through the din.

He was back as soon as she turned off the water and opened the door. "Hurry up," he said, the steam swirling around him.

Marjorie stood wrapped in a towel, rolling up her hair in fat curlers and reaching into a jarful of clips to fix them in place. "Okay, okay," she answered. "Why don't you sit down and take a load off your mind." She motioned to the bathtub. He sat down on the edge, glum, knowing it would be a while.

"The guy that's taking me out tonight's real nice," she said, pleased at having an audience. When all of her hair was set she fitted a blue scarf around it, which made her head look upholstered. "I met him at the office, a new guy. He's taking me to dinner and a show. Not bad, huh? The last show I saw was *Music Man*. It must have been five years ago. I took your grandmother. That was a mistake. She didn't like where we sat. And Robert Preston was sick that night." She fit a stray hair under the scarf with her finger. "It's nice to meet someone with a little class for a change. I'm tired of losers."

"Yeah," he muttered, thinking of the long routine she'd go through before being ready: the shiny eye shadow (blue, to match her scarf; he bet she'd put on a blue dress, too—she was very particular about those things); the gizmo that pinched her eyelashes and the little brush that made them darker. She began putting on lipstick.

"It's been so long since I've met someone nice," she mumbled toothlessly, keeping her mouth still as she applied the lipstick in broad, oily strokes. "I think you'll like him. Shit, did I smear it?" She turned to him for confirmation. Matthew shook his head, knowing it would mean a delay if he nodded. It was going to be a hard day, he reflected. It always was when she had a date coming up. But what was worse, he knew, was the day after, if the evening hadn't gone well.

"You know why I get stuck with losers?" she went on. "Because I don't know how to tell them to bug off. I can smell a loser a mile away. It doesn't matter. A guy tells me I'm the first person who's given him the time of day and I feel I can't let him down. What happens? I coast along until he drives me crazy."

"Was TJ a loser, too?"

"Your father?" Her face fell serious. She studied it in the mirror for a moment, then brought a tissue between her lips to blot them. "No," she said, "he was no loser." She threw the tissue bearing the bright red imprint of her lips into the toilet bowl and flushed. "But he thought I was."

By the time Matthew decided to go into Woolworth's after her he'd lost sight of the blue scarf. The store held a din of Saturday

shoppers. The air was heavy with the smell of french fries from
the luncheonette counter. The old wooden floor creaked under-
foot: the place reminded him of a gymnasium. The salesladies
with their smocks were busy arranging merchandise. They were
mean and old and never wore lipstick on their grey lips. He
wandered up and down the aisles, keeping his eye out for the
blue scarf.

He thought about the men who came to take his mother out.
He'd be in the living room watching Jackie Gleason, the door
bell would ring, and some man would be standing there with
flowers, asking if he was the Matthew the guy'd heard so much
about. Marjorie would yell in from the bathroom that she'd be
right out. Until then Matthew had to sit with the man. Some
were nice, most of them kept straightening their ties or had these
holes on their face or looked around the apartment in a way that
made Matthew think they wished they were somewhere else. His
mother was right; most of them were losers.

Around the time Gramma got sick Marjorie stopped going on
dates and for a long time after that she never went out at night.
Then Matthew began waking up Friday or Saturday nights,
hearing voices in the kitchen. (He'd been moved into Gramma's
old room.) The radio would be on low, the refrigerator would
open and close. His mother giggled a lot, then said they had to
keep it down because her kid was sleeping. The man's voice was
deeper, solid, like something you hit against in the dark. It
resonated through the walls right into Matthew's mattress and
didn't let him sleep. He'd convince himself that he had to go pee
and glance into the kitchen on the way to the bathroom. He'd
slip past and see the man from a few hours earlier, now with a
glass in his hand, his tie off and his shirt open, eyes red and
watery. Sometimes his mother would be sitting in his lap, or else
they might be kissing. Everything in the kitchen would be quiet.
Matthew'd watch. Sooner or later his mother would stop and say,
"Wait, he's out there." How did she always know? he'd wonder,
hopping back to his room, grinning.

Back in bed, Matthew would wait to see if the man left or
stayed. If the front door closed, it meant he'd left. He'd sense his

mother creeping toward his room. His door would open a crack and let in a sharp cone of light from the hall. She'd peek inside and wait for Matthew to say, "I'm up," which he usually was. Then she ventured in and sat on his bed, smelling of perfume and whiskey, still in her dress, but her shoes off. Her makeup gave her raccoon eyes in the darkened room. She'd demand to know what he was doing up at this ungodly hour. "You didn't mind that I was out?" she always asked him. Matthew always shook his head no. (Having a sitter made him feel like a baby, he said.) Then she gave her report. Either the guy was a creep, which meant he was good-looking but nothing else, or else he was a drip, which meant he was boring. "I'm just too good for 'em," she'd conclude. For a while she'd sit without saying anything, staring off into the darkness. Finally she'd kiss him good night and walk to her room.

If the man stayed over Matthew kept awake, his ears pulled to the rumble of the man's voice, which charged the darkness around Matthew's bed with a strange electricity. By morning, he'd be gone. Matthew woke early, threw the beer bottles into the trash, and sponged the sticky rings off the kitchen table. Sometimes he found things: a cigarette lighter, keys, combs. Once a man left a tie hanging over the back of a chair. Marjorie let him keep it. She stayed in her room most of the day. Just as it was getting dark, she drifted into the kitchen to make herself coffee, still in her bathrobe, splotches of makeup giving her a ghostly look, saying nothing. He'd see the same man for a couple of Saturdays in a row until he stopped coming. Then there'd be a new one.

There was the blue scarf, two aisles over. He found her tearing open a package. She was applying makeup to her eyes, then looking into the mirror of the sunglasses display. It was all because of tonight, he guessed. But why was she always doing things like this? She tossed the package away and chose another. Matthew watched from behind a pillar, praying she would stop before one of the ladies caught her. His eyes darted around in case one should be swinging near. He decided to go look at the turtles and then come back and demand to continue on to the sneaker store.

The Woolworth's turtles were crowded together in their grimy tank beside the houseplants. They looked wasted and hollow and paddled feebly through the brown water churning with sediment. It wasn't right, he thought. He'd once complained to one of the ladies in the smocks, but he was told that it wasn't any of his business if he wasn't buying. He imagined them scooping out the dead turtles and heaving them into the garbage like rotten fruit. Something like that had happened at school. A girl had brought in a turtle for the Nature Corner but lost interest. The turtle went unfed, its water fouled. Matthew'd watched the turtle weaken day by day. He wanted to take it home. Marjorie had objected. One morning it was found dead. A boy chucked the soft animal into the wastebasket. Matthew mourned the turtle in its coffin of crumpled milk cartons the whole day. Why was it that the wrong people were allowed to have things that they shouldn't? He headed for the cosmetics department.

"What do you think of this color lipstick, Matty?" Her lips bore a coating of bright pink.

"I want to go," he said.

"Soon. Is it too bright?"

"You're going to get into trouble if you do that."

"It was the sample. Tell me." She grew serious, held her lips still and looked straight ahead.

With her two shades of green eye shadow, her bright blue scarf and the lipstick, she looked like an exotic bird. "It smells like bubble gum."

She shook her head, reached into her handbag, and gave him some money. "Go buy yourself something at the luncheonette counter. I'll be through in a minute."

Matthew slumped away. Something had happened to her after Gramma died, he thought. Sometimes, after a man left the apartment he'd hear her crying softly. She could be angry with Matthew one moment and then give him ice-cream money the next. She stayed home from work more than she used to. He'd return from school and she'd be in bed watching TV and eating cookies.

He climbed up on a stool. A man in a white uniform with one of those hats like the ice-cream men was scraping the hot metal plate they cooked the hamburgers on.

"What you want?" he asked.

He had darkish skin and a mustache. A Spanish, Matthew thought. Matthew pointed to the orange drink spraying up and around in its square fountain. The man took a cone-shaped paper cup, fitted it into a metal holder and filled it. Matthew gave the man a nickel and a dime.

"What's wrong with you? You feel bad?" the man said.

Matthew was too surprised to answer and shook his head no. The man was leaning over and smiling. He chewed gum. Something made of gold hung around his neck. His dark hair shone like the leather of his mother's pocketbook.

"How old are you?"

"Ten."

"That's nice. You sure nothing's wrong?"

Matthew told him about the sneakers. The man looked at his watch.

"It's a little past four. You got enough time."

"She wants to buy some stupid makeup for her date tonight."

"Your mama's going out on a date?"

Matthew nodded his head.

"What kind of date?"

"With some guy."

The man smiled. "Where is she?"

"Somewhere over there," said Matthew, pointing over his shoulder. "She always says she's going to do something, then she never does. If I don't get them today I'll have to wait another whole week."

"Is that her with the blue scarf?"

Matthew nodded.

"She pretty. You got one pretty mama."

"How come you say 'mama'?"

"It's how I learned it."

Two girls slid onto stools beside Matthew. The man went off
to make make french fries for them. Matthew sipped the orange
drink and watched him. The man's sleeves were rolled up to
make thick bands over each muscle. He had a bouncy way of
moving. He surprised Matthew by slipping a plate of the french
fries in front of him, winking. Then the man went somewhere
else. Matthew turned around but he couldn't see the scarf.
Maybe she was done.

"Tell you what," the man said, returning. "You go over and get
your mama. Tell her if she finishes real fast, I'll give her a free
Coke."

"Oh yeah?"

He winked again. Matthew slid off his stool, heading for the
aisle with the cosmetics. He saw the blue scarf; his mother was
coming the other way around the back of the store. A tall man
with a heavy, square face walked right beside her.

"Wait up," Matthew cried.

Marjorie spun around and started toward him but the man
pulled her back by the wrist. "Let go," she shouted.

They reached a door. Matthew ran toward them. "Mom?"

She turned toward the man. Her voice shifted to a confidential
tone. "Look, I didn't mean to yell." She gripped Matthew's hand
rather firmly. "This is my son." She began to lead him away but
the man blocked her.

"Save it," he said, opening the door. "Get in. Junior can come
too. He might learn something."

They walked into a tiny, brightly lit room. The door clicked
shut behind them. Inside there was a desk with a phone and
chair, nothing more. The man sat down, his belly bunched up
before him. He pulled out a pad, slipped a sheet of carbon paper
inside it, and began writing. Marjorie kept her glance firmly on
him and away from Matthew.

"One lousy lipstick," she muttered.

"I don't care if it was one stick of gum. Stealing is stealing."

Matthew's eyes shot up to her. She went to light a cigarette.

"Not here you don't," said the man.

"What's happening?" Matthew said.

"I'll tell you later," Marjorie said, through gritted teeth.

There was a knock.

"Yeah?" grumbled the man at the desk.

"It's Sal." The doorknob jiggled. The man threw his pen down and opened the door.

The luncheonette guy stood in the doorway. His eyes met Matthew's, then he looked at Marjorie.

"What's up?" said the guy behind the desk.

"Can I talk to you for a minute?"

"Let me get this report filled out first."

"Wait." He stepped into the room and closed the door. He looked Matthew. "She your mom, right?" he said, motioning to Marjorie.

Matthew nodded his head slowly.

"You know him?" Marjorie asked Matthew, beginning to look frightened. He nodded.

"Listen, Mel," Sal said to the man, who'd sat back down. "Couldn't you let them slide this time?"

"Why in the hell should I?"

"She didn't really mean to do it."

"How do you know what I meant to —"

"Can it!" Sal said to her, suddenly sharp.

The man behind the desk laughed. "You see, the gal don't want your help." He turned to Marjorie. "You got some ID on you, Lady?"

"Wait, Mel. What she swipe?"

The man produced a shiny gold tube from his pocket and rolled it across the desk. "This."

Sal picked it up. "I take care of it," he said, pulling out a bill from his pocket. Marjorie was about to say something but Sal put up his hand.

The other man regarded the money quizzically. "That still ain't no reason to let it slide."

"Look, you know I help you before, right? I got you a couple of good ones, that mother and daughter team, right? If you catch her again, she's yours. But this time let her go."

Marjorie stepped forward. "Mister, I don't know what you think you're going to get from me — "

"Mind your own business," Sal said.

The man looked at them both. Then his eyes fell on Matthew. His mouth curled into a self-satisfied grin. "Okay," he said slowly. "I don't know why Sal's put in his two cents for you. In my book you ain't worth it. Sal's a good guy so I'll play along on one condition." He looked directly at Marjorie. "That you tell Junior exactly what you did."

Marjorie let out a whimper.

Sal faced her. "I think you should do it," he said.

"Who are you?" she said. "What's going on?"

"I work at the luncheonette counter. Your son told me what a nice mama he got so I wanted to help, okay?"

She looked at Matthew. "I swiped a lousy tube of lipstick," she said.

"You going to tear that up, Mel, okay?" Sal said.

"Maybe I should save it for the next time."

"There ain't going to be no next time," Sal said, looking directly at Marjorie.

"Thanks," she said with averted eyes.

The man opened the door. She ushered Matthew out.

"Could you wait a moment," Sal whispered to her.

"I'm in a hurry. I have to go buy sneakers for my kid."

"Just for a moment."

She motioned for Matthew to wait, then turned to Sal.

Matthew saw him say something to her. She barely looked at him. Then she smiled, reached into her pocketbook, and wrote something on a piece of paper. She took Matthew's hand to leave.

"Hey, Junior! Catch!"

Matthew turned around. Sal threw him the lipstick but he dropped it. He picked it up, wishing Sal hadn't seen him miss it.

2

Matthew stood on the blistered asphalt in front of the old pier building, hopping back and forth from the pinch of his new sneakers. The sky was clear, the sun very bright, but a chilly wind seeped right through the canvas of his shoes. It was still too cold to be wearing them, he realized. Justin had already scrambled up the concrete block and stood before the loading dock.

Matthew'd passed by this strange building on his way to the park and often wondered what was inside it. It looked like a giant, rusty shoe box that jutted out over the river as though it had been pushed off the street. His mother said she'd break both his legs if he ever went there, but she didn't say why. Its rows of smashed windows gave it a mean appearance although it was too old and rundown to look really scary. Way up near the roof, sturdy, proud stone letters spelled out the name of a shipping line. Sections of the metal walls had rotted away, leaving gaps resembling the sharp-edged holes punched into soda cans.

He'd gotten to know Justin several weeks before. They went to the same school, same grade but different classes. They met when they were both on the late line, one day when Matthew had spent too long trying to get his mother up for work. Pretty soon Justin was coming over almost every day. Justin had some strange ways. If they disagreed, Justin's face puffed up as if he'd swallowed a cloud. He'd shake his head and stare at the ground, not saying anything else but not listening to Matthew. Whenever they laughed, Justin kept laughing longer and louder. He was always tripping Matthew, or waiting around a corner to scare him. Yet at home, when his mother was around, he was different. He let Matthew try her stethoscope, made them Kool-Aid, and taught him how to do headstands. "Justin likes you," Carlotta had whispered to Matthew one day as he was leaving. "You can come over anytime."

Justin was a loser, Matthew decided. He seemed to have no other friends. But this morning Matthew was glad when Justin's knock gave him an excuse to leave the house. Last night, Marjorie had gotten all fixed up to go out with the guy who'd been taking her out to the theater ("This time I'm going to be ready when Rob comes," she'd announced) but he never came. She'd waited until nine o'clock, poured herself a drink—something clear from a big bottle, not beer—and drank it at the kitchen table. Then she went into her room to undress, taking the bottle with her.

"Let's go in," said Justin.

"It looks like it might fall down any minute. You been inside before?"

"Sure."

Matthew didn't know whether to believe him. That was another habit of Justin's: lying. Not real big lies, just things that weren't true. For example, saying he knew how to ride a motorcycle or that he was once in Florida. Under Matthew's questioning, Justin claimed that Florida was in New York, which made him distrust Justin from then on. Despite Justin's boasting, Matthew envied his daring. It had been Justin's idea to come down here. Nothing seemed to scare him. Matthew began to understand why: it wasn't bravery but not knowing any better. He'd dared Matthew to dart through cars along Ninth Avenue to get across. Matthew said it was too dangerous. Justin said that if anything happened, his mother could fix him up since she was a nurse.

"Prove you been inside," Matthew demanded. "Tell me what it's like."

Justin bit his lip. "It's like being at the bottom of the ocean," he said.

"How do you know what that's like?"

"I just do!" He crouched down. The garagelike door had been rolled down almost to the ground, leaving an opening. "I'm going in," he announced, and began crawling through. Matthew had no choice but to follow.

"Holy," said Matthew, on the other side, standing at one end of a great, binlike space. Light streamed through openings in the roof with biblical majesty or pierced through chinks in the walls like stars. Stanchions stood in rows along the gullied concrete floor. Far above, trusses spun arch after arch like steel echoes that faded out of sight at the far end. A tinkly staircase zigzagged up to the crumbling shelf of a mezzanine.

"Your face is all dirty," Justin said. "You look like a bum."

"Yours too!" They started to laugh, setting off a storm of reverberations.

"What is this place?" Matthew said.

"It was a fort," said Justin. "Look at all the bullet holes."

"I don't know," said Matthew. "Maybe it was a very old Woolworth's."

"Race you to the other side," shouted Justin, taking off.

Their footsteps were monster thuds. They ran past stanchions, pogo sticks jumping out of their way. Matthew was surprised at Justin's speed. They closed in on the panel of sunlight that marked a doorway all the way at the other end, squeezed through at the same time and wound up tumbling onto the pockmarked concrete terrace of the pier outside. Matthew landed on his back and Justin on top of him, his head pillowed by Matthew's belly. They lay laughing on the cold ground. Each shake of Matthew's belly made Justin giggle more, and each of his giggles pumped another laugh out of Matthew.

When they stopped Matthew asked Justin if he'd really been in the pier building before. Justin hesitated. "Tell me the truth," Matthew commanded.

"No," Justin said, growing still. "But I wanted to."

"My mom told me I couldn't come here."

"She boss you around a lot?"

"Nope," Matthew said. "My Gramma used to; then she died." He paused. "What about your mom and dad?"

Justin sat up. "They both let me do what I want," he said, staring out ahead of him. Then he turned to Matthew. "Let's not tell anyone about this place so it'll be all ours," he said.

★

They returned to the pier building almost every day after school. If they found a bum pissing in the corner they'd scare him so he'd piss on himself. Or else they'd tank up on water and have peeing contests to see who could go the farthest. There were always plenty of bottles to smash and chunks of concrete to send thundering against the walls. They found hypodermic needles (Justin identified them), even a little money. They made up stories to tell their mothers where they'd been.

The best part was the mezzanine, which they named the attic. To get to it they had to climb the string of metal steps that clung precariously to the wall. Each step sent out warning creaks the moment it bore any weight. The staircase wobbled as though the screws holding it were ready to pull through their holes. Matthew held his breath with each step, set as little of his foot down as he could, as if to lessen his weight. The bannister swayed free of its moorings at the slightest touch. He felt like he was sneaking up on someone.

Once they'd cleared the last step, they were in a sunny garden of junk. Most of the roof had fallen away. Heaps of moldy plaster and fragrant rotting wood had fallen off the exposed roof beams. A hole in the floor opened up the cratered moonscape of the ground floor to view. Beyond the hole the attic assumed something of its original appearance. A recognizable corridor separated two rows of small rooms — offices, suggested Matthew, jail cells, thought Justin. They housed desks whose wood was rippled from water damage, file cabinets fuzzy with rust and clumps of soggy paper. The river smell was everywhere, a caretaker making the rounds. Each day they chose a new office to occupy, climbing over the crags of wrecked furniture, sitting on the windowsills, the traffic of the West Side Highway on one side or the river's calm on the other.

One day, on the river side, they heard a noise.

"Someone's here," said Justin.

"Just a bum."

"No. It came from one of the rooms."

Matthew slipped off the sill.

"You gonna look? You crazy?" Justin asked.

"You scared?"

"No!"

"Then let's go see what it is."

"I don't feel like it."

Matthew hopped down and walked past him, smug with satisfaction at showing Justin up. He climbed outside into the corridor, crept up to the doorway of the next room, and peeked in. He saw no one, slid past to the next. It was empty as well. The suspense left him light-headed, and his fear almost made him laugh. Poor Justin, he thought, scared of everything. Soon only the large room at the end was left to be checked. He heard something as he neared it and squeezed close to the doorway to catch his breath. He looked in. This was the largest room, emptier than the others. He saw nothing unusual, and crept in, looking from side to side. He went the whole length of the room and turned around. Then he saw. In a far corner, two men stood facing each other, their arms locking them tightly together. They were kissing. Their pants were rolled down to their ankles; Matthew made out one hairy leg pressed between the other's two, spread slightly apart. He froze, his heart leaping. They didn't look at him. He prayed they wouldn't and began the long walk back out, moving as silently as he could. Just before he reached the door, one man turned to him. His gaze wouldn't let Matthew move another inch. Matthew noticed a tattoo on the man's arm. The other had a mustache. They smiled at him.

"Where are you going?" the man with the tattoo said. His voice was a soft clap to Matthew's chest.

Matthew stared at them, waiting as long as his nerve would let him, then he sped into the corridor. Justin waited by the stairs.

"What'd you see?" he asked.

"Nothing."

The next day Matthew returned, his legs aquiver as he climbed to the attic. But the room was empty. He trudged back into the street. He found a tin can to kick out of his way.

Seven

1

"Hey Red, you put the whole thing in ass-backwards!"

Frank's voice boomed through the garage like something thrown against the wall. Justin heard it all the way in the changing room in back. He struggled to undo a shoelace, trying to get out of his shoes so he could put on his garage clothes. He'd gotten there late and was out of breath after sprinting from his house. His belly, heavy with cookies, wedged tightly inside his pants. Every time he was ready to leave for the garage his mother appeared with something for him to eat, asking him dumb questions about school or how he was feeling.

Changing in the back room was the worst part of working at the garage. The single bulb hanging from the ceiling shed a grimy light on the sweating cinderblock walls. Pictures of naked women were taped to the doors of the battered lockers. Bull's-eyes had been drawn on their nipples, and penises at their crotches. "Red was here" was written on one of them. The moments between taking off his dungarees and getting into his overalls left him feeling clumsy and unprotected. He never knew when one of the other guys might catch him like that.

"Hey, man, Don't pull that shit on me. It was you who told me to do it that way," Red shouted.

His uncle was always arguing with one of the guys who worked there. Red had threatened Frank with a wrench once. The shoelace wouldn't come free. Justin panicked and tried pulling off his dungarees but the pants leg bunched over the shoe. He stood with his pants half off, his one stockinged foot on

120

the chilly concrete floor. The damp air wrapped his wobbly flesh in goose pimples.

The hood of a car slammed shut. Someone was coming. Justin pulled frantically at the tops of his pants. Something ripped, and his pants pulled free. He threw them into his locker, reached for his overalls and stepped into them just as the door scraped open. A short, wiry man with bright red hair stomped in.

"Fucking fatface," he yelled behind him. Justin raced to zip himself up. "Whaddaya got to hide?" Red sneered, throwing open his locker. He took a long swallow from a small bottle, then slumped down on the bench. His hair was a mat of tight red curls that seemed to glow, and his rubbery face was splattered with freckles. He was often in a bad mood; Justin thought it might be because of all those freckles.

A moment later Frank boomed in. "What the hell you think you're doin, Red? Get back there and finish that carburator. We got to get it done today." He noticed Justin. "Hey, Champ. When you get in?"

"Couple of minutes ago," Justin mumbled, heading for the door.

"Okay, okay. Take it easy." He patted Justin on the shoulder.

Red watched them. "Leave it to Beaver," he sneered.

"Shut your trap and get back to work," said Frank. "I'm not paying you to sit on your ass."

"For what I'm getting paid it's the most you can expect."

Justin slid past, glad to get away from them. Frank never yelled at Justin. He spoke to him the way he did to Carlotta, careful not to say anything that would make Justin change his mind about working for him.

Justin had forgotten about his uncle's offer. Then, the way home from school one day, just as he'd passed the garage, his uncle happened to step outside.

"Hey, Champ. Long time no see." Carlotta had told Frank she didn't want want him coming over for supper anymore. "You got a minute? Let me show you something." He led Justin into the garage. "Guys, say hello to my nephew, Justin," he said, beaming and putting his arm around Justin. The guys eyed him suspiciously. Frank led him over to a car. "Watch this," Frank said. He flicked a switch. There was a grinding whirr, then the car began to rise. "You put a car up on one of these things, it's like giving it an x-ray. You see everything—engine, axles, brakes, muffler." The car was nearing the height of Justin's head. "A car ain't so different from a person: every part has a job to do, and if something goes wrong, the car gets sick."

Justin followed the car's motion, hardly blinking from excitement. The thick shaft came into view, pushing up from the floor, shiny and striped with lines of grease. The car came to a halt. Frank motioned for Justin to come with him underneath. Justin hesitated. "Cmon, Champ. It won't fall."

"What's that thing?" Justin pointed toward the chassis.

"That's connected to the steering wheel. It makes the wheels turn."

"And that?"

"That's for the exhaust."

"How come the car stays up there like that?"

Frank explained. By the time he was finished, Justin was smiling.

"Would you like to let her back down?"

"Yeah!"

Frank showed him to a little box mounted on a pedestal. "Throw that lever."

Justin did. The car began to sink. When the wheels touched down Frank said, "Tell you what. You work here, and I'll let you work the lift whenever we need it. How's that?"

Justin said yes.

He came twice a week after school. He broke open the cartons of Pennzoil and set them up on the wire rack. He stacked tires, held the flashlight while one of the guys worked inside a hood, swept his uncle's office in the front. He went for Frank's White Owls and his coffee, cleaned the tools, submerging them in a depth of cool gasoline, working the gunk loose with his fingers, then pulling them out, a dull silver. Each day Frank presented him with two quarters, which Justin put into a Tropicana orange juice bottle under his bed. He promised himself not to spend any of his earnings until he'd accumulated ten whole dollars. He wasn't sure what he'd spend the money on, but there were several possibilities: a pizza all for himself, a model motoring set, a Schwinn bicycle, although he didn't know how to ride yet.

Two guys worked at the garage besides Red. There was Bud, a huge guy with droopy eyes and large hands, who had a slow, slurry way of speaking. Red nicknamed him Dodo. Bud didn't seem to mind. He admired Red because of the stories he told about women. Bud let Red boss him around although he could have crushed Red with one hand. Ernie was a tall, good-natured guy with a pointy nose; the others came to him for help. He'd been working there longer than the others. Justin liked him the best. Red and Justin were enemies from the very beginning. Red called him Frank Junior. He'd send Justin to get a wrench without warning him about oil on the floor near the pegboard, or he'd hand Justin the clamp of a battery cable, knowing the insulation was shot, waiting for Justin to double back from the shock. But Justin loved the garage. He liked the bright blue overalls Frank had bought for him, the way his hands were almost all black by the time he finished working, and the gooey pink soap he got to wash them with. Frank was always surprising him with a Hershey bar or a bag of M&Ms.

Just before quitting time they all filed into the back room, but Justin dawdled, finding something to do so he wouldn't have to undress in front of the others. He'd come in when they were almost ready, and he'd take a long time to wash his hands, further delaying taking off his clothes. He listened to them talking, usually about girls.

"I knew something was gonna happen last night cause she was jumpy the whole time we was in the movie," Red was saying one evening.

"The same chick from last week?" Ernie said.

"Yeah."

"I thought it was hands off with her?"

"Not last night!" He put out his palm for Ernie to slap.

"You gave it to her good, huh, Red?" said Bud. He held his fists before him and swiveled his hips.

"Take it easy, Bud," said Ernie.

"People like him shouldn't think of reproducing," said Red. Bud looked puzzled. "Hey, Dodo, you know I'm joking, right?" He winked at Bud. "Anyway, I told her I'd drive her home. She lives all the way out in Canarsie. I said I had to get my old man's registration first. We went back to my house. My folks were away for the weekend. I said we should go up and have something to drink. The minute she was up there, she knew what the score was."

Justin listened at the sink, working the soap through his fingers slowly. Red described everything in detail. how he'd gotten her down to her panties in his goddam parents' bed, how he sucked on her titties, how he stuck his fingers right up inside her and she felt like jelly.

"Then right at the last minute, the bitch clamped her legs together tight as a goddam vise." A menacing tone crept into his voice. "I told her she was getting it no matter what so she might as well enjoy it. She started crying. I didn't care, I rammed it the hell in."

"Did she scream?" said Bud, a ridge of tongue slipping through his teeth.

"Nah, she liked it, goddammit. I felt a little bad for her afterwards. But it was her own fault. She shouldn'ta started what she couldn't finish."

Ernie and Red slapped palms again.

"How about you, Champ?" Red said, turning to Justin suddenly, his freckles glowing like a thousand teasing lights. "You gonna get yourself some pussy too?"

Justin stared at Red's bare chest, the color of paste. It was strange how the freckles stopped just around the base of his neck. Red made a grab between Justin's legs. "Champ's got a hard-on! What do you know? I didn't even think you had what to get hard."

"Leave the kid alone," said Ernie.

Finally they were gone. Justin changed. On the way out he passed the naked woman with Red's name on it. He looked at the woman's smiling face, at her hands holding up her breasts as though they might drop otherwise. He imagined Red coming down on her and her smile becoming a scream. Justin's thing hardened.

He understood what they were talking about, almost. He'd mixed up "tits" and "balls" at first and didn't understand about what there was to shoot ("I must have given her a quart," boasted Red). But a month of listening to them had given Justin a rough picture of things. He noticed how their voices shifted when they talked about it, different from when they talked about sports or cars, lower, like it was a kind of secret.

One day, cleaning out his uncle's office, he found a magazine full of pictures like the ones taped to the wall of the back room and some with men lying on top of the women. His thing stirred. So this was it, he thought. He heard his uncle coming, and slipped the magazine down his overalls. That night, after work, he took the magazine to the park to read. His eyes widened before the glossy, unbelievable images; women with mean smiles, with blond hair and red lips and big, big titties. He'd noticed these on women before; he used to like resting his head against his mother's. But he'd never seen them showing. As the weather grew warmer he began noticing the women around him more and more, each with this secret beneath their coats. He watched them sitting in the park, imagining what lay just beneath their dresses, the dark space their legs led to. Justin wasn't exactly sure how it looked under there, since the magazines never showed it.

Mornings before school, he began observing his mother as she slid behind the partition, damp and fragrant from her shower, in her bathrobe. When she took it off and hung it over the partition, she sent a wavy silhouette against the tufted cloth, and he knew she was completely naked. One morning he surprised her in the bathroom just as she got out of the shower, determined to get a better view. She shrieked and pulled the plastic curtain around her. He pretended it was an accident and left, ashamed but exhilarated, feeling a little like Red.

★

"Sit down, Champ," said Frank, motioning to the chair beside his desk. It was after five. The others had already gone, the garage was quiet. Justin thought of the magazine he'd taken with him, hidden under his jacket. Frank leaned back in his swivel chair, took a long puff of his cigar, and let out a leisurely blue plume. "How you doin?"

"Okay," said Justin.

"That's good, Champ."

Give me my money, thought Justin.

"You know, sometimes I don't know what I'm doing here."

He had a habit of saying things that made Justin ask, "What do you mean?" Today Justin wasn't going to. He wanted out. He wanted to go to the park, read his magazine, and get home before his mother asked him why he was late.

"I gotta go," he said.

Frank gave him a weak smile. "I know, I know. Just listen to me for a moment. I got no one else to talk to." He rolled forward in his chair. "I like you, Champ. I hope you like me, too."

"Yeah," said Justin, looking away from his uncle's lopsided eyes.

"I'm glad somebody does. The guys that work here sure as hell don't."

"You yell at them too much."

Frank was surprised. "Too much? I don't yell at them enough. If I didn't keep after them they wouldn't do a damn thing."

"Ernie would."

"All right, Ernie. But that's not the point. I can fire the other jerks tomorrow, nothing stopping me. There'd just be two jerks to replace them. The world is full of jerks and most of them ain't smart enough to do anything else but fix cars. I know I ain't no Einstein either. But I'll tell you something. I don't gotta go begging to nobody. As long as I got this garage I can stand on my own two feet." He gestured to the water cooler, the Goodyear Tires clock, his beat-up desk. "It ain't much, but's it's mine. That's why I put up with all those jerks. My old man never gave me the time of day. I was the rotten egg. My brother Ralph, your father, he had everything handed to him on a silver platter. He was the fair-haired boy, his shit didn't stink. Now don't get me wrong, Champ. I ain't saying nothin against your father." He clopped off a tube of ash from his cigar and stared at it. The overhead lights hummed. It was almost five-thirty. Now I won't have enough time to go to the park, Justin thought.

"But, let's face it," Frank continued, louder. "The guy was a prick. That's why I couldn't wait to sell all that stuff in the apartment. I didn't want it, it reminded me of him. I was glad to get rid of it right after — " He stopped himself, and looked over to Justin, who was staring at him. "Let me tell you something, Champ, and I want you to remember it." He paused. "There was only one person who ever gave a hoot about me. You know who that was?" Justin waited. (Would he have to say, "Who?") "It was your mother. My own flesh and blood made like I didn't exist. Fool Frankie, my brother called me. But not Lottie. She was better than anyone I ever knew. She cares about people. Now I know she hates me." He fell silent.

Justin stood. "I really gotta go now."

Frank pulled out a five dollar bill from his pocket and handed it to him. Justin hesitated. "Take it," he said.

Justin stuffed the money into his pocket and left. He ran several blocks, all the while patting to make sure the magazine was still there.

★

"Ain't you gonna change?" Red said.

Justin had begun to undo the snaps of his overalls, figuring the others were ready to go. Bud was already dressed. Red just had to put his shirt on.

"Lemme alone," Justin said.

"Lemme alone," mimicked Red.

"I never seen him change," said Bud. "What'sa matter, you ashamed?"

"We're all guys," said Red.

"Maybe he ain't got nothin there," said Bud.

Justin wished Ernie were there. Ernie would have stuck up for him. Red would have told another of his girl stories and would have forgotten about Justin. But Red never told them if only Bud was there; he thought Bud was too stupid to understand.

Red snatched Justin's pants off the bench.

"Hey!" Justin shouted.

Red dangled them before him. The moment Justin made a grab Red tossed them over Justin's head to Bud. "Saloogie!" he cried. Bud tossed them back.

Justin jumped up after them. His overalls dropped to his ankles. Horrified, he went to pull them up. Bud was behind him and pushed. Justin tumbled to his knees. Their laughter rang above him. Red waved the pants like a bullfighter's cape, just out of Justin's reach. The ends of Red's belt dangled around his waist, the buckle flashed before Justin's eyes. Justin lunged for it and pulled. Red was spun against the lockers, Justin fell back the other way, stunned, the belt firmly in his hand.

Red came at Justin. "You gimme that or I'm gonna stomp you . . ."

Justin snapped the belt across Red's naked belly. Red howled and fell back, his skin branded with a reddish stripe. He collapsed in half around it. Bud made a grab for Justin; Justin brandished the strap at him.

"Get away, Dodo!" he shouted.

Frank entered. "What's going on?" He caught sight of Red. "Jesus —".

"I'll kill you, you little bastard," he whimpered, staggering toward Justin. "Look what the bastard did!" He displayed his stomach.

"He stole my pants," said Justin.

"Get dressed, you," Frank said to Red. "Then come into my office."

"Why?"

"I'm giving you walking papers. Get a move on. Bud, you can go home now."

"That little prick stole my belt."

"You ain't one to talk about stealing," said Frank. "I've had my eye on you. Get moving, Bud."

Bud slid past obediently. "See you around, Red," he said.

★

Justin sized up the metal drum filled with oily brown water, trying to decide whether he should attempt to get it to the sidewalk by himself or ask one of the others for help. Frank had told him not to do it alone. But Ernie and Bud were busy and Fong, the guy Frank hired to replace Red, was off somewhere else. Frank wasn't there, either. Justin decided to chance it. He braced his hands along the rim, saw his face reflected in the rainbows of grease on the surface. He heaved one side of the drum slightly.

"Sure you can handle that?" Bud shouted.

"Sure." Since Red had left they'd gotten to be friends and Bud respected him. Justin began shifting the drum slowly from side to side, letting the water come to rest in between. When he'd gotten it almost to the streeet, he paused. Not bad, he thought. His arms ached a little but it wasn't too much farther to the curb. His uncle would be surprised to hear he'd managed it alone. He rubbed his fingers together and began again.

At that moment, Frank entered. "Hey, I told you . . ."

Justin panicked. The bottom rim met a patch of grease. The drum lurched out from under him. A torrent of dirty water lapped across the floor, washing around Frank. The drum bowled across the garage floor until it hit the Pennzoil rack, sending the cans to the ground like salvos.

Frank charged over to him. "What the fuck did you do?" He gave Justin a shove that sent him sprawling into the water. Ernie, Bud, and Fong were watching. Justin fought back tears.

At the end of the day Frank apologized. "Do me a favor, Champ," he said, handing Justin another five dollar bill. "Don't mention this to your mother, okay?"

Justin took the money.

The next time he saw his uncle on the way to the john with one of his magazines rolled under his arm, he took a small screwdriver from the pegboard and told the others to get ready to see something good. He crept up to the bathroom door and waited. From inside there was a splashing stream. Then the magazine rustled open. Soon Justin heard something moving back and forth. A watery murmuring filled the tiny john. Justin inserted the screwdriver between the door and the frame, lifted the latch.

"Now," he whispered as the door swung open. Frank sat on the toilet, pants rolled down, a weasly grin on his face, one hand on the open magazine pressed on his knee, the other grasping the reddened bulb between his legs.

"Wha — ?" He looked up, fumbling for his pants. "Close the door, goddammit. Close the fucking door!"

The garage shook with laughter. Justin joined his coworkers, a hero.

2

Gramma's wheezing was a saw rasping back and forth through the hole in the living room wall, where Matthew slept. She was in the next room, coughing and spitting. Water sloshed in her throat, shchlshchlshchl. It poured out of her mouth and nose and ears, out of her ass, it spilled onto the floor, dirty and stinky. Matthew huddled deeper in his blanket. The wall began to crack.

Help me, she said. She was drowning. Her hand clawed against the wall as she tried to stay afloat, but she was too fat. Matthew could save her if he ran in. But he didn't want to.

Footsteps, wet, heavy feet clomping toward the living room. Water started pouring into the living room, it swirled around the Castro where Matthew lay and heaved the bed up, it washed around the TV. Matthew held onto the edge of the bed, fearful of being tossed into the steaming soup.

Gramma burst into the living room. She tore away part of the door frame. Her wet bathrobe was pasted to her bazumbas like sauce over dumplings. Yellow egg slime bubbled out of her mouth, her arms looked like pudgy torpedos. She wants to tear out my lungs, Matthew thought. Hers are no good anymore so she wants mine.

She came over to his bed and shook it like a rug to throw him off but he held on. I saw what you do at night with your filthy little thing. She climbed into the Castro, it bobbed up and down like a raft. They were swirled out of the apartment, into the hallway, and down the stairs, floor after floor, faster all the time. She kept trying to grab him and push him overboard, but he held on. They rounded the last landing to the ground floor. The bed whooshed down the hallway to the front door. It was locked, they were going to crash. Gramma made a last lunge at him. He closed his eyes and shouted a curse.

Get away. You're doody!

She vanished.

Matthew sprang from sleep, panting. The room wavered around him, he was sweating. It was the same dream again. He'd had it often since Gramma died. He was sure it came from sleeping in Gramma's old bed. He'd asked Marjorie for a new one because he slumped in the hole she'd left in it. He went to the bathroom to rinse the morning guck from his mouth.

On the way he stopped before the door to his mother's room. She'd been out with someone last night but he didn't know who. She'd acted strange the whole day before, the way she usually did when she had a date coming up — dropping things, throwing clothes out of a dresser drawer to find something, shouting. When Matthew asked if she had a date, she told him to mind his own business. Around five, when she usually started getting ready to go out, she announced that she was sending him over to her friend Joan's house for supper.

"You can play with her son Richie, he's your age," she said.

Matthew said he wanted to watch Jackie Gleason.

"Just take the bus up Eighth Avenue," she said, pressing some change into his hand. "You can watch Jackie Gleason over there." By the time Joan drove him home, Marjorie was gone. There was a note on his bed. "Be good, sweetie," it said. "See you tomorrow. Mom."

This morning her bedroom door was half open. He peeked in. She looked tiny and gentle in the middle of the room's chaos, like a girl from a fairy tale fallen asleep in the woods. On the days she had to go to work, she underwent a transformation in the morning. She was thin and pale on her way to the bathroom before her makeup but emerged wide-eyed and talking in a rush, as though the lipstick and eye liner had given her speech and sense, like cartoons where the man drew a character into life. In her dress and high heels, she was tall, complete. But Sundays, when she stayed in bed, she remained small.

Just as Matthew put his mouth to the bathroom faucet he heard something. A snore? His mother? He listened again. It hadn't come from her bedroom. He shut the water, tiptoed to the living room, then drew back. A man lay asleep in his underwear on the Castro. His clothing had been neatly arranged on the club chair. The blanket lay on the floor below his feet. His skin was dark against the white sheet, his black hair came to a little point at the back of his neck. Each breath lifted his shoulder blades up out of his dense upper back, then sank them back down. His legs and arms were thick and furry, his feet extended just over the edge of the bed. (Matthew's feet hadn't been able to reach it, even when he'd stretched his arms out from the other end.) One arm was hooked around the pillow as though it were the shoulder of a friend. Matthew's palms became clammy where they pressed against the door frame. The man began turning around. Matthew waited, terrified of being seen, unable to look away. The man's face came into view. Matthew recognized him: the Spanish guy from Woolworth's.

Matthew was back in his bed and under the covers, shaking and out of breath before the man yawned.

★

Bits of bread crust clung to the tangle of hair on Sal's bare chest. Slivers of shell caught in seaweed, Matthew thought. Nearby, the buried treasure of his gold cross. Ridges of purple veins rose out of his forearms. His muscle came up when he lifted his coffee cup. Matthew's throat tightened each time he glanced up from his plate across the table.

"If you let your eggs sit there long enough we'll be able to use them to plug the leak in the bathrooom," said Marjorie. She sat beside him in her Levis and a shirt.

"You didn't eat anything, either."

"You know I never eat breakfast," she said with a sly smile. "But Sal here went to all the trouble to make this nice food. The least you could do is eat it." She smiled at Sal.

I don't want any of his stupid food, Matthew thought.

Matthew was mad. She'd snuck this guy into the house behind his back. Look at her, he thought, hair brushed, dressed, even some liptstick on, and it's Sunday and not even twelve o'clock. She was putting on a show for this guy. The eggs bore a mantle of bright red sauce that looked delicious. Matthew was hungry, all right. But he wasn't going to eat this guy's food.

"Don't force him, Jojo," Sal said. His large white teeth flashed between plum-colored lips.

He already had a nickname for her.

"I'm not hungry," Matthew said.

"Stop playing games, Matty. You're always hungry."

Look who's playing games, he thought, glancing at her red lips. Was she wearing the lipstick she'd tried to filch? Sure looked like it.

"What is this stuff, anyway?" Matthew said.

"It's called huevos con salsa," said Sal.

Matthew plunged his fork in.

"Be careful, it's — "

Matthew downed a mouthful. A moment later he sprang for his milk. "That's hot!" he said, chugging it down.

Marjorie held back a laugh.

"Eat some bread," Sal advised.

"Why didn't you tell me it was hot?" Matthew shouted.

"Pipe down," Marjorie said.

"You did it on purpose," Matthew said.

"Sorry." Sal said. "Here." He broke off some of the bread for him and watched as Matthew ate it. "Your mama tells me you like turtles."

Matthew kept eating.

"Sal is talking to you, Matthew."

"Yeah," he said.

"I seen turtles as big as this table when I was a kid."

"Can I have some cereal?" Matthew asked.

Marjorie shook her head.

"You don't like it, Matto?" said Sal.

"Why can't I have some cereal?"

"Sal asked you a question."

Matthew glared at him. "You Puerto Rican or something?"

"Matthew," said Marjorie.

"Are you?"

Sal started to answer, but Marjorie put her hand up for him to stop. "That's enough, Matty."

Matthew scraped the sauce from his eggs with his fork. He saw Sal watching, took his napkin, and wiped away what was left. The eggs were good, not runny like Gramma's or rubbery like his mother's. He saw the two of them smiling at each other. "You're lucky Gramma isn't here," he said to Marjorie.

"Sure am, Kiddo," Marjorie snapped. "And one more crack like that you can go to your room."

Matthew returned to his eggs. The sauce had etched a warm path down his throat and into his stomach. Anytime his eyes fell on Sal, his insides gently glowed. He examined the sauce. There were little brown flecks in it. He snuck a little onto his fork and tasted it again. It wasn't so bad. But if this guy was so great, how come she didn't want Matthew to see him when he came over last night? What was the idea of shipping him off to Richie's? He glanced at them. They were smiling at each other again.

"You a piano player?" Matthew said.

They turned.

"I work in Woolworth," Sal said. "You know that, you see me there . . ."

"My real father was a piano player."

"What the hell are you talking about?" Marjorie said.

"My grandmother said that the only reason he stuck around with her was because he thought he could make a buck off her—"

"That's enough!" Marjorie said.

"But as soon as he found someone who could sing better than she could he left—"

"You little shit!" she said, springing up.

"Jojo," Sal said, taking her arm.

"I should wash your mouth out with soap!" She went to hit him in the face. Matthew jerked away and his eggs were swept to the floor. She broke into sobs. "Get out of my sight, you monster," she said, falling back into her chair.

Matthew saw Sal taking her into his arms as he ran to his room.

★

Sal began coming to the house almost every Saturday evening. He had two suits, a dark one and one made of something that could shine in the light. His hair was slicked back into lacquered grooves. The tap of his pointy shoes in the hallway alerted Matthew that he was almost there. Matthew kept to the sofa, his eyes firmly fixed to the television screen. Sal remained in the kitchen. Marjorie always tried to be ready on time. She never wore her high heels; he figured out why. After they left the apartment he'd run to the peephole and watch them walking down the hall. Even in flat shoes she was taller.

He returned to the sofa, confused and a little sad, fell asleep on the Castro watching movies on television. He'd wake hours later, the screen blank and buzzing, his hands wedged into the warmth between the sofa's cushions. He felt himself being lifted into a cloud of beer and sweat. Sal's arms locked beneath Matthew, and he was carried to his room. He fell back to sleep imagining Sal carrying him to bed over and over again. In the morning he awoke to the sound of Sal's energetic toothbrushing (the reason why his teeth were so white, Matthew guessed). Then the front door closed; Sal would be off to mass. When he returned, he started their breakfast. Soon the kitchen filled with the rustle of frying.

"Don't you get tired of cooking all the time?" Matthew asked one morning, watching from the kitchen doorway.

"As long as people like what I make, I don't mind. Do you like what I cook?"

"Sort of." Sal gave Matthew a spoonful of the sauce to taste.

"It's good," Matthew said.

Sal squeezed his arm. "Matito," he said.

Matthew went a little tight in the stomach.

When breakfast was ready there was a plateful of doughy churros crusted with sugar, a mound of fluffy eggs joined by thick slices of chorizo and strong, oily coffee that emboldened Matthew's milk.

"I think I like Sal," Marjorie said to Matthew one evening. "So you better be nice to him."

"I am."

"Do you call making that stink that first Sunday nice?"

"How come you snuck him in like that?"

"I was nervous. Also a little embarrassed. You know, about the lipstick."

"Why does he call me Matito?"

"It's a Spanish nickname. He uses it because he likes you, even though you acted like a dope."

Friday afternoons Marjorie stopped off at a bodega on the way home from work to pick up what Sal would need for their Sunday breakfast. Saturday morning they vacuumed and dusted and straightened around the house. Marjorie put up fresh curtains in the kitchen and sent Matthew with a bundle of her old clothing to the Salvation Army. She bought herself two new dresses. "What do you think?" she said, showing them to Matthew. "I got these special because Sal doesn't like low necklines."

She also bought a toothbrush, which hung beside theirs in the bathroom.

3

April sunlight through the planking scored the soft earth below the bleachers. Justin found his usual spot in the corner and pulled out the magazine from under his jacket. "MY HUSBAND SHAMES ME AND I LOVE IT" was slashed across the chest of the woman on the cover. She lay on her back on a furry pink bed in a black bikini. Her blond hair cascaded over the edge of the bed in stiff waves. Her legs were parted, her crotch obscured by a second masthead which read "CONFESSIONS OF A CORPORATE HOOKER." Justin opened the magazine at random.

> *Hump me, baby. Stick me good with your red hot poker, and hump me to hell . . .*

How big was it in there? he wondered. He couldn't imagine his mother lying there like that.

Footsteps clattered above. Heads telescoped through the slats. Justin stuffed the magazine back under his jacket and ran toward the other end. Kids starting jumping down around him like locusts from the sky.

"What are you doing here?" A blond-haired kid stood right in front of him.

A kid with a pockmarked face pulled the magazine out from Justin's jacket. "Hey, look what I found!"

The blond-haired kid snatched it away. "Where'd you get this?" The others clustered around.

"Stole it."

"Yeah?"

Justin heard the admiration in his voice. "I always steal them."

"From where?"

"Secret."

"You live around here?" asked a short kid.

"Yup."

"We never seen you. What's your school?" said another.

Justin told them.

"That's only for punks. We all go to Sacred Heart," said a kid with glasses.

The blond-haired kid stepped forward. "You know who we are?"

Justin shook his head.

"We're the Bloodhounds. This here's our fort. Only Bloodhounds can come here."

"It ain't yours, it's the city's. Gimme back my magazine."

"Too late. It's Bloodhound property now."

"We take what we want," said the small kid.

"If you're tough you can be a Bloodhound, too," said the blond-haired kid.

"He gotta have a nitiation, Kevin," said a tall kid.

Kevin smirked. "You don't gotta tell me how it works. If it wasn't for me there wouldn'ta been no Bloodhounds." He turned back to Justin. "Well, you wanna do it?"

"What if I don't?"

"Then you can't stay in the park."

"Who's gonna stop me?"

The circle tightened around him.

"Okay. What I gotta do?"

"First answer some questions," said Kevin. "You got any friends who are niggers?"

"No."

"You sure?"

Justin shook his head, thinking of that strange guy Matthew hung around with.

"You better not have. We hate niggers. Niggers is overrunning everyplace. They ain't allowed in this park. Any nigger who tries to come here gets slashed."

"With what?"

They exchanged ominous smiles.

"With this," Kevin said, reaching into his pocket. A long blade flashed through the air between their faces. Justin jumped back. Kevin laughed. "You scared?" The others laughed in chorus. "There's one nigger who's going to get it for sure," he said.

"What he do?" Justin asked.

"He tried to call the cops on us," said one kid

"He thinks he owns the park," said another.

Kevin pointed to a scar across his cheek. "You see this? Know where it came from? I got it when the nigger tried to mess with me."

Justin made a run for it. Kevin stopped him with the point of the knife. "Anybody we ask to join the Bloodhounds gotta join." He moved in closer. "You ready?"

"For what?"

His eyes narrowed. He smiled. "The nitiation," he said. The others held him fast. "Get his jacket off."

They had it off quickly and wrestled him to the ground. A kid pinioned each limb immobile. Kevin removed his jacket with an exaggerated slowness, prolonging Justin's terror. He held the blade so Justin could see it.

"What are you going to do?" Justin said.

"You'll see," said Kevin, lowering himself down over Justin's middle. His legs clamped tightly around Justin's hips. "We're gonna become blood brothers, you and me. Every Bloodhound is blood brothers with me. Make a fist," he said. He brought his fist beside Justin's. Justin squirmed as he lowered the knife. "Keep still. It's too late. We found you in our fort so you gotta become one of us." Kevin looked at him through glassy eyes, a lifeless smile on his lips. He placed his fist besides Justin's. The knife hovered right above the corded veins of their wrists. His face had tensed to a dark red, as though the slightest pinprick would have made it spurt blood: an angry sun surrounded by a frightening orbit of faces.

"Oh no—" Justin shut his eyes. A screaming blur closed in around his head. The blade lanced both wrists with a single swipe, leaving a furrow of blood behind. Kevin pressed his wrist against Justin's, his body rock back and forth slightly, as if mixing their blood together. Then he pulled away. "You're a Bloodhound now," he mumbled, exhausted, standing up.

They released Justin. He stared at the flower-shaped smear of blood on his wrist.

"Press your other wrist on it or else you'll bleed to death," the kid with the pockmarked face said softly. "I'm Mike."

"We call him Pebbleface," said the short kid, whose name was Tony. He pointed to a kid whose eyes appeared gigantic behind thick eyeglasses. "That's Eugene."

"I'm W-W-Walt," said the tall kid.

Kevin snapped the knife shut. "Who are you?" he said.

Justin told him, his eyes still on his wounded wrist.

"Can you really get more of those magazines?" Kevin asked, picking up the magazine. Justin nodded limply.

"Hey, what's this?" He held the magazine open to a picture of a large Negro man pressed on top of a white woman. Kevin drew out his knife in a rage and sheared the picture to pieces. "Goddam niggers," he shouted, hurling the magazine against the wall.

4

Sal kept to his knees for a long time after the rest of the congregation had taken their seats. His face was buried in the rough bowl of his hands. Wisps of Spanish escaped between his fingers. When he was finished, he rose and looked up at the altar, his face as ruddy as a boxer's. Matthew could see he'd been crying.

After the service Matthew asked him why.

"I was thinking about how my father must have felt when he realized my mother had grown old."

Several Sundays before, at breakfast, Sal had asked Matthew and Marjorie if they would like to go to mass with him.

"Not that again," said Matthew.

"I'd rather sleep," said Marjorie.

"How about once, Matito?"

The Sunday after that they left the house before breakfast. Sal set a brisk pace up Amsterdam Avenue that had Matthew trotting to keep up.

"Gramma used to go to the church around the corner from us," Matthew said. "Why don't we just go there?"

"I know that one. There the walls gossip about what was said in the confession booth."

They passed block after block of apartment buildings brooding along the street in the still May morning. "Why do we have to go to church and hear some old guy tell us how bad we are?" said Matthew.

"That's not the reason I go. My father never goes, even though he very religious. He say the church is full of liars who put on a clean shirt on Sunday for mass. But the church is the only place I can talk to him."

"You mean God?"

"No, my father."

"You said he lives far away."

"He does. So I go to the church, get down on my knees, close my eyes. I try not to think of anything, nothing, like my head is filled with sky. If I'm lucky, he comes around. He helps me. Sometimes he talks about how things are going down there where I come from. The other day he complained that my mother was getting too fat. I'd go crazy if I couldn't talk to him. I almost go crazy right after I moved here. I was living in a shithole over on West Forty-eighth Street, a rooming house full of scum. I worked as a freight operator. Some days I felt like taking the elevator to the top floor and letting it drop. I couldn't do it because there was a safety brake. I was going to church two, three times a day. I ask my father what should I do."

"What did he say?"

"He say I should get another job and move someplace nice."

"If you miss him so much why don't you call him up?"

"It's not that easy."

"Why not?"

"He's far away."

"Take a jet," Matthew persisted.

"You don't understand," Sal said, stepping up the pace, making it hard for Matthew to do any more talking.

Matthew started going with him every week. He liked hearing Sal's stories. They took Broadway back home after the service. By then the solemn, cool streets had come to life. Sal pointed out all the places he'd worked as a short-order cook, where he'd seen a woman run over by a cab (one of those Checkers, big as a tank), where a man had jumped off the roof of the Ansonia Hotel and landed in a baby carriage.

"Yeah?"

"Funny thing was, the carriage was full of tomatoes! Hey, look across the street." He pointed to the Regency Theater. "That's where I took your mother out for the first time. It was a Doris Day picture. Your mama loves Doris Day, don't ask me why."

"You going to marry my mom?"

"I don't know. Think I should?"

"She told me she'll never get married because all men want to boss her around."

Sal frowned. "Your mama thinks the whole world is out to get her. Including me sometimes."

Sal had lived on the Upper West Side since coming to the United States. People were always stopping him on the street to say hello. Sal introduced Matthew to them as his Matito. Matthew liked it. But he wondered; did Sal expect him to say Dad?

Sal often talked about where he came from, a place whose Spanish name Matthew never remembered. The women there burned candles to make men love them or to give them sons. The flies were as big as can openers. People chewed on the leaves of plants that let them see the stars during the day.

"How come you left?" Matthew asked.

"I had to."

"Did you do something bad?"

"Everyone does bad things. The only ones who get caught are either unlucky or poor. I was both." Then he began walking faster, a signal for Matthew to stop asking questions, or risk making Sal angry.

Matthew knew he had a temper. Once Marjorie had made fun of Sal going to church. He'd thrown dishes to the floor. A mineral glow was in his eyes, as though he no longer saw through them. His large hands gripped plate after plate as Matthew and Marjorie ran for cover. "It's a shame that he's so crazy," Marjorie said to Matthew after Sal had gone. "Otherwise he'd be perfect."

Matthew knew those hands. He remembered how they had saved him from an ambush of the Bloodhounds. The gang had surprised him one day in the park after school. Before Matthew knew what was happening, he was surrounded. The ice-cream cone he'd been eating was flung away. His school books were torn from his hands. He was thrown down, his legs and arms immobilized. His shoulder throbbed from where it had hit the ground. Kevin sat on his stomach. The heels of his hands dug into Matthew's arms. Sal had appeared out of nowhere, rising behind Kevin's head like a giant. He pulled Kevin off and threw him to the ground. Kevin lay squirming, then tried to get up and run. Sal pursued him and shoved him back down. For a moment it looked as thought Sal would plunge his foot into Kevin's stomach. On the way home Sal's hands twitched like machines that couldn't be turned off. As they passed the statue Matthew remembered what kids said about the devil living right underneath, and he shuddered.

★

One Sunday Sal told Matthew about the Chapel of the Bones.

"It started a long time ago. There was a man in the village, whose real name I forgot but who was called El Ojo, the Eye. He was what you'd call an eccentric. People thought he was loco because he went around talking to himself. What they were most afraid of was his eyes. No one ever saw them blink, not even his wife. That might not have been so strange except that, as he got older, he began telling people what their souls looked like, and it was usually bad news. So-and-so's soul was as dirty as a rag, someone else's shivered, another's smelled like horse sweat. It wasn't so unusual for someone in the village to be talking about someone else — the people there were known for their gossiping. But El Ojo wasn't doing it behind their backs: that was the difference. What was worse, he was usually right. People started leaving the village so he wouldn't get too close a look at them. Those who stayed avoided him. Even his wife, loved by everybody and known for her goodness, started fearing him. She went around wrapped in both her skirts, even in bed, thinking it would prevent him from seeing her soul. In the warm weather she sweated terribly but refused to take anything off. 'You smell like a goat,' El Ojo complained, 'and that's worse than having a dirty soul.'

"Finally, the people of the village did what scared people always do: they went to the priest. But the priest was more frightened of being exposed than anyone else. He visited El Ojo in secret and begged him to stop all his troublemaking. The age of mystics, of San Benedicto and Santa Teresa de Avila, was over, he said. The church had since become modern. 'Priests can go to college,' he said. But El Ojo wasn't impressed.

" 'So you don't believe me, is that it?' he said. 'Well, I see what I see. I happen to know, for instance, that your mother doesn't have a shoulder bone.'

"The priest was furious. How dare anyone talk about his mother in such a way. 'The poor woman will be ninety-two,' he said. 'Let her live in peace.' The priest was very attached to her, everyone knew. There were even some stories. 'If you keep this up, I'll have you excommunicated.'

" 'If you do, Padre,' said El Ojo. 'I will be forced to give an exact description of your soul to my wife, a good woman but one not known for her ability to keep a secret.' He looked the priest right in the eye. Then he winked.

"When the priest's mother died, her son performed the requiem mass. All during the service he couldn't keep from looking at her in the coffin. People felt sorry for him, a man of his age carrying on like that about his mother. What they didn't know was that he was itching to find out whether what El Ojo had said was true. But what could he do? It was a sin to disturb the peace of the dead.

"On the night the village was celebrating the Feast of the Virgin, the priest, who'd had his share of wine, slipped a knife under his robe and went off to the cemetery, determined to find out once and for all if El Ojo really had the power he claimed. But it was impossible to lift the heavy slab from his mother's grave. There was only one person who might help.

" 'Okay, I will,' said El Ojo. 'But if you see that was I right, you must let me have one of her bones.'

" 'That's blasphemy! What are you planning, devil worship?'

" 'Bone first, talk later.'

"Together, they got her out. The priest was too squeamish to take a knife to his poor mother so El Ojo performed the operation, sneezing from the dust that sifted through the hole cut in her papery skin.

" 'It certainly doesn't take very long, does it?' observed the priest, turning away.

" 'Look,' said El Ojo cheerfully, wiping his hands. 'No shoulder bone. See for yourself.'

" 'I believe you, I believe you,' said the priest without looking.

" 'Now can I have my bone?'

"The priest nodded.

" 'Which one may I have?'

" 'Take what you like, only hurry up. Holy Mother of God, I can't bear to stay here a moment longer.'

"Out of convenience, El Ojo took the left shoulder blade. 'And that dungeon below the church where they used to imprison heretics, it's empty, isn't it?' he asked as they left the cemetery. Again the priest nodded. 'There I will build my Chapel of the Bones.'

" 'Your what?'

" 'Una Capilla de los Huesos.'

" 'But why?'

" 'When I look at people I see all that has come before them, which is what souls are made of,' he explained. 'The grandmother they got their jaw from, the blood of fathers and grandfathers flowing in their veins, the dust of earthquakes in their bones. I no longer see their bodies, but their spirits, swirling in a sea of the dead, not heaven, and not hell, but in a place no living person can describe. I yearn to have a place for such communion with the spirits.'

" 'What about the church?'

" 'The church,' sneered El Ojo.

"The priest thought for a moment, then shook his head. 'No, I can't let you do this,' he said.

" 'You'd better, or else I'll tell my wife about you and the slender doe-eyed son of Señor Rosario.'

"The priest began helping El Ojo with his project. Slowly, he began to understand. The people noticed a change in him. He stopped talking about sin and fire and hell during his sermons. Instead, he urged them to go into the desert like San Jeronimo and meditate on the bleached bones of animals. Most figured he missed his mother.

"Each Sunday, for the rest of their lives, the two of them had their own service in the secret chapel. El Ojo's wife thought he was fooling around with Altagracia Ruedo, who owned the village panadería. Before the priest died he passed the secret on to the next priest and he passed it on to the next. El Ojo initiated his son into the mystery. It went on like that for generations."

"Who's in charge of the chapel now?" Matthew asked.

"No one."

"Why not?"

"Because I'm not there."

Matthew stopped. "You mean you would be digging out people's bones if you weren't here?" He thought of Sal cutting the sausage for Sunday breakfast.

Sal nodded his head. "Why not? Doctors do it all the time." He laughed. "No, I wouldn't have kept on doing it."

"Did you ever go to the Chapel of the Bones?" Matthew asked.

"Of course. My father started bringing me down there when I was your age. To get there you had to go down these narrow stone steps. They were damp and slippery so we went very slowly. The draft always blew the priest's candle out. My father gave me the bones to carry. Finally we reached the bottom. Hundreds of bones were pressed into clay on the walls. Some were arranged in rows. There were pairs of hip bones, like butterfly wings, and leg bones going up and down in a zigzag. The priest said a prayer over the bone, and they set it in place. The first time I was there the candle went out before they were through. I was so frightened I ran up the stairs but I tripped, knocked my head on the stone steps, and konked out. When I came to, my father was beside my bed, whispering to me not to tell anyone what I'd seen. Then I started having strange dreams of fire and people with black spots all over them. I even had them during the day, when I was awake. I was afraid to leave the house. Anytime I heard someone speak it sounded like echoes. I couldn't eat. I didn't want to drink. My mother was so worried, the house almost burned down from all the candles she lit. But my father knew what was going on. He brought me back down to the chapel. As soon as I was before the bones I started shaking. I felt very, very old. I felt centuries of happiness and sadness inside of me, of people being born and dying. I could see very far. I was crying, but I felt very happy. My father kissed me. He died not long after that, knowing that I understood."

"Your father died?" said Matthew.

"Yeah."

"You mean all this time you've been talking about your father and he's been dead?"

"Yeah."

"Why didn't you say so?"

"What difference does it make?"

"What difference does it make?" Matthew shouted.

"He's the same person now as he was before he died."

Matthew thought of meeting Sal for the first time in Woolworth's. He seemed so different now. "How come that El Ojo guy liked dead stuff so much?"

"Because the dead are closer to their souls than the living. My father used to say that people's souls were more interesting than the bodies attached to them because they didn't talk so much."

"Right after Gramma died I kept having bad dreams," Matthew reflected. "Maybe it was her soul trying to get me. Do you really believe all that stuff?" he asked.

"Yeah, and I'm gonna tear this arm off right now cause I need a bone real bad!" He went for Matthew's shoulder.

Matthew laughed. "It's spooky, though."

"You're not scared of me, are you?"
"Only when you start throwing plates."

5

Carlotta hung up the phone. Her sister Marion in Montauk had just called, wanting to know if she and Justin would be coming out for Memorial Day weekend this year, as they had the last. Carlotta was grateful for the invitation. Her unit at the hospital was understaffed, and work had left her ragged. It was the middle of May but it felt like a muggy August. In the past couple of weeks Justin had grown surly and detached. He'd lumber into the house after working at the garage, his face smudged like a miner's, chocolate caked at the corners of his mouth. He'd wolf down his supper in moody silence, scribble a page or two of homework, then head for the television set. If she tried to interfere, they'd quarrel. If she came to his bedside at night, asking if he wanted to talk, his scowl warned her away.

In the two months Justin had worked at the garage, he'd changed into another child, one she hardly knew anymore. He'd grown fatter. His cheeks had massed into jowls and his belly ballooned out under his T-shirts. His shoulders had broadened, and he'd begun to look more masculine. He was entering that phase, she knew. But the horrible swagger in his walk was no work of puberty, nor was his habit of working up a cord of spittle and aiming it into the kitchen sink. She felt as if she was about to lose her child forever, and Frank was speeding the process along.

We'll talk out at Montauk, she told herself, moving from the phone. It would be good to get away from the city. Justin liked the water, and he'd be able to play with his cousin Stevie. She imagined herself and Justin walking along the beach. She felt an anxious twinge in her stomach. Certain things might be easier to talk about there.

It was her day off. Justin was at school. She thought of buying herself a dress to wear out at Montauk. She folded up the partition and set it out of sight behind her bed. Maybe Frank had been right. Perhaps Justin was feeling cramped living here and had to find a way to show his masculine bravado. They'd been in this apartment almost three years; she'd gotten the old place out of her system. She could ask the landlord if there was a bigger apartment in the building.

She began making the beds. She fluffed the pillows and set them in place. She hadn't slept with a man since Ralph, but she still slept with two pillows. Was she nostalgic, or lonely? She went on to Justin's. When she pushed his bed from the wall she saw his jar of money. She'd watched its contents grow like an hourglass, marking the time Justin had worked for Frank. Little of the earnings had been spent; Frank supplied him with all the sweets and presents Justin wanted. Two months ago Justin didn't want Frank coming for supper. Now they were like brothers. She pulled the open end of the sheet taut, then slipped her hand under the other to redo the corner. Her hand slid over something smooth. She pulled it out.

TEENAGE VIXENS

She flung the magazine to the floor. Her stomach soured. She imagined Frank's face, sloppy with pleasure at plying Justin with what he knew would irk her. He'd always tried to provoke her when they lived in the same apartment, hadn't he, leaving condoms on the bathroom floor, slipping raw frankfurters under her covers. She could destroy the magazine, of course, but there'd be more. She could prohibit Justin from working for Frank. But that hadn't worked the first time. Justin would defy her and sneak off to the garage. Maybe that was what Frank wanted: to instigate Justin's rebellion against her in order to show her where Justin's affection truly lay. Wasn't that the whole idea of having Justin work at the garage, to win him away from her?

By then she was bristling. She'd moved from the old apartment to get away from Frank. She banned him from her house. Now he was weaseling his way back into her life, this time using her son to get back at her. It was cowardly and wrong, but it was working. She recalled the morning several weeks ago when Justin had barged into the bathroom, finding her naked. The sheepish smile he wore was an exact copy of Frank's. Who'd put him up to that? Since when did Justin have an interest in such a thing? He was all of eleven. She could have hurled that jar of coins out of the window. No, she cautioned herself, don't do that. Don't give him a reason to hate you. But she allowed herself the pleasure of tearing the magazine in half and throwing it in the trash. She decided to put fresh sheets on Justin's bed and didn't want the magazine touching them. The instincts of a nurse, she reasoned. Or a prude. Well, maybe. But she'd be damned if Frank would be the judge of that.

Carlotta yanked the sheet off the bed and got a fresh one. When the bed was made, she ran her palm against the taut sheet. She liked the feel of a freshly made bed, so cool and smooth. She caught sight of something bright-colored on the floor—a torn piece of the magazine—and her pleasure diminished. It wouldn't be all that long until Justin started . . . She drew a cover over Justin's bed, as if to mask the rest of her thought. She picked up the scrap of paper and recalled the day she'd found the wardrobe key among Justin's things.

Another secret, she thought. So many.

Memorial Day was two weeks away, she told herself. There was plenty of time to prepare what she would say to Justin out at Montauk. Plenty of time to talk.

Eight

1

"The way we do it is one of us goes to the guy wearing the uniform by the door who rips the tickets," Justin said. They huddled in a doorway against the drizzle. "You tell him you have to go in and look for your little sister."

"Why me?" Matthew said.

Justin thought for a moment. "Because you look like you really got a kid sister." He grinned. "Besides, I've already pulled this on them so they'd know something was up if they saw me. Look, all you gotta do once you're in is open up one of the side doors for me, okay?"

Justin had told Matthew they'd be able to get into the movies free. He figured Justin had some kind of pass. He hadn't said anything about sneaking in.

"I don't know," said Matthew.

"Why not?"

"What's playing?"

"Pirate picture."

"I don't like pirate movies."

"We don't have to stay for the whole thing. But there's nothing else to do today."

"It was a dumb idea to play hooky on a crummy day like today."

Justin sneered. "I knew you couldn't do it."

"You sure it'll work?" said Matthew, hurt.

"Sure."

"What happens if the guy asks how come I'm not in school?"

"Tell him you go to a Catholic School and they got the day off."

Matthew headed off. The light from the marquee made him feel conspicuous. He wanted to turn back but he knew Justin was watching.

"Ticket, Sonny?" said the man at the door.

"I don't have one."

The man pointed to the street.

"I just want to find my sister."

"What's your sister's name?"

Matthew searched the furry peaks of the man's eyebrows for an answer. "Just lemme find her."

"You don't even have a sister, do you?"

"I do too!" Matthew said, suddenly angry. "My mom wants her to come home because. . . because they're taking my father to the hospital. He's so sick he's gonna die."

The smirk turned icy as the man stepped aside. "Okay, but make it out before your old man croaks."

Matthew ran across the huge yellow flowers of the lobby carpet and through the doors. A giant ship sailed over chilly, blue water on the screen. The movie matrons' flashlights swept up and down the aisles. Those ladies were even meaner than the ones in Woolworth's. They wore boxy shoes that looked heavy enough to break your shin if they were to kick you. They were all very old and their skin gave off a ghostly glow. Matthew imagined that they never left the theater but lived in tiny rooms in the basement like mummies.

He was halfway down the side aisle, heading toward one of the red exit signs, when a beam of light struck him. He fell into an empty seat. The matrons didn't like people walking around. As soon as the light had passed he crept up to the nearest door and pressed down on the brass bar. The door opened with an incriminating click. He was caught in a pool of grey light from outside. There was no one there, he pulled the door shut. Flashlights came at him from all directions. He raced to the last door all the way in front of the theater. This time Justin flew in, like air filling a vacuum. The matrons began closing in.

"Follow me," Justin whispered. They raced across the front, then up the center aisle, past rows of turning heads. Matthew collided with one of the matrons along the way. Her scream echoed through the theater, sounding as though she'd been strangled. They leapt up the large lobby staircase, took a smaller flight of stairs to the balcony, high up under the great dome of the movie house, then sank into seats up in the very last row.

"Look," said Justin, pointing with satisfaction to the confusion far below.

Matthew looked down. This is how it was when they first were friends, Matthew thought. That was before Justin worked at the garage, before he'd started bragging about all the money he made and the things his uncle let him do. Matthew didn't know anything about cars, he hated listening to Justin talk about butterflies and alternators and crankcases. "It's like the attic up here," he said.

Justin smiled.

"Guess what?" Matthew said.

"What?"

"My mom's got a boyfriend."

"She gonna marry him?"

"I don't know. They fight a lot."

"What about?"

"Stupid things. She says when he goes to church it reminds her of my Gramma.. He says that she never thinks about what she says before she says it. Then she tells him he should stop acting like her father. I like him. He said he's going to take us to the country this summer. We'll live in this house and go swimming every day. You like to swim?"

"I don't know how. Hey, you know what my mom did? She took all my money away and made me put it in a stupid bank. She's been acting strange a lot. She's always asking me, 'What's wrong? What's wrong?' She don't like it that I work at my uncle's garage, that's all. She's a real creep."

Talking about the garage again, Matthew thought. He looked at the screen. Two pirates were dueling up and down the deck of a ship.

"Bet you that guy makes the other one fall off the ship," said Justin.

"He could just swim around to the other side and climb back on."

"Sharks would get him first."

Matthew followed the bright crisscross of metal. "Are you afraid of when you're going to die?" he asked.

"I'm not going to die," said Justin.

"Oh, yes you are. They'll put you in a box just like they did to my grandmother."

"She died on account of she was old."

"Kids die too."

Justin paused. "Did you see when your grandmother was dead?"

"Yup. She looked like she was sleeping."

One of the pirates forced the other overboard. A second later an iron light swept over them.

"Look at the two of them," said a voice, "sitting together like little girls."

"Holy," said Justin.

A second beam strafed them. They sprang from their seats, grabbed their jackets, and tumbled toward the other end of the balcony. When they got to the head of the main steps a man was waiting at the bottom.

"Right this way," he said in a steely voice, looking at Matthew. "You and your little sister."

The matrons swept up behind them. Down below, the lobby was filling up with spectators. "Go on, get yourselves down those steps, you little sons of bitches," said a matron.

"Don't you call me that," said Justin, thrusting himself at her, his eyes dark and angry. Her flashlight dropped from her hands, he scooped it up. He looked as if he was going to hit her over the head with it.

"Get the old fartface," someone shouted from below.

The man was coming toward them.

"Sandwich," shouted Justin. They ran down on either side of him, slipping past his grabbing hands, through the lobby, out one of exit doors, into the crowds on Eighth Avenue, and came to a halt several blocks later.

"She shouldn'ta called me that," Justin said.

"You still got the flashlight."

Justin stared at it, as if wondering where it had come from.

"Aren't you boys home from school a little early?"

They turned. Mr. Sloane stood before them, his umbrella poised like a walking stick.

"Half day," Justin snapped.

"That so," he said, turning to Matthew.

"Hello, Mr. Sloane," said Matthew, avoiding his glance. "This is Justin."

"I know." He glanced at the flashlight. "A modern day Diogenes, no doubt, searching for truth in Hell's Kitchen."

"How do you know who I am?" Justin said.

Mr. Sloane smiled thinly.

"Mr. Sloane is a piano player," said Matthew. He felt uncomfortable seeing the two of them together, sure that neither would like the other.

"Tell me, young man," Mr. Sloane said to Justin. "How is your friend doing, the one with the scratch on his face and the chip on his shoulder? I believe the youngster's name is Kevin."

Justin glared at him.

"The one that tortured the squirrel?" asked Matthew.

"The very same."

"What are you two talking about?" asked Justin.

Matthew turned to Justin. "You mean Kevin's your friend?"

"A word to the wise," said Mr. Sloane, about to leave.

"Can I come over to the house tomorrow after school, Mr. Sloane?" Matthew said.

Mr. Sloane's eyebrows arched up like horses trying to throw their riders.

"What house?" asked Justin, looking at both of them.

"The House of Lords, the White House, the House of Blue Leaves, the house that Jack built, exactly which house are you referring to, young man?" he asked in a stony voice. "In the case of your cohort Kevin it might very well turn out to be the house of detention." He cast an angry glance at Matthew. "In yours, the doghouse."

"Mr, Sloane, I —"

He left.

"What was he talking about?" said Justin.

"Is that true what he said about you and Kevin?"

"What if it is?"

"We're enemies."

"Yeah?" asked Justin, suddenly anxious.

"Mr. Sloane told me. You got to be crazy to be friends with someone like him!"

"Well, is he your friend, that nigger?"

"Don't you call him that!"

"Well, is he?"

"What if he is?"

They glared at each other.

"What's that about a house?" said Justin at last.

"What house?" said Matthew. But he could tell from the sly smile on Justin's face that he suspected something.

2

"Keep quiet, Mr. Bubble," Carlotta said, steadying the swing of the IV bottle hanging beside his bed.

His face wrinkled with mock recognition. "Nobody wants the wisdom of a poor old alky," he said.

"You can talk all you want after I get you hooked up here."

"By that time it'll be the end of your shift and you'll be gone. And who will I talk to then?" He motioned to the empty bed beside him with a broad theatrical gesture. "Benson over there didn't have the decency to wait until after I was discharged to die. A rat deserting a sinking ship."

The bottle played with the light like a prism. "Keep that arm of yours still or I'll never be finished."

"Exactly my intention," he said.

She took hold of the little chamber midway down the tube, counted the drops passing through it to the sweep of her watch's second hand, and turned the chamber's knurled dial until she was satisfied with the flow. "There," she said. "Now you're okay."

"I was okay before I was connected to this contraption. Don't you think I'm a little too old to be having an umbilical cord?" Mr. Bubble—his real name—had been an actor for many years until his drinking made it hard for him to get work. Once he'd been handsome. With his broad build, bushy mustache, and oval-shaped bald head, he looked like a turn-of-the-century boxer. His sarcasm reminded her of Ralph's.

"Sometimes you carry on like an infant."

"I do it on purpose to bring out the maternal instinct in you." He grazed her arm. "What's wrong? You've been looking miserable these days. The last time I was here you were fresh as a cling peach."

"I'm tired."

"I know it's not my place to tell you such a thing but I am your patient and my well-being is, after all, somewhat dependent upon yours, wouldn't you say?"

It was Mr. Bubble's third time in the hospital. He seemed locked into the inevitable cycle awaiting middle-aged alcoholics: bingeing, getting sick, drying out, and then bingeing again. It would go like that until his liver was completely consumed. This time he'd been up in the ICU before his condition stabilized. In the six months since he'd been there last he'd aged so much. His face had grown hollow, his skin had become scaly and taken on a decidedly brownish tinge, he'd lost weight. The sweet, cornlike smell of his breath told Carlotta his condition was worse.

"So you're not going to tell me what's eating you, is that it?" he said.

"I can't take this weather. It's still June but it feels like August."

"A flimsy explanation."

"Maybe I seem sad because I'm not happy to see you here again."

"I'm only doing it for your own good. Do you think I would be here otherwise? As soon as you stop looking like Whistler's

Mother, I'll check out." Carlotta smiled shyly. She liked him, although a part of him frightened her, the part that seemed bent on destroying himself. Sometimes she had no patience for his patter, which seemed like a cheap diversion from what he was doing. She wanted to shake him to his senses but she knew he'd make a little game out of it.

"Poor, pitiful Sister Carlotta," he went on. "You're so good and I'm so bad." He went to pinch her cheek, a gesture which, he said, made him feel like her English uncle. She pulled away, his hand pursued. The IV needle worked out of his arm and fluid snaked across the floor. "Oh my," he said. "It looks like I've sprung another leak."

"One of these days . . . " she said.

"The candy strippers here don't like me," he reflected as she began adjusting the flow once more.

"They don't like it when you call them that."

"It's just a joke."

"Maybe they don't find you funny," she said when she was finished.

"That is as unlikely as a pope without a hard-on."

"How would you know?" she said.

"Tell the truth," he said suddenly serious. "You're angry at me for being here again. I can tell."

"I'm disappointed. Just before you were discharged the last time you told me you knew someone who could get you work doing commercials — "

"Things don't always work out so neatly, you know. Well maybe for you they do." There was a smugness in his voice. She knew he thought that she lived her life according to a set of schoolgirl rules, where prudence and foresight made it possible to avoid complications. Why, she thought angrily, just because she didn't drown herself in whiskey?

When she washed her hands at the nurses' station, she looked at her reflection in the mirror above the sink. The harsh light revealed every tiny wrinkle. Below each eye lay a soft gully of blue, the result of sleeplessness. She drew her fingers across carefully as though her skin might peel away if she pressed too hard. In six weeks she'd be a grand old thirty-three, she told herself. When she'd mentioned that to Mr. Bubble, his face puffed up with exaggerated surprise. "What?" he said, "You look young enough to play *National Velvet!*"

And in six weeks and two days it would also be the third anniversary of Ralph's death. Birthday, deathday. The two dates seemed to knit closer together each year. The coming of the warm weather was enough to trigger a murmuring anxiety in her which rose with each degree of the thermometer. The heat waited for her each morning like a grim reminder of what time of year it was. She had to force herself to get out of bed. The days stretched out, long and vaguely threatening, as though anything she did might flare up into disaster. Justin was sullen in the morning, ready to start throwing accusations at her any minute. The twenty minutes it took her to walk to the hospital left her listless, her insides dried to chalk. Mr. Bubble was waiting with his barbs.

When her sister Marion had picked her up at the station in Montauk, she'd said, "Where have you been, Lottie, in the land of the living dead?"

The weekend had been miserable. Justin had complained about the long train ride out. "Uncle Frank could have driven there in his car much faster," he said. Carlotta's arms erupted with a vicious sunburn. Marion's husband had come down with a stomach virus. Justin and Stevie had had a fight within the first few hours when Stevie wanted to use his snorkel mask first. Justin swung a punch that knocked the wind out of him.

"Are you out of your mind?" Marion said to Justin as she helped Stevie to his feet. "Why did you have to hit him like that? He's half your size."

"I want to go home," he said.

Monday, when they were supposed to leave, he disappeared. Marion finally called the Beach Patrol, who found him atop a high dune on a remote stretch of beach, staring out into the water.

Carlotta left the hospital and started down Ninth Avenue. Summer turned the city into a great, sweating gymnasium, she thought, with everyone stripped bare and forced to act out their lives in full view of everyone else. Children elbowed by, their hands sticky from melting ice-cream cones, rushing to keep pace with a mother who seemed eager to be free of them. Everyone swam in the same thick, heavy air, pulled along by the street's dirty current. Just before West Fifty-seventh, the street began a downward slope. Carlotta imagined the flood carrying everyone away, all the way down to a great drain at the end of Manhattan. They'd be sucked into it and spat out into the ocean along with all the rest of the city's sewage. The emergency room was crowded with the victims of the season: people cut open with knives or broken bottles, people who'd put poison into their veins or had their limbs crushed under tires, people who didn't know what to do with themselves in the summer. Mr. Bubble had been just another victim of the season.

As soon as she got home she pulled off her uniform, leapt into the shower, and threw on the cold water full force to tear away her skin's gummy film. A pleasurable shiver drove deep into her pores and cleared her head. Then she dried off and retrieved her uniform from the bathroom floor. It looked as though she'd thrown it off in the heat of passion. She shook her head. That would be the day, selecting a partner from the hordes of the great unwashed along Ninth Avenue, on the way home from work. She picked up the damp uniform. No one since Ralph, she thought, letting the uniform swing at the end of her finger. Then she threw it in the hamper, put on a cotton shift, fixed herself a pitcher of iced tea, closed the venetian blinds, and sat down in the dim kitchen. She had an idea.

Tonight, after supper, she would try once more to talk with Justin. She'd tempt him toward reconciliation with his favorite meal, macaroni and cheese. It was really too hot to be using the oven, but she would. There was a box of marble cake mix in the cupboard; she'd whip that together as well, since she was baking anyway. After they finished eating she'd pull out her old anatomy book from nursing school, show him that breasts and naked bodies could be more than pornography. It was a little corny, she thought, but she was corny and, anyway, she had to start somewhere with him.

She set to work, pleased at her plan. By the time the macaroni was done she was sweating again and took another short shower. Only when she came out did she realize that Justin should have been home a half-hour ago. She went to the window. The sky had greyed around a diminishing orange ball of sun. The street was empty. She thought of calling the garage but she shrank at the thought of hearing the pitying tone of voice Frank would use with her. She was reluctant to have him know that she was scared, and surely she'd hear Justin's tramp up the stairs any minute. She returned to the kitchen. The top of the macaroni and cheese looked dried and unappetizing. The smell of marble cake cooling on the counter gave the apartment a false sweetness.

The doorbell rang.

Frank stood with his arm around Justin. "Sorry, Lottie," he said. "The kid worked so hard I took him out for a little something." Justin huddled beside him. A crust of what looked like dried mustard clung to his lip.

She pulled Justin inside. Frank moved to follow. "Get out of here," she said, closing the door. She stood before it, unable to face Justin, wishing there was somewhere in the apartment she might escape to.

Justin skipped around nervously, waiting for her reaction. Frank began pounding on the door. "Let me in," he shouted, "let me explain." Justin went toward the door.

"Get away," she ordered. "Get into your pajamas and go to bed."

"It's too early."

"Do as I say," she said. The pounding went on. She imagined herself being hounded for harboring a criminal, pushing Justin out of the door and crying, Here, take him, take what belongs to you.

"Lottie, please!"

"Get out of here or I'll call the police!" she shouted.

Later, she lay down but couldn't sleep. She went to the kitchen table and lit a candle instead of turning on the overhead light so

Justin wouldn't wake up. She took out her anatomy book and opened it. In the flickering light she looked at the pictures of men and women, their inner organs exposed, their functions explained. On the glossy paper they seemed to be a supremely capable race: a logical skeleton, smooth bundles of muscles, feathery nerves carrying supple electricity. Everything was necessary, everything inevitably right. She closed the book.

★

The next day she walked around the nurses' station, dizzy and weak from the night before. The other nurses gave her sympathetic smiles when they saw her refilling her coffee cup. She couldn't eat, and her empty stomach complained from all the coffee. Mr. Bubble was off the floor all day for tests. She was grateful; she wouldn't have been able to put up with him that day. But just before the end of her shift he was wheeled back. Ugly purple splotches on his arms marked the work of an inexperienced technician.

"I feel like I've been ground up into sausage," he said when she came to check his IV.

Carlotta nodded without taking her eyes from her watch.

"They used me for target practice down there."

She hung up a fresh bottle.

"Did you hear what I said?"

"I'm trying to get this done."

"The hell with the goddam tubes. Is that all you're interested in? Talk to me."

"Try to sleep. You've had a rough day."

"Stop talking to me like a kindergarten teacher."

"I want to get home, Mr. Bubble. Let me look at that arm of yours."

"What's so important about my arm? My liver's already shot."

She lifted his bony wrist and inspected the injection site.

"Where are my pills? I want something for pain."

"The med nurse on the afternoon shift will give them to you," she said, beginning to count drops.

"That's it, ignore me. I'm just an old alky, that's all."

"Nineteen, twenty, twenty-one . . . "

"You sound like you're counting off the years of your life."

"Twenty-five, twenty-six, twenty-seven," she continued, louder. She was beginning to sweat.

"Twenty-six, pick up sticks, twenty-seven, go to heaven," he sang.

"Stop it, for Christsakes!"

He yanked his arm away. The chamber slipped from her hand.

"You know what your problem is? You think that if you can control something you'll be able to understand it. You're not here because you want to help anybody, you just like being around people who are worse off than you are."

"I'm not interested in hearing a sermon." She pulled the plastic chamber back.

"Poor little candy stripper," he said. "You wish the whole world would be sick so you'd be able to make it better. But what happens with the people who don't want you to cure them? What about the jokers who like being sick, like me? You can't handle that, can you? You don't like it, it's not orderly, it's not clean." His voice broke into a chuckle that followed her down the hall after she left his room.

It wasn't until she was halfway down in the elevator that she realized she'd hung the wrong bottle. "Holy Jesus!" she said, slapping the button to return to her floor. The hallway was empty; the afternoon shift was getting report from the head nurse in the nurses' station. She slipped back down the corridor.

Thank God none of the other nurses saw me, she thought.

She was weak with the thought of having to face Mr. Bubble again. But he was already sleeping when she came in, as though exhausted from his abuse. She removed the bottle and replaced it with one containing his medication. Miraculously, he didn't wake up. Yet something inside made her wish he had. Then he would have known she'd made a mistake. He would have seen just how well she had things under control.

On the way out she met Pat Hinks, from the afternoon shift.

"I thought you were already gone," she said.

"I — I left something in one of the rooms." Carlotta said.

3

Matthew walked up the street over the viaduct. He looked around. When he was sure no one was watching, he pulled back the fence that separated the sidewalk from the beginning of the slope. He put one foot through at a time, then pulled in the shopping bag he was carrying. The fence snapped shut like a bear trap when he let go. He began walking through the dense overgrowth. In the winter the path to the camp had been dangerously exposed. Mr. Sloane had the men dump a barricade of garbage at the entrance to keep away the curious. But now it was nearly buried under a protective baffle of weeds. Ephesus compared the slope to the jungles of Africa, but then he found a way to compare everything he liked to Africa, a place he knew only by name.

Most afternoons Matthew was over at the house, helping out. Work had gone very slowly until now. Mr. Sloane told Matthew he sensed the men were getting impatient. It had taken months to empty out the rubble from inside, sneaking it in small batches to dumpsters that belonged to the nearby warehouses. (They'd left the yard the way it was as a kind of camouflage.) Then came the work on the foundation, digging a little moat around it, painting the old wooden stanchions with tar, pouring in bucketfuls of gravel, and covering it all up. Quite a few of the cross beams had to be replaced. Only then could Skip begin to work on the roof. All that had taken years. But since the warm weather, much had been done.

Matthew knew how far along the path he was by the smell of Ovid's soup. Fragrant tongues of meat and spice flicked their way through the leaves to meet Matthew halfway. Ovid's soups never smelled the same twice; it depended on what the others brought back from the Ninth Avenue markets: less-than-perfect produce, scraps from a kosher butcher who was a little perplexed when

Ephesus spoke to him in biblical Hebrew, and Matthew's offerings, usually chicken bones. Today the slope smelled of tomatoes.

"Soup is the most wonderful thing on earth," Ovid would tell Matthew. "It's a bunch of different things that gets changed into something better. Take a carrot, a potato. They nice, but ain't really so much by themselves. Stick 'em in a soup, they get dressed up. This world's full of soups, all different kinds. Course they all don't look like eatin soups, but soups they is. Blood's a soup, now ain't it? Air too. The ocean's a mighty soup. And the earth," he said, motioning with his ladle to the ground, "that's about the most beautiful soup there is." He leaned over and whispered to Matthew. "That's why I always put a little bit of it in when I cook." He winked.

There was another reason for Ovid to cook soup all the time, Matthew knew. Mr. Sloane had arranged for a restaurant in the theater district that specialized in "home" cooking to buy three batches of the soup a week. Ephesus hauled it over, carrying the huge pot on his back in a harness fashioned from upholstery webbing.

"I hope you not be bringing any more of that spicy stuff," said Ovid as Matthew set down his bag. "The last time the man in the restaurant complained, said he wasn't runnin no Mexican place."

"These are mostly from what my mom cooked, not Sal."

"Are they still quibblin?"

"Yeah."

"They's having lovers' quarrels. I ought to fix them some of my wedding soup. It'll help." He reached for the bag. "Well, let's see what you got for me today." He upended it over the pot. A cage of bones slid into the bubbling water. Ovid poked them under with the ladle. "You know, there is one problem bout livin in a soup such as we is. You know what that is?" Matthew shook his head. "You never know who you gonna bump into in the pot!"

"You mean like Skip?"

Ovid nodded his head.

"Is he still away?"

"Yeah, he staying at the house these days. Pity he don't go no farther. Look, here Ephesus."

They turned. A tall black man appeared hauling a carton over his shoulder that he lowered to the ground with a slight rattle. "Joe was there today," he said. Joe was a black man who worked at the nearby A & P and didn't mind the odd case of this or that disappearing off the delivery ramp. Ephesus stood back up. He was a giant wiry man, even taller than Mr. Sloane and very strong. He wore old-fashioned overalls and heavy boots. His crown of white hair gave him a grandfatherly appearance. In his younger days he'd worked laying rails for the Union Pacific. Mr. Sloane said he was over seventy.

"Hello, Matthias," he said. "Do we have some work waiting for us in the pot?"

"A little. Are yesterday's bones finished yet, Ovid?"

Ovid fished out one bone with the ladle, looked at it, and nodded.

One day Matthew had come to the camp and asked if could build a bone chapel in the cave where the men slept.

"You mean like a chapel where you go and pray?" asked Ephesus.

"But with bones on the wall," said Matthew.

"Bones?" said Ovid. "Anybody who gots bones should talk to me."

"You must be one of those poor, retarded kids those ladies collect money for," said Ancil.

"Why you want to build a church?" said Ovid.

"So I can pray to the spirits."

"I don't want no spirits where I sleep," said Ancil. "Ants is enough."

Ephesus held up his hand. "Let the boy explain."

Matthew tried to gather together all of what Sal had said during their walks home from the church. No matter how he tried, his explanation didn't sound right. The men looked at him, sympathetic but puzzled. He realized that he didn't understand it all himself. What did spirits have to do with bones, anyway, he thought, especially with the ones from supper? Sticking bones onto the walls of a church cellar seemed a little silly, when you came right down to it, and hanging them up in a cave — not even a real cave but a concrete hut built into the slope, which once housed relay equipment for the railroad — seemed just as silly.

Still, Matthew had felt something those Sunday mornings, alone with Sal at the breakfast table after Marjorie went to lie down on the couch. Sal had Matthew close his eyes. "Feel the force that comes from deep in the ground and enters you each time you breathe," Sal had said. Matthew breathed obediently, thinking of the air shaft, the river, the viaduct, all the deep places of the neighborhood — was that what Sal meant? Matthew didn't know but the squeak of Sal's chair made Matthew smile, knowing Sal was near. And it was for Sal that he wanted to build the bone chapel.

"You don't have to say another word," said Ephesus. "I understand. The bones of the dead. Spirits of generations out of the black heart of Africa and the Ten Lost Tribes of the Falashim, all of them bearing the wisdom of the Bantu, the prophecy of the Zulu. All of that will be enshrined in this temple, a new station of the celestial underground railway, freeing our souls from the slavery of the body."

Ancil winced.

"A temple such as the one at the court of Timbuktu, a temple of—"

"Chicken bones," Ancil said. "This child wants to string up chicken bones where we have to sleep. I'm beginning to think maybe Skip was right about us after all."

Ephesus put a hand on Matthew's shoulder. "You have received a divine wisdom from your friend Sal. We shall hearken to it. Up until now we have been a ragged band of men lost in the wilderness of the white man. Now we will be able to invoke the help of the black God of Moses."

Ancil looked at Matthew. "I thought kids your age liked stealing hubcaps. But who knows. Maybe if you were, you'd want to stick them up on the wall, too."

Ephesus took a flask from his pocket and offered it to Matthew. "This will build up your constitution in the days to come and make you fit to do our work." Matthew took a sip. It went down like a hot wire.

From then on Matthew scraped all the bones from the supper plates into a bag and hid them behind the iceberg that had built up in the freezer. He brought them to Ovid, who cooked them clean. Then Matthew and Ephesus went to work. They found a piece of cyclone fence to stretch around the ceiling of the cave in the back, the space Ancil confined them to. They attached the bones with piano wire from Mr. Glaubach's shop.

"Okay, Matthew," said Ovid, lifting up a ladleful of ivory-colored bones. "They's yours."

4

They had Justin back up against the wall under the bleachers. The magazines he'd brought from the garage had been thrown to the ground.

"Don't talk like you didn't do it," said Tony.

"We saw you," said Eugene.

"He thinks we're d-d-dumb," said Walt.

"Traitor," said Pebbleface.

"You're all lying," said Justin, his voice flecked with fear.

Kevin stepped forward, his nose within an inch of Justin's. "Traitors gotta be punished," he said.

"I ain't no traitor!"

"We saw you with that kid who's the friend of the nigger," said Tony.

"Admit it," said Walt.

"I ain't admitting nothin."

"Don't try to get out of it," said Eugene.

Kevin pulled out the knife, switched open the blade, and held it just below Justin's chin. "Is that kid your friend?"

Justin said nothing.

"We ain't got all day," said Tony.

The point of the knife pricked Justin's Adam's apple when he swallowed. He shook his head no.

"Swear," said Kevin.

"Swear what," he said, trying to move his mouth as little as possible.

"Swear he ain't your friend."

"Swear it on your f-f-father's life," said Walt.

Justin bit his lip. "My father . . . he's . . . I ain't got no father!"

"Your mother's then, said Kevin.

Justin's tongue felt dry enough to snap in two.

"Well?"

"I can't talk with the knife there," he said, stalling for time.

Kevin lowered it.

"He's afraid that if he says it, his mother's titties'll fall off," snickered Tony.

Justin broke free and rammed his fist into Tony's face. The little kid fell against the wall, and a bright swatch of red broke from the side of his mouth.

Kevin grabbed Justin, the knife at his belly now. "Come on, swear. Swear on your mother's life that nigger-lover ain't your friend!" His teeth dug into his blue lips.

"I swear," he began.

The point pricked his belly button.

"Spit it out," said Tony, clambering back up. His pulpy mouth was shaped into an angry grin.

"I swear he ain't my friend or else . . . Wait! I gotta say something secret." He looked at Kevin.

"Don't believe him," said Tony.

"Shut up," said Kevin. "Okay, what is it?"

Justin leaned over to Kevin. "The nigger, he got a house somewhere. Let's go and . . . let's go and wreck it."

Kevin snapped the knife shut. Then he smiled. "That's good," he said. "That's real good."

Nine

1

Carlotta took a Kleenex from her purse and wiped off the mica-flecked surface of the stone bench before sitting down. The cleanly chiseled letters spelling out Ralph's name on the stern marble slab reminded her of the inscription on a public building. She stared at it until it began to look like gibberish. The cemetery stretched around her, a careful composition of smooth lawns knobbed with stone, a little, gated city, complete with named streets (Cypress Lane, Martin Luther Road), tiny monumental houses, and a guard at the entrance. Cemeteries were good places for people like her who wanted things to be neat, she thought. A cluster of black some distance away marked mourners at a burial. She suddenly felt conspicuous in her nursing uniform. She imagined the mourners sweating in their funeral clothing, as she had when Ralph was buried, on a sweltering summer day like this one.

The smell of the damp earth freshly opened spread through the thin air quickly. Carlotta remembered what Mr. Bubble had said about going to cemeteries: like going to church except you got to see the last reel. He described his ideal funeral: it would be held in a used-car lot and advertised as a close-out sale. Every tire-kicking sucker in the East would show up. They'd have him set up right in the middle of it and pipe in "Pennies from Heaven" on the loudspeakers.

Carlotta's head ached. The bus had taken her past steaming asphalt acres of parking lots beside the shopping centers along Route 4. Bamberger's and cemeteries, that's what came to mind when she thought of New Jersey. She'd found herself on that bus, hardly knowing how she'd gotten there, unable to recall the walk from the hospital. Earlier that day, just before she went off her shift, Mr. Bubble had died. He'd been prepped for his liver scan and was on the cart, ready to be taken down. She was there when they coded him. She had left the hospital, knowing she couldn't bear to return to her steaming apartment. But being on the street was too much. Where to go? Central Park? Too many people. She got into a cab that took her to the Port Authority bus terminal and bought herself a ticket, slapping the money down on the counter as if she were drunk. She climbed onto the bus, grateful for its sterile air conditioning and dark windows, which filtered out the world. The tiles of Lincoln Tunnel reminded her of the hospital; she was relieved when they reached the New Jersey side and began climbing the concrete curves over the Hackensack marshlands. She got off the bus — she'd remembered the stop even though it had been nearly three years since she'd been there — and walked through the cemetery gate. The plot was tucked into a far corner but she remembered where it was, too. She hadn't cried to see the grave; she'd studied it, a generous grey piece of marble and a handsome bed of glacial ivy, all as she'd remembered it. Why shouldn't it have been? She'd picked out the slab and paid for it and sent a check to have the ivy replanted each year. The grave was no labyrinth waiting to trap her for all eternity, as she sometimes imagined it when she considered going to the cemetery. It was a simple piece of stone inscribed with what she already knew: Ralph's name, and the dates of his birth and death.

She heard the burial service being read in a man's whispery voice. Nothing else in the world made a sound. The cemetery corresponded to her idea of a monastery: fresh air, silence, and everybody doing the same thing. It was strange how Mr. Bubble's death had driven her to Ralph's grave, yet at the ticket counter it had made perfect sense. Carlotta looked at Ralph's name again. Carved into stone like that, it had a stability that didn't suit him.

After he'd died she had promised herself to visit the grave regularly and to take Justin there. Yet today's visit had been her first since the burial. She'd soon decided against bringing Justin to the grave, since he was sleeping so badly. She herself had lost the need to have any more contact with her husband. He'd prepared her for separation by staying away; his death had simply fixed things. She hadn't been able to grieve. Instead, she'd felt only relief. She'd strained to believe in her marriage, as devoutly as a young novice might believe in her decision to take vows. Ralph's death had freed Carlotta from hers. He'd joked about her living in a convent; his death allowed her to leave it.

The cemetery made her think of the old apartment. The ornate tombstones might have been all those end tables and fern stands left behind by Ralph's mother. That large old gravestone near the mourners resembled the wardrobe with its pillars and pediment. Why had she kept that thing? It had been a bad seed brought from the old apartment and planted in the new one. It had grown and spread its poison. She'd wanted to make a clean break but hadn't been able to. She knew why, of course. She would have been forced to admit that her marriage had failed, and Carlotta had always been careful to protect herself from failure. She'd been determined to preserve what had been good, what she had loved. But it had been a mistake to keep it. She looked down at the cemetery grass and thought of the apartment's broadloom carpet, also green, like the still surface of a pond covered with waterbeads. She loosened her shoes and took them off, looking around to see if any of the mourners were watching. Taking your shoes off in a cemetery was probably considered a sacrilege, but, she told herself, her feet were clean. The grass felt prickly and firm beneath her stockings; it wasn't the soft, giving grass of a house lawn. Frank and Justin used to roll around on that carpet. With Ralph away, Frank took more interest in Justin. Frank was a loner; Justin became a playmate. He bathed Justin, took him to the park, and stayed with him when Carlotta began working at the hospital once more. Out of Ralph's shadow, Frank bloomed. He cleared the clutter from his room and repainted it, enrolled in an auto mechanics course at Voorhees, and began working out at a gym. He took Carlotta and Justin to Bear Mountain and Jones Beach in his Plymouth. He began eating with them again, remembered each of their birthdays with presents. One night Carlotta looked across the supper table at him. In the space of several months he seemed to have been totally transformed. His hair was combed into shiny waves. He wore a nice shirt that showed off the attractive bulk of his arms. "You're a good-looking guy, Frank, do you know that?" she had told him. "You ought to find someone who'll appreciate you." Frank had looked away, his face darkened.

The mourners had begun to disperse toward the road. The shovels of dirt had been spilled, the cemetery people would attend to the real job of burying the dead. Carlotta recalled the peculiar sense of leaving Ralph at the end of the service, there in a place neither of them had ever been to before. Ralph always hated New Jersey. It would have made more sense to bury him on the beach, where he died, like soldiers who were buried near the front, or pioneers on the trail, each one lying below a hastily erected cross. This little, perfect city had never been his, she thought. She rose and followed the mourners out toward the gate.

Back in Manhattan, it had grown mercifully cooler. As she went about getting supper ready, Carlotta became aware of a sharp sweetness in the air. She checked the kitchen cabinets, then the garbage. In front of the wardrobe, the smell intensified. She went for the key and opened the doors. Nothing looked awry. She parted the clothing. The bottom was layered with candy wrappers, red pistachio shells, potato chip bags, the work of a careless camper in the woods. She herself hadn't looked inside the wardrobe since the winter, when she'd thrown in some camphor nuggets. That was around the same time Mrs. Cleary had found Justin inside. She'd assumed that after Justin began working in the garage he no longer thought about . . . Daddy.

She shut the door, hoping he wouldn't notice she'd been there; she thought of how a bird, sensing its nest has been tampered with, will abandon it. She stood thinking for a moment, then went to the calendar above the sink and circled a date. I'm going to have a birthday party, she told herself. It's been so long since I've had one. Frank'll be there too. It'll be the three of us again, just like old times. Then she did what she hadn't been able to do since Ralph died: she cried and cried.

2

School was out. July dragged on and on. Frank had little work for Justin and then only in the morning. Kevin had disappeared and the other Bloodhounds didn't know where he was. Matthew never wanted to do anything with Justin. Justin saw him around the neighborhood, carrying bags of things he wouldn't show to Justin, or else saw him in Woolworth's, talking to the Spanish guy behind the counter who gave him free french fries and soda. Justin knew Matthew was over at the nigger's house, helping him fix it up. Where the house was, was supposed to have been a secret, but Justin found it out: he'd followed Matthew there without him knowing.

His mother was acting even stranger than before. She walked around the apartment like a robot. She hardly ate. She talked to herself. At night, she paced. Once he woke up to find her standing at the foot of his bed, looking at him. Other times, she cried. It made him crazy to live in the same room with her.

"Nothing today," Frank told Justin when he came by. Frank gave him a little money and told him to keep out of trouble. Justin considered what to do as he walked down the street. He had nowhere to go. Just walking made him sweat. Heat collected in the folds of his dungarees; he longed to be in the cool garage. He decided to go to Kevin's house and see if he was there. Kevin had warned all of the Bloodhounds never to come by where he lived. Today Justin decided to chance it. He had a good excuse ready: he was going to tell him where the nigger's house was. Inside Kevin's building shouts fell from an upper floor. Justin followed them up the stairs and down a hallway. He crouched by the door.

"Get offa me!" A kid's voice.

"Get back here!"

"Lemme outta here!"

Justin listened. It was Kevin, he thought, unbelieving.

"Don't you talk to me like that, you lowlife." There was a slap. Now a woman. "We warned you not to pull nothin again."

"I didn't do it!"

"So the guy in the store made it up, that it?"

"Don't hit me!"

Another slap. Kevin whimpered. Someone ran.

"Where do you think you're goin?"

"Get back over here, you."

"Lemme outta here!"

"We already told you, you ain't leavin this house until school starts."

"Mom, tell him to stop!"

There was a crash, then the sound of scuffling feet. The door flew open. Kevin ran into the hall. His father trudged after him, a balding man in soiled pants and an undershirt. He brandished a gleaming vacuum cleaner pipe. Kevin's reddened eyes met Justin's. His mouth hung open, sharpened by surprise and anger. Kevin plummeted down the stairs. His father went as far as the landing. "You stinking lowlife," he bellowed into the stairwell. Kevin's footsteps grew fainter until the front door slammed.

"This ain't a show," said Kevin's father, motioning with the pipe. "Now get the hell out of here."

Kevin was waiting when Justin came out. "I ain't never going back there again," he said. "They can both rot in hell."

"What was going on?"

"They been keeping me cooped up in the house since I got caught taking stuff from a store. That was a week ago. They take turns watching me. They even put locks on the windows so I can't climb out the fire escape. It's so hot in there. They're out of their minds."

"Where are you gonna stay now?"

"I don't care. I'll sleep in the park."

Justin showed him the money he got from Frank.

"Let's get some candy," he said.

Kevin downed his candy bar with sloppy bites as if he hadn't eaten in a long time. "You're my friend," he said. "The others are just assholes. They'd stick me if they could. I don't trust none of them. Tony's a cockroach, Eugene got blubber in his brains. The only reason I let Pebbleface stick around with me is on account of the money he steals from his mother. Walt, he's the dumbest of them all. He said the way you get babies is when a guy and a girl piss in the same glass." He balled up the candy wrapper and tossed it away.

Justin looked at him. "You really get that scar fighting the nigger?"

"Who told you I didn't? I — " His anger broke off in midsentence. "My old man did it to me one night with a broken bottle when he was drunk." He fell silent for a moment. "You ain't going to tell nobody about what happened with my parents, will you?" Before Justin could answer Kevin reached into his pocket. "Here," he said, giving Justin the switchblade. "Take it."

"Huh?"

Kevin pushed it into Justin's hand.

"Why?"

"Cause you're my friend."

Justin backed away. "And what if I take it?"

Kevin smiled. "Then it's yours. Cmon, already." He shoved the knife into Justin's hand, then watched as Justin put it into his pocket. "And remember," he said. "This is just between you and me, okay?"

★

That night, Justin waited for the shifting in his mother's bed to stop. When all was quiet, his hand crept down between his bed and the wall, worked its way beneath the mattress. The knife was still there. He pulled his fingers against its smooth casing. A pulse of power moved through him.

When his mother had come over to his bed earlier, he was scared she'd noticed the lump in the mattress where the knife was hidden. But she'd said nothing. At first he thought she might start telling him another of her stories about Daddy, the way she used to do. But it had been something about some dumb birthday party she was having for herself next week. She'd had this goony smile on her face the whole time. Usually she never smiled. She talked about the two of them turning over a new leaf, about Uncle Frank. Justin was suspicious. He thought she might have just been saying all those things to trick him and that any minute she'd reach down and pull out the knife. She had good eyes, he knew; she saw everything. He hadn't been able to sneak the magazines away for too long. But when she was finished she bent over and kissed him good night.

Justin pulled his hand back out. He thought of Kevin sleeping in the garage. It had been Justin's idea to sneak him in there when he said he was afraid to return home. "If my Uncle Frank catches you then I don't know you," Justin had said, figuring Kevin would balk. But to Justin's surprise, he'd submitted. The little window in the back of the garage was open. Justin warned Kevin to be out of there before his uncle or the others came. He told him about the blanket in one of the lockers. Justin remembered the sound of Kevin's voice that afternoon, as frightened as a girl's. He thought of Kevin's father with his dirty pants and vacuum cleaner pipe and got a queasy feeling. How long would Kevin be able to go on sleeping in the garage? he wondered.

He reached down for the knife and pulled it out. Under the covers, he opened it. The blade was as wide as two fingers. He brought his thumb across its edge to test its sharpness. The drag of his skin against the metal proved it. Then he slid his thumb the other way, the sharp way, not enough to get cut, just enough to insert a thread of pain under his skin. He switched thumbs, did the other one. Slowly, he brought the blade against his arm, stropping it gently, tracing the rise of his biceps with it, leaving a trail of goose pimples behind. His body began to swirl with pleasure beneath the movement of the blade. He tried it against his face, his legs, releasing warm tendrils of sensation. He peeked under the covers. His thingy was getting hard. He saw the knife poised near it, a barricuda and an eel bumping noses.

Carlotta let out a shout in her sleep. The knife jumped forward, nicked the taut satin of Justin's penis. He let out a yelp of pain, then gulped it back down, and felt his insides tear as the scream tried to escape.

3

Skip kneaded the back of his head as he stood in the doorway. He peered down the alleyway to see if one of the kids was waiting on the street. He didn't see them. In the alley, all the garbage that had been there the day before was still in place. If there were just some rusting cars it'd be like living in the Ozarks. The old flabby cat he'd named Bertha was grubbing away at something. Skip had never seen an uglier animal. He had always believed that no animal or plant could ever be ugly, only people. Bertha, with her crusty eye and oily fur, had proved him wrong. His brain was doing a tap dance after his spring into wakefulness. It was certainly too early for all this activity. Each limb hurt in its own special way. His joints didn't mind complaining, either. A narrow shaft of sunlight was all that made it down into the alley, but it knew just where to aim the glare into Skip's eyes. Worst of all, his back, which was never in A–1 condition, felt like it had been fed through a drill press. He rubbed his head some more. One moment he'd been lying peacefully in his bed. The next moment, Pearl Harbor.

He felt ashamed. No matter how much he'd drunk, he'd never fumbled guard duty like this before. Whenever Sloane complained about his drinking, Skip had told him, "The only bad thing about liquor is if you can't hold it. I can." Well, what was Sloane going to say when he found out that two punk kids had given him the slip?

A fresh river breeze against his legs reminded him that he had no clothes on. It didn't matter; there was nobody looking at him except Bertha, and they had long ago decided not to have too much to do with each other. The honest sun revealed his every detail mercilessly: a middle-aged Negro with skinny legs, dry skin, a modest, still serviceable musculature, and some paunch, but nothing out of line for a man of his age and experience. He slapped it with his hand just to make sure. Considering the abuse he'd given his body, it might have been much worse, he decided. Still, the sun didn't miss a trick. There were those big old Donald Duck feet of his. Well, who looked at your feet, anyway? If they did look down thataways, then it was really something else that was on their minds. And, he told himself, there were some people who still found him good-looking, Donald Duck feet and all. He chuckled to himself and gave his belly a scratch. Then he pulled the door shut and headed back to bed. On the way his foot came down on a sharp chunk of plaster that knifed through his naked sole.

"Damn!" It ain't right, he thought, hobbling back to his bed, a door set up on a base of cinder blocks, just high enough off the ground so he could have a little advantage over the rats. He wanted more than anything to fall back to sleep, but the sun through the cracks in the walls wouldn't let him. Besides, it was too hot. He began to feel like a dog left in a parked car with the windows rolled up. He rummaged around in a box beside his bed, found a length of cigarette to smoke and sat up.

All in all, things were going better now that he was living in Sloane's gingerbread house than they were when he was still with those colored beatniks under the boardwalk. Even though he hated to admit it, the house was coming along. Ephesus had got the plumbing in and together they'd plasterboarded most of the walls on the first floor. The back windows were already in (and protected by some boards nailed over them) and so was the new flooring. It would take time, but look how long it was taking them to finish the Bruckner Expressway. The place would be nice when it was finished. He'd planned to set himself up on the second floor, far away from Sloane and his ragtime piano. And Ovid could sleep in the kitchen for all he cared. Ephesus was fine to work with; he had some strange ideas—all religious people did, Skip thought—but deep down Ephesus was all right and, what's more, the man knew how to drink. If Ephesus wanted to have a room to himself for that voodoo bone business, he could,

Skip decided. He glanced at the cigarette butt and decided to retire it. He was about to flick it somewhere.

"Heh, heh, you is funny," he muttered, carefully tamping the glowing butt against one of the cinder blocks.

Who'd have guessed he'd wind up in a place like this, he thought. After leaving the viaduct he'd gone up to live with his brother over near Mount Morris Park. "You still camping out?" his brother said. Skip got work setting up chairs for conventions in the big midtown hotels, then driving a van for a wholesale sewing machine supply outfit. Finally he worked in his brother's liquor store. You had to ring a bell to get into it. The counter and all the bottles were behind Plexiglas. There was one little window you put your money into and another where you got your bottle. He watched the people coming in for their little bottles of Jim Beam or their big bottles of Gordon's looking like they'd hardly be able to get the bottle open, let alone hold it in their hands long enough to drink from. He certainly had nothing about black folk drinking. But it scared him to see these kind of folk. Then it scared him that it scared him, because he realized how different from all of this he was. He'd grown up here, lived here, and it wasn't all that long ago that he'd been one of those people shuffling up to the window in the Plexiglas. Bad as it was, it was better than lots of other places. Now it seemed like Mars to him, and the people might have had pointy ears and tails, they seemed so strange. Maybe he'd grown too soft for it. Or maybe it had just grown too strange. Either way, he knew he had to go back to Sloane's place.

He examined the sole of his foot. A little blood squeezed its way through the puncture. "Guess that's how what's his name felt getting hung up on that cross," he said. Skip and his feet. They'd sure been through a whole lot together, running, hustling, getting stepped on, hopping to. They might of been the only real friends he had. "I could just kiss you two if my back didn't hurt so much to bend," he said. "But on the other hand, you is pitiful, letting a pair of milk-faced punks outrun you." His toes wiggled in shame.

By the time Skip had gotten wind of what was going on, the kids had made it all the way to the back part of the house, where most of the work had been done. He was so out of it that when he heard voices he thought he must have been dreaming.

"We can light it here," said the first voice.

"You think it'll take?" asked the second.

"Sure, the whole place's made of wood. It'll go like paper."

He didn't like that dream one bit, sprang to his feet, and bounded to the back of the house, pitch dark because of the good walls. He grabbed one kid, a fat one, and trundled him against the wall. The kid squirmed like a butterfly getting pinned down.

"What the hell you doing in my house, Lardy Ass?" Then he noticed a second kid sneaking around behind him. He threw Lardy Ass across the room, figuring to hurt him just enough to scare him. The kid ran out. Then Skip blocked the door. He didn't want the second one getting away.

"Come out, you little cockaroach."

The room smelled of the wood he and Ephesus had just sawed the other day. It killed Skip to think of someone being here who didn't belong. He moved toward a pile of planks. A figure darted past. Skip grabbed him by whatever he could get his hands on; it turned out to be an ear.

"What in hell are you doin in my house?"

"Get offa me!"

Skip dragged him to the door to get a better look. "Hey, I know you!" Skip took one look at Kevin's face and memory did the rest. A room with a cross over the bed. Skip lying next to a white woman whom he'd met at the liquor store, pushing forty, too washed out to be pretty, but with a good bit of spunk in her. Right in the middle of things, a mean-looking boy — the same one he had hold of at that moment — charging in with an ice pick in his hand. There was hardly no ice in that room to pick, so the kid tried to use it on Skip's chest instead. The woman flying out of bed, not a stitch of clothing on. None too easy for the boy to take, to judge from the look on his face. And the whole time she was screaming, screaming.

Kevin stared, transfixed by Skip's nakedness.

"I want to know what you doing in my house?"

"It ain't yours."

"Well it sure as hell ain't yours." Skip looked at him. "What in God's name is the matter with you? Ain't you got nothing better to do than going around being mean all the time?"

Kevin broke free. Skip lunged after him. A shaft of pain across his back crippled him and he fell against the wall, helpless. He stayed there, sweating, praying for the spasm to pass. By the time he'd made it to the door, the kid was gone.

That sure is something, Skip thought, deciding to get out of bed. He swung his legs to the floor. So much meanness in such a small amount of space. "Kevin came into the world being mad at it," his mother said to Skip one afternoon as they were getting dressed. Well, Skip might have have felt sorry for Kevin, living dirty the way he did, living poor, his father crazy, his mother carrying on with someone like himself, but he didn't, because Kevin was just too mean to feel sorry for. What was he doing, running in with an ice pick? Was it his business if his mother had a little fun? Her husband didn't sound like no Romeo. Skip felt a little bad about the whole thing; he'd probably have to put a stop to it now. Damn, a man like him could sure get to feeling lonely sometimes. He wondered what the others did when the need arose. Sloane played the piano, probably. Ephesus was too old for that kind of stuff. Ancil felt too bad about only having one arm to try and get women. And Ovid, well, Ovid was still a boy. Someone would have to sit down and have a word with him.

This Kevin number would have to be dealt with, Skip thought. Too bad Lardy Ass had to get mixed up with someone like him. Lardy didn't seem to be too big on the smarts. He decided to keep half an eye on the fat boy. He looked down at his toes. "You think you guys been busy lately? Wait till you see what I got planned for you now!"

Ten

"I hope you like it, Lottie." Frank leaned forward in his chair to give Carlotta the little white box wrapped in shiny green paper. The birthday cake he'd bought sat on a platter between them on the kitchen table under a shiny mantle of icing. The package glistened in her palm like a lizard.

"Thank you, Frank," she said.

Justin regarded it with suspicion. He'd sensed something strange about this party of hers from the beginning. It didn't make sense. She never had birthday parties. She'd asked him what he wanted to eat that night. He wanted macaroni and cheese, but was afraid to ask for it after what had happened. Then she suggested it herself. Frank sent him home from the garage early. She had Justin take a shower, and, when he came out, fresh clothes were waiting for him, as though they were going somewhere. She'd had her hair cut short, too. Frank appeared in a white shirt and light-colored pants, smelling of Old Spice. He smiled as he spoke to her. Had he forgotten that she'd slammed the door in his face two weeks ago?

The meal had been the quietest Justin ever remembered. Frank didn't mention the garage once, so neither did Justin. Without warning, Carlotta let out a laugh in the middle of the meal. Frank looked up in alarm. She wiped her mouth and grinned.

"I don't know why, but I was thinking of the time we drove upstate and I leaned out the window and the wind blew the chewing gum out of my mouth." She giggled.

Something was going on, Justin was sure. He didn't like seeing the two of them together. He didn't like seeing Frank there in the house. He belonged in the garage.

Carlotta lifted off the wrapping paper and opened the box. Inside, a snowy pearl on a silver chain lay nestled in cotton.

"It's lovely, Frank."

Justin asked to see it.

"Let your mom put it on first," said Frank.

Carlotta handed it to him. "Will you?" Frank fitted it around her neck and closed the clasp.

"What do you two think of it?"

Frank studied the pearl, as if trying to make sure it was the same one he'd picked out at a Seventh Avenue jeweler's the week before.

"Is it real?" said Justin.

Frank laughed. "It ain't fake. Look who's talking. How come you didn't get your mother a present? You got all that money I gave you."

"That's all right," Carlotta said. "I've been putting it away in his savings account." She served the birthday cake with scoops of ice cream on top.

"It's nice to be here again, Lottie," said Frank.

"I'm glad you came." She got up and switched on the fan. "Let's go into the living room," she said. "It's cooler there."

Frank settled himself on a chair. Justin sat at one end of his bed and Carlotta at the other.

"In honor of my birthday I want to tell you a story," she said.

"What's going on?" said Justin, unable to control his discomfort.

"I just want to tell—"

"I don't want to hear no stories."

"Let your mother talk," said Frank.

"The one I want to tell tonight I've never told before, Justin. I've tried to, but I've never gotten it right." She smiled, the skin around her eyes wrinkled in a way that made her look older. "It's about you and me and Uncle Frank and—" she took a breath "—Daddy."

Frank shifted in his seat.

Carlotta fingered the pearl. "These days I've been thinking a lot about Daddy. Maybe you wondered why I was acting so strangely, Justin."

"Lottie." Frank's voice sounded higher than usual. "I thought we were supposed to have a birthday party."

"We are. But I'm not the only one who has a birthday around this time. I've already had my party. Now it's time for Daddy's."

"You mean . . . Ralph?"

"Yes."

"His birthday wasn't around this time; what are you talking—"

"His . . . anniversary," said Carlotta.

They faced each other. Now it would happen, thought Justin, now some explosion would come. But Frank looked away. "What is this, show-and-tell?" he asked.

"If you don't want to listen to it, you don't have to," she said calmly.

"What are you going to tell him?"

"The truth. He's already heard enough lies."

"I never lied."

"We both did."

"Look at him," Frank said. "He's scared shitless."

Justin had curled his knees up to his chest, held by the stave of his clasped arms. His head bent low and he stared down into the dark crevice against his body.

Carlotta turned to him. "Do you remember those things we used to talk about before you went to bed?"

He nodded without looking up.

"There came a time when you didn't want to hear them anymore, remember?"

He nodded once more.

"Why was that?"

He didn't answer.

"One night when I tried, you pushed me away, do you remember?"

He lifted his head.

"I couldn't sleep that night," she continued. "I was sure you knew exactly what it was I couldn't tell you."

"You're talking in riddles, Lottie . . . "

"Look at me, Justy." She waited until their eyes met. "I want to tell you about what happened to Daddy. Do you want to hear it?"

His lips trembled. "Daddy?" he murmured.

Carlotta nodded. Justin stared at her without speaking.

"Why does this have to be tonight?" Frank said. Patches of sweat stained the front of his shirt.

"It should have been done a long time ago."

"But it wasn't, so why dig it up now?"

"Because from now on I want to start getting a decent night's sleep. That's not too much to ask for, is it? A good night's sleep. And I want my son to have it too."

"No one's blaming you, Lottie."

"That's all right, I do a good enough job of that myself." She folded her hands together. "What's worse, having a nightmare when you're asleep or awake?"

The room had grown dim. Frank went to switch on a light.

"Don't. It's nicer like this." She turned to Justin. "A week or so ago I made a mistake in the hospital. It was a little one and I fixed it in time. My patient didn't even know about it — no one did, but it scared me. Soon after that, the patient died. It wasn't my fault, he was going to die soon anyway; he'd been drinking himself to death for years. But I liked him and it made me very sad. Afterwards I had a crazy idea: what would have happened if I'd made a really big mistake, like giving him the wrong pills or forgetting his shot? It happens. Like that baby who died because they fed it salt instead of sugar. What if he'd been younger and I did something wrong that might have killed him? I couldn't get it out of my head. Just the thought of causing someone to die was frightening. And do you know what I did afterwards? I went to the cemetery to see where Daddy is buried."

"The merry widow," Frank muttered.

"I went there because I kept thinking about something that happened before we moved here. Maybe you can remember it too. I want you to remember it." She paused. "It was in the summer. We all drove to the beach."

Justin's head lolled back slightly, as if bouyed up on a current of thought.

"We went in Daddy's car, the one you said was the same color as the holey cheese. You were sick, you remember?" she asked, coaxing him. "You made a pukey in the car."

"Daddy," murmured Justin.

"The kid doesn't know what you're talking about," said Frank.

"When we got to the beach I said you couldn't go in the water and you cried. Then Daddy said if you were quiet he would take you in for a little bit so you could see the waterman."

Justin looked alert.

"What?" asked Frank.

"Tell him, Justin."

"The waterman lives in the ocean. He eats the toes of the people who get too close," he said softly.

"The kid's talking like a baby," said Frank.

Justin stared into empty space between them. His mother and his uncle grew vague in the room's dimness. A distant rustling of water dissolved their voices.

"We almost had an accident on the drive out there. Ralph nearly hit someone," Frank grumbled.

"He was still tired from driving in from Chicago the day before. If you hadn't started drinking so early you could've driven. I even asked you to."

"If I hadn't started drinking I wouldn't have been able to stay in the same car with the prick for two hours at a stretch."

"Frank, I don't want you slinging mud at him again tonight."

"Why not? We're playing Truth or Consequences, aren't we? Why don't you mention what a prick he was to me the whole morning, trying to get me not to come along. He couldn't just say bug off. He never came out and told you straight off what he was thinking. He was a slippery talker. But I knew he couldn't stand the sight of me. He asked me only because he wanted to prove what a nice guy he was."

"What else do you remember?" Carlotta asked her son. "Justin! Look at me!"

He turned but seemed to be looking at some point beyond her.

"We got to the beach and walked to where there were no other people, do you remember? Daddy said the sand was as hot as oatmeal, and you took a handful to taste."

"The guy was a real comedian," said Frank. "You make him out to be the happy father. The only reason he planned this little outing in the first place was because he had a guilty conscience about staying away so long. You were about as happy to see him as I was. The kid could have cared less. Tell her, Champ. You said you wanted to play Bulldozer with me in the sand, right?"

"Then Daddy set up the big green beach umbrella—"

"You left out the part about Ralph making a stink about how I drunk up all the beer on the drive out."

"You had. You must have gone through most of a six-pack before we reached the expressway."

"Big deal. I told him we could get more at the beach."

"So you made me go with you to get it."

"It wasn't at gunpoint."

"You should have heard yourself carrying on about how far it was back to the concession stand."

"It was bad enough having to haul the creep's beer. Maybe I wanted company."

"You were looking for the chance to get me alone."

He laughed sharply. "I had all the chances I needed in the apartment while he was away. I didn't have to do it just then."

"You were drunk," she said, keeping an even voice. "And you wanted to make a fool out of Ralph."

"That's a load of crap."

"Oh? Then why did you wait until Ralph went into the water to go for the beer?"

"Stop talking like a high school sophomore. It was you who asked me to come along to the beach. You think I wanted to? You think I wanted to hear him go on for an hour about the wonderful deal he had cooking in Chicago? He didn't ask me once about how the garage was doing."

"It wasn't a signal for you to start your little fairy-tale romance with me again."

Frank's eyes narrowed. "You set me up, Carlotta. That whole last year we were living in the apartment you set me up."

"How? By treating you like a person? No one else had done that before — not your father, not Ralph. At least that's what you said. Was that setting you up? Maybe you weren't used to being treated that way, and it was too much."

"You talk as slippery as Ralph used to."

"You tried to make me into a girlfriend. But I wasn't, no matter how bad things got between Ralph and me."

"How many nights did I have to listen to you carrying on about how you felt like a widow with Ralph being gone?"

"As many as you went on about feeling like a leper, without friends . . ."

"And the time that broad called up, asking to speak with Ralph, and then hanging up?"

"I was ready to die. I needed someone to hold, someone I could cry to."

"Someone to kiss, even if it was only Ralph's fat, ugly kid brother."

"I never said that about you!"

"Maybe someone to sleep with, too . . . "

"Maybe once. Enough to know it wasn't good for either of us." Her voice left the room ringing.

Frank's thick voice deadened it. "Maybe more than once. Tell the truth, Lottie. You were afraid. That was the only reason it wasn't good for you, at least not afterwards. But it was good for me, Lottie. It was very good for me. I wanted you more than anything. Too bad you weren't ready for the follow-through. Just my tough luck, right? Maybe if I was someone else you might have let me down easy, but I was only Ralph's kid brother — "

"I told you no, what else did you want to hear?"

" — the ugly duckling who'd be grateful for whatever I could get. You knew I wouldn't make a stink no matter what you did with him. You knew Ralphie was going to come home sooner or later. You figured that would end it clean. But even grease monkeys get disappointed sometimes." He leaned forward. "Face it, Lottie. The only reason you wanted me to come along that day was so you could air out your guilty conscience and parade in front of Ralph as the good wifey."

Justin looked at them. The rustling in his head grew louder. There was water, waves, a beach, a dark beach. He couldn't see them anymore.

"You were drunk."

"Yes, holy mother, I was drunk. I was drunk off my ass. That was why it all happened, is that it?"

"It helped."

"You're either a goddam fool or you've been telling those stories for so long you don't even don't know the truth anymore." He was shouting.

"You wanted to hide it, not me. It was my idea to tell Justin—"

"You're not telling nobody nothing. You want to keep things clean." He got up from his chair. Carlotta stiffened. "You still want to tell one of your Daddy stories. Tell it to Justin; I don't want to hear it." He stood in front of her. "Look at me," he said.

She raised her eyes slowly.

"I loved you, Lottie. I won't ask you if you loved me, you probably wouldn't have the guts to admit it. Maybe I was drunk and couldn't keep from holding you again, pulling you down behind a dune, even with the kid right there." He touched her face.

The light switched on. Justin stood before the wardrobe, his hands wooden at his side, leaning forward, as if trying to hear something. His eyes glimmered, sparking back and forth from Carlotta to Frank like a loose connection. Frank's hand pulled away. Carlotta reached for the pearl around her neck. Justin began grinning horribly. Frank stepped toward him.

"Uh-uh," said Justin, shaking his head back and forth as if it were out of his control.

Carlotta stared at him. "Justy?" she said.

He kept on grinning. "Hump me baby. Stick me with your red-hot poker and hump to me hell! Yeah!"

"What's got into him?" said Frank.

"Hump me, hump me, humpa humpa." Justin thrust his hips back and forth, not taking his eyes from them. "You want to give it to me? Yeah? I'm gonna give it to you, yeah. I'm going to give it to you good—"

"Stop it, Justin!" Carlotta said.

"He stuck it to her, yeah! He stuck it to her, he stuck it to her good—"

"The kid's gone crazy."

Justin gripped the handles of the door and began pulling.

"Get away from there," said Carlotta, getting up.

"Daddy," Justin said to his reflection in the mirrored door. "Can I come in?" The door began to creak.

"Get away!" she said, reaching for Justin. He flung her away with a fierce jerk of his arm.

"Are you there, Daddy? Will you come to me now?" Justin went on, his face tightening as he pulled harder. "If you do I'll be able to save you so you won't drown." The door snapped open. Carlotta gasped. Justin grew calm. He lifted his hands to touch the clothing. "Daddy," he whispered. "I saw you swimming out there. They were gone but I saw you. They left you alone but I saw you." He stroked a jacket and began to cry. "I tried to save you. I ran as fast as I could. It was so far. The oatmeal hurt my feet. How come you swam so far away?"

"Come on, Champ," said Frank, coming up behind Justin. "Let's go—"

Justin spun around and saw his uncle's crazy eyes coming at him. He reached into his pocket. A silvery spurt flew at Frank, a red stripe cutting into his hand. He let out a cry and stumbled backward onto the floor.

"Frank!" shouted Carlotta. She grabbed a towel from the bathroom to wrap around his arm, kneeling beside him. His head rested against her shoulder, his eyes half closed. Justin stood before them, moving the blade back and forth as though preparing for his next jab. He saw his mother's eyes following the knife's motion, as if hypnotized. The pearl dangled from her neck, teasing him, daring him to destroy its calm, white perfection. His mother opened her mouth to speak, and he lunged the knife toward it. Carlotta shrieked. Something held his ankles fast. Frank had grabbed them. Justin kicked free and ran from the aparment. His cries filled the hallway.

He raced to where Matthew lived and hammered on the door. His knocks boomed through the building. Other doors opened but not Matthew's. He looked down at the open knife still gripped in his hand. His knuckles were red and swollen, the skin smudged and bearing a trace of blood. He snapped it shut and went back down the stairs. The sky hung low and starless. A block away he met Kevin, looking scared and sickly in the purplish glare of the street light. Neither wanted to return home; they headed for the garage to sleep. They walked for a long time without speaking.

"Look," Justin said. "There it is."

Mr. Sloane's house stood in a lightless pocket in the middle of the street between brick buildings on either side. It rose up out of a dense patch of weeds; its peaked roof speared the night. They went up to the fence. The boarded up windows in the front were dark glasses shielding eyes that kept watch.

"Goddam," shouted Justin, giving the fence an angry shove. The fence heaved back and forth with a jingly clatter.

"Get your little asses the hell out of here," said a voice in the darkness. They beat it away from there fast, as though the sidewalk were snapping at their heels.

PART THREE

September

Eleven

"Now hold on, boy. You is sputtering like a firecracker," Ephesus says to Matthew. They step over the charred wood in the alley on the way to the street, sidestepping pools of water left by the fire trucks. Ephesus closes the gate.

"Why lock it now?" Matthew says. "The house has already been messed up."

"It don't need to get any more."

Matthew looks at the burned house as Ephesus slowly threads a length of chain through a bedspring, fastening it to one of the shopping carts. Matthew had walked through the burned building in a daze, still buzzing from the Bloodhounds' latest ambush, dreading the moment when he'd come upon what was left of Mr. Sloane's piano. He found nothing. "Where is it?" he'd shouted.

"Where's what?" Ancil said, throwing charred wood into a pile.

"The piano."

"What piano?"

"Mr. Sloane's."

"There was never a piano here."

"I saw all of you pushing it down the street last week."

"You mean that nice new copper piping we got? A cop tipped off Mr. Sloane about where a bunch of it was laying around doing nothing. We went and got it but we didn't want to advertise it. The piano's sitting safe and sound in the shop. Now why don't you give a hand with this wood."

Ephesus snaps the lock and they head for the corner, opposite the green soldier. Matthew remembers that day back in March when he'd seen Kevin for the first time, when he'd met Mr. Sloane. Mr. Sloane had warned him about Kevin then. Now it seemed that Mr. Sloane hadn't heeded his own warning.

"I'm sure it was Justin and the rest of them who did it," Matthew says.

"You already done told us that, Matthias."

"Well, what are you going to do?"

"Right now you and me is going to the temple." That was his name for the bone chapel.

"A bunch of creeps try to burn down your house and you're not going to do nothing?"

"I didn't say we wasn't going to do nothin, I only said we wasn't going to do it now. And, anyway, I don't call going to the temple doin nothin. I needs to think. I needs to clear my head for what's comin next. You could use a little head clearin yourself. Now quit getting so fired, you heatin up the air and Lord knows it's hot enough as it is. And anyway, what do you think we should do? Find those two and shoot them?"

Matthew thinks of the squirrel swinging on the pole.

"Call the cops."

"Now you know Mr. Sloane would not be for that. We look after ourselves, we don't need nobody else tellin us right from wrong."

Matthew sighs. Ephesus was just another version of Mr. Sloane. All the viaduct men were, in a way. When Matthew first met them they all seemed different from one another. He was surprised at how such a group had come together. (Accident and luck, Mr. Sloane had explained. He'd met Ovid, for example, in a barbershop where Ovid's job was to steam the towels; he'd fallen into conversation with Ancil after Ancil handed Mr. Sloane a handbill for a fortune teller.) Skip seemed to be the outsider, but Mr. Sloane said the only difference between Skip and the others was a matter of style. "Skip's from New York," he explained.

Back at the camp, Ovid stands beside the pot. "You doin a soup run today?"

Ephesus nods, continuing on to the cave. He pulls open the metal door. Inside it's dark, damp as a cellar and smelling of roots and rust. They walk past all the beds to the rear. Ephesus lights a candle and places it on the coal stove. The candle sheds an ivory glow on the rows of bones climbing the walls around them. ("Just like the angels over the doors of Saint Patrick's," commented Mr. Sloane with a wry smile.) They sit down cross-legged on a piece of carpet. Barely one section of the fence is covered; even that much has taken weeks. The bones look like bows tied onto the fence. It's hard for Matthew to imagine communicating with the souls of dead people here, maybe it only worked with human bones. He's disappointed with the way the bone chapel turned out. After Sal was gone, it hardly mattered to Matthew. Ephesus encouraged him to keep on with it. Matthew sees him close his eyes, getting ready to do what he calls "sittin deep." His head leans back slightly, exposing his great nostrils. He appears to rest on his thick white hair as though on a cloud. His large hands cap his knees, his body falls nearly still.

When his eyes open, he removes a flask from his pants pocket, drinks, then offers the bottle to Matthew.

"Hey," Matthew says, swallowing a healthy mouthful. "You're not wearing overalls." He points to the Ephesus's pants. Little gold flecks run through the deep brown of the fabric. "They're new, aren't they?" Come to think of it, the others have been wearing new clothes, too.

"Ain't no reason why the servants of the spirit can't look good."

Matthew has another drink. His head begins to glow. The gold flecks in Ephesus's pants swim like fish. "I hope you don't let Kevin and Justin get away with it," he says.

"No bunch of hoodlums gonna wreck what we have built."

"You sound like it's no big deal."

"We calm cause we know just what we gotta do."

"What's that?"

The door pulls open. Mr. Sloane steps into the cave. "Are you gentlemen finished with your spiritual ministrations?"

"Come in, Brother," says Ephesus.

"Has everything been worked out?" he asks, sitting down beside Ephesus.

Ephesus nods his head.

"Good." He turns to Matthew. "As you know, we have a score to settle. You say you know those responsible for trying to destroy our house. We need your help in trying to find them." He speaks with the smoothness of velvet lining the sheath of a dagger. His gaze ignites the alcohol in Matthew's belly. "Will you help us?"

Matthew nods.

"You said it was that boy Kevin and your friend Justin —"

"He's not my friend anymore!"

"It was just a point of reference. Now, tell me, how are you sure it was those two?"

Matthew thinks. "Remember that time you were hauling those copper pipes, the time I thought it was a piano? Kevin and Justin were watching you. That's how they found out where the house is. I swear I didn't tell them, Mr. Sloane."

"I believe you."

"And something else. Justin got Kevin's knife. They must have made some kind of a deal, and it must have been a real important one or else Kevin wouldn't have given his knife away."

"So you think the deal was for Justin to help burn the house?"

Matthew nods. "If I were you I'd just bump them off."

"Here," says Mr. Sloane, producing a gun from his inside pocket. "Use this, and make sure to do it so that no one will find out."

Matthew shrinks away. "Where'd you get that?"

"That shouldn't interest you. I thought you wanted to do some bumping off." He smiles and replaces the gun. "Revenge may be sweet but it is quite costly. Now, where was I? Oh yes. You think they made some kind of deal. But how do you know it was Kevin who decided to burn the house? Maybe it was Justin's idea."

"Kevin said he wanted to kill all the niggers, I heard him that day he jumped me. I never heard Justin talking about niggers until he met Kevin. He's dumb. He'd do whatever Kevin told him."

"Can you describe these two charming boys?"

"You know what Justin and Kevin look like, Mr. Sloane."

"Just double-checking."

"Kevin's skinny and mean-looking. Justin's fat."

"The skinny one, what color hair does he have?"

"Yellow."

Mr. Sloane turns to Ephesus. "Skip might drink like a fish but he knows what he's talking about."

"Skip?" says Matthew.

"Justin and Kevin paid him a visit just before the fire." He reaches into his pocket once more. "Do you recognize this?"

"The flashlight Justin took from the movie! Where'd you get it?"

"We found it in the alley near the house."

"Well that proves it — "

"To whom? The police?"

"They could fingerprint the flashlight."

"And what would they find? My fingerprints. Skip's. They'd probably say I burned down my own house to get the insurance money. As if anybody would have insured that house."

"Well, what are you going to do then?"

"We is goin to do what we gotta do," says Ephesus.

"We can't talk about it yet," Mr. Sloane explains.

Matthew looks down. "You don't want to tell me because of that time I let Justin know about the house, right?"

"What's done is done," says Mr. Sloane. "You've helped us, and you're the only outsider who has. We trust you, and I want you to remember that. Otherwise I wouldn't have gone and brought you to the house that first day. You understand?"

Matthew nods.

"We like you, Matthias," says Ephesus.

"We have one more job for you to do. It might be a lot harder than running back and forth to Mr. Glaubach's shop for tools or carrying those heavy ceiling beams. I want you to tell Justin that, if he knows what's good for him, he'll stay away from Kevin."

"I don't want to see Fat Face ever again."

"It don't gotta be no social call," says Ephesus.

"What if he doesn't listen?"

"Then it'll be his problem."

"What if he asks me why?"

"Tell him anything you want except what you've heard here. Will you do that for us?"

"Yes," Matthew says.

"Good," says Ephesus, getting to his feet. "Now how about us having some of Ovid's dirty soup?"

Matthew motions to Mr. Sloane's pocket. "Are you really going to use that?"

"Go ask a policeman the same question. His answer will be the same as mine."

"How come you don't like cops?"

"Maybe because I grew up in a part of the country where some of the ones I saw had two uniforms. One was blue like the ones here. And the other was white with a point on top and two holes cut out for the eyes."

The supper is a somber one. They eat in silence around the dying fire. The only sound Matthew hears is the clack of their spoons against their bowls. Skip's there, too, but even he can't liven things up.

"If we don't look like a bunch of bachelors at a church supper!" he says.

Matthew looks at the odd assortment of men beside him. They sit on crates, except for Ephesus, who squats on the ground. Their bowls are poised on their laps. They too are wearing new, fancy clothes. Ovid can't get his trousers closed all the way; he leaves them half unzipped, holds them up with a pair of suspenders. Ancil's found a vest and a derby that's way too big for him. Matthew feels like crying, happy and sad at the same time. These men are his true friends, he thinks. Why are there always some creeps messing things up?

*

It's dusk by the time Matthew leaves. The empty street is quiet except for the draw of fans. He passes by his own house and looks up at the windows of his apartment, dark because his mother's at her rehearsal and won't be back until late. No sense going home, he thinks, wishing she were there just then. He keeps on walking, not knowing where to, his bellyful of Ovid's soup keeping him to a slow pace. He thinks of Asa, whom he hasn't seen since the fight last week. He's tried to visit him. Asa's mother came to the door, opening it only as far as the chain would allow. Matthew could hardly see her. She told him that Asa was going to his old school now. She peered at him through worried, nervous eyes, as though she thought it was Matthew who had beaten up Asa.

He hears Mr. Sloane's words in the cave earlier. His heart grows heavier. He'd betrayed the viaduct men with his big mouth. He hadn't meant to, but he had. It had been the same with Sal. Matthew works something loose from his tooth: a fleck of stone. So Ovid really did put dirt in. Sal and Ovid would probably get along well, cooking together. He'd like Ephesus, too. He wonders where Sal is at that moment. Still in the country? Far away? Matthew'd returned to Woolworth's over and over again but they told him the same thing: he'd left and nobody knew where he went to. Matthew raced to the mailbox every day before his mother did, in case a letter from Sal was there. But no letters came.

A kid turns the corner up ahead. Kevin? Justin? He freezes. His fists clench, his legs coil tight. He imagines hammering off the peak of Kevin's jaw like plaster or boring into Justin's blubber. No, it's someone else. Matthew slumps down on a stoop, exhausted. He remembers what Mr. Sloane said about warning Justin about Kevin. He didn't dream someone like Mr. Sloane would ever hold a gun in his hands. Yet how calmly he'd pulled it from hiding. Did he always carry it? Did he have it that day when he chased Kevin and the others from the squirrel? Is that why they were so scared of him? Matthew gets up, his limbs still tense. He nears the river. A slight chill gloves his throat and prickles his arms. At the mailbox on the corner of Twelfth Avenue, he stops. Cars rumble overhead sporadically. Across the street, a single

light marks a deserted stretch of broken asphalt. Just beyond it is
the pier building.

A figure appears at the edge of the light. Matthew follows it
with his eyes until it disappears into the building. His legs lock
in a moment of panic. He leans against the mailbox, wondering
what to do next. The neighborhood drops away around him;
only the pier building remains. He's never forgotten those two
men up in the attic. He takes a deep breath, pushes himself up
off the mailbox, and steps into the gutter carefully as though it
were a sheet of ice.

Up close, the pair of loading docks jut out like the paws of a
sphinx. Broken glass glitters on the asphalt, a scattering of
diamonds. He hesitates. A fine sheen of sweat cools his face and
the back of his neck. He leaps up onto a loading dock and, with
instinctive caution, checks to see if anyone is following. The
round-topped mailbox across the street looks like the last
milestone along a road that's taken him many months to cover.
He turns to face the opening and prickles with a pleasurable fear,
the fear he'd felt walking into the pond at night, waiting for its
dark, enveloping chill. He crawls underneath the opening.

Inside, darkness floats over him in gentle ripples. Breezes
finger him. The sense of his own daring emboldens him. He
drinks in the dank, powdery air. He imagines the two men there
in the darkness, half undressed, waiting for him. His eyes adjust.
Surroundings surface. Figures slide in and out of view. A face
veers by, another. He walks to where he thinks a wall must be.
Whispers pull at him, feet shuffle past and leave chalky echoes.
As he approaches the wall, a frieze of arms and legs take shape.
Closer, T-shirts glow above the white rings of socks. Two faces,
dull images cut in fluid stone, press together, two chests and two
bellies. A hand slips up and down a bare arm, sculpting it.
Matthew's brain sings with excitement. He's really seeing this.

Matthew walks on, anxious to see the next shadowy diorama,
as though he's in a gallery of his dreams. He sees a man crouch-
ing, his face locked between the legs of someone standing. The
standing man draws hoarse breaths: the other's head slides back
and forth. A hardness between Matthew's legs begins to rise, his

heart beats as though plated with zinc. He aches with the nearness of what they do, a translation of what he's done by himself in his bed a hundred times before, made more real, yet more unbelievable, by seeing others doing it together. He brings a bit of spittle to his hand and slips it down into his underwear. His legs part to accept the wonderful, wet glove. The standing man's breath begins to erupt in choppy gasps. A choked cry presses through the other's lips. Matthew steps closer, his breathing thickens as he strokes himself. The man reaches over, slides a hand down the back of Matthew's pants, and clamps his backside with thick, warm fingers. The man begins to quake, he lets out a cry, squeezes tighter. Matthew's insides collide, grow dense and shimmering, his knees buckle, hot tears squeeze from his eyes, he falls against the wall. A thousand moments later, he pushes himself back up, shivering slightly. He peers into the emptiness around him. Where is the man who touched him? He wants to find him. But the darkness has consumed him.

His nose is suddenly alert, refracting the smells in the air like a prism splitting light into color. The river's musk billows around him, laden with iodine and garbage. It mixes with the pungent rot of the streets and the sewers, with mud, dirt, and earth — the smells of the deep places: the river bed, the air shaft, the cave under the viaduct. He brings his hand to his nose and smells it there, too.

Someone passes before Matthew, leaving a cinnamon trail of after-shave lotion. The figure slows, comes near. Matthew sees the spread of a man's chest, the muscled drape of his arms. Matthew presses close; his face comes up as high as this man's chest. He rests his head against the purring belly, breathes in the smell of his shirt, sweet with cigarettes. A hand cups his face, tilting it upwards. A dark face peers down. Matthew reaches around the man's waist, his hands strain to meet at the other end. The man's legs and stomach are so hard, it's like holding the soldier in the park. The man strokes the back of Matthew's head.

You are precious to me, Matito. I love you. I want to be your father. Will you be my son?

Yes.

I have a secret. I want you to know it because I love you. It is about me. Should I tell you?

Yes.

Do you promise to tell no one?

Yes.

Not even your mama?

Not even her.

Matthew's chest presses the hardness under the man's pants. He feels the man's pulse quicken. Matthew's beats unevenly against it, as though racing to keep up. He feels himself pulled closer.

Look at me, Matito. Can you see me?

Yes.

You sure?

Yes.

I killed somebody. I did. With my own two hands. With these hands.

Who?

A woman. A very beautiful woman, someone I loved.

Why?

I thought she loved someone else. I was too crazy to think. I didn't want it to happen. Will you forgive me, Matito?

Matthew begins to cry. The man squats, his face drops beside Matthew's. He lays the warm weight of his hand on Matthew's neck. "What's wrong?" he says "You scared? I'm not gonna hurt you." Matthew stops crying for a moment, surprised at hearing a voice.

"You okay now?"

Matthew throws his arms around the man, begins to howl once more. The sound of his cries blows up and fills the darkness.

"We better get you out of here." He gives Matthew his hand. "We can go out through the side," he says, steering Matthew with his shoulder. They reach a ragged hole in the wall. The man goes out first, waits for Matthew to follow. As soon as he's outside he takes off into a wild run, away from the man's voice, which thins like the watery edge of a dream left behind in sleep.

★

"Sweetheart," Marjorie says, springing toward Matthew as he walks into the house. She throws her arms around him in the doorway. "Where the hell were you?"

He trembles with surprise. The smell of the pier building and the man's after-shave lotion is still strong in his nose, the man's touch feels branded onto Matthew's skin. He's terrified that somehow she might smell it too or see a hand print on his shirt. She leads him into the blinding light of the kitchen and they sit down. Her eyes swim in a pool of black, her lips are a faded red. The smudged makeup makes her face appear out of focus. Her pocketbook lies open like a cornucopia, makeup and tissues and nail files spill out. There's sheet music and a bottle of whiskey, too.

"What's the matter?" he asks.

"First you tell me where you've been."

"Over at Asa's," Matthew says, avoiding her glance.

"Is he feeling better?"

"Oh yeah, a whole lot better. His parents transferred him back to the Jewish school after what happened." He slips a little truth into his story just in case.

"You shouldn't have stayed there so long. I really got worried when I called up Justin's mother and she told me you weren't there. She sounded very unhappy."

"Did you sing good?" Matthew says, eager to change the subject.

She smiles and shrugs, reaches for the bottle. "What difference does it make?" She takes a swig, then slams the bottle back down on the table. "I'm a fool," she says, shaking her head. "Oh, before I forget." She lunges for her pocketbook. I have something for you. No, wait, close your eyes and stick out your hand." He does. "Hey, what have you and Asa been doing, digging ditches?" Matthew sees the smudges on his palm. He rushes to the kitchen sink to wash them before she gets suspicious.

"Okay." He takes his seat again and she places a package wrapped in a red napkin in his hand. It's a glass ashtray with the word Jack's on the bottom. A lady treble clef sits on a piano holding a champagne glass and singing. A bass clef man plays the piano.

"Thanks, Mom. I can use it to keep pennies — "

She takes a letter out of her pocket and throws it on the table. "Do you know what this is?"

Matthew puts the ashtray down.

"As long as you own up to snooping through my mail I won't take that ashtray and crown you with it."

"Sorry," he mumbles.

"Apology accepted." She takes out a second letter. "This is the follow-up. It was waiting for me when I got home. If you weren't in the coal mines with Asa you could have given me some sympathy." She hands it to him. "Can you read Greek?"

> *After you and Matito go I didn't know what to do. I stay up there by myself. I think alot. I even think I go drown myself in the pond. Then my father came. When you will learn, he tell me —*

"Hey! It says he's coming here tomorrow night!" Matthew cries.

"I know," she says, leaning her chin on her hand. "What am I going to do?"

"He's coming! Sal's coming!"

"At least one of us is happy. I'm going out of my mind."

Matthew reads the line again.

"He sure picked a wonderful day to return. Tomorrow's the gig at Jack's, you know."

"What are you going to do?"

"Sing my ass off and hope Jack likes me."

"I mean about Sal."

"Sal," she says, shaking her head. She takes another sip from the bottle. "Just when I thought I was doing okay. Now I can just go and forget about tomorrow. I won't be able to sing worth shit." She looks at the letter. "I can't believe his father came all the way from wherever that was, just so Sal could have a shoulder to cry on."

"His father's dead."

"What do you mean, he's dead?"

"He is."

"But Sal wrote — "

Matthew explains.

"That man gets more impossible by the day. But I still love him, you know that, Matty?"

"Good."

"That's easy for you to say. You know, there's something I've been meaning to ask you. I thought you two were buddies. How come you snitched on him?"

"I thought it would make you two get married quicker. He said he didn't want to marry you until you knew."

"Well, you got to hand it to Sal, he's honest."

"Why'd he hit you?"

"You remember that night? You'd told me about Sal that afternoon. All during supper I kept trying to decide if I should say something to him, but I figured I'd better keep my mouth shut and mull it over. The whole time you were swimming with him I couldn't stop thinking about it. Don't go crazy, I told myself. Don't lose your temper, no matter what. Then you ran in crying, I thought something must have happened between you two. I thought that maybe he did something to you, and I got scared. When he finally came home he was drunk as a lord. Didn't you hear him? I don't know how you could have slept through his carrying on.

"I told him to keep it down since you were trying to sleep. I said I didn't want him sleeping there. Then he started talking to himself in Spanish. He said he wanted to talk to you. I told him no. I was really scared he might hurt you. When I tried to stop him from going into your room he . . . hit me." She rests her forehead in her hand and stares at the table. Her eyes grow red. "I always swore that the moment a man ever laid a hand on me I would leave him . . ." Her voice dissolves into sniffles. "But I really didn't want to leave Sal."

Matthew goes and puts his arm around her. "He scared me too, sometimes," Matthew says, remembering the Bloodhound ambush. He pauses. "Do you want him to come back?"

"I don't know what I want anymore."

Twelve

1

In the dark, the door of the nigger's house looked like an old-fashioned wooden grave marker to Justin. Any second it would open. The nigger would come out.

Get the matches, Kevin says, opening the can of oil.

Justin's hand digs into his pockets trying to get the matches.

Hurry! I hear someone coming.

Justin can't find them. He hears footsteps.

Come on, Kevin shouts.

Justin looks in another pocket, then another. His pants have a thousand pookets and he must look through all of them.

He's coming, shouts Kevin.

The door opens.

Justin heads down the staircase of his apartment house, shaking his head to dislodge the picture stuck in his brain like a slide jammed in a projector. He dreams it when he goes to sleep and thinks about it during the day. His stomach goes queasy each time: he can almost smell the oil. It's Saturday, the sun's out: a perfect day not to have to go to school. But the neighborhood crawls with danger. Since the Bloodhounds have found out that Justin gave Kevin's knife to Matthew, they've sworn revenge on him. He never knows when they'll come after him. Walt's jumped out from between parked cars, a length of pipe in his hand. Pebbleface and Eugene have given him chase from the schoolyard. Pipsqueak Tony seems to materialize out of thin air. The only Bloodhound Justin hasn't seen in a while is Kevin. Justin figures Kevin's just biding his time.

Then there's the nigger. Since the fire he's had his eye on Justin all the time. At first, Justin thought it was the same guy he and Matthew ran into the day they snuck into the movie. But it's another one. Justin sees him everywhere. He's skinny enough to hide in the shallowest doorway or use a lamp pole for cover. Justin'll be walking down the street, he'll suddenly have the feeling of being watched. He'll turn around to see two eyes fixed on him like shotgun barrels. Somehow, there's always enough time for him to escape. After a while Justin's sure it can't be pure luck. The nigger must be letting him get away on purpose, but why? That scares him almost as much as the thought of getting caught.

To top it off, the nigger is wearing Daddy's clothes. Justin thinks he knows how the nigger got them. Two days after his mother's birthday party, Frank went to the apartment when nobody was home. He smashed the mirrors of the wardrobe, stole the clothing, and dumped it somewhere.

Carlotta told Justin he wasn't to set foot in the garage again. Justin doesn't really want to, mostly because he's afraid of what Frank might do. But he misses work. He misses Frank. A couple of days after his mother's birthday, Justin saw Frank in the garage, still wearing a bandage around his wrist. He must have cut Frank bad. He really hadn't meant to cut him. It was something about the way Frank and his mother looked at each other that night, and those eyes . . .

Matthew hates him now, too. Justin's sure. He misses Matthew most of all. Matthew was a better friend than any of the Bloodhounds ever were. The night he'd run downstairs after cutting his uncle, it was Matthew that Justin really wanted to see, not Kevin. That had been a horrible night. He and Kevin huddled together on the damp, hard floor of the garage with only a single blanket. Kevin put his arms around Justin. "To keep warm," Kevin had said. Justin hadn't wanted him to. "Why not? Ain't you my buddy?" Justin turned over on his side, Kevin pressed in close, his oily breath warm against Justin's neck. When Justin returned home the following morning, stiff and tired, Carlotta was waiting for him. She wore the clothes of the evening before. The pearl was gone. Her eyes were red and swollen.

"Give me that knife," she said. Her lips hardly moved as she spoke. Justin refused. Calmly, too calmly for him to anticipate, she pulled him across her knees. He struggled, but her strength surprised him. She had his pants down before he knew what happened and beat his backside raw with her bare hands.

Justin opens the front door, looks both ways. When he's sure the coast is clear he steps outside. It feels hot as July. The way he sees it, there's only one way to extricate himself from the mess he's in: get rid of the knife. He's decided to give it to Matthew to let them be friends again. The Bloodhounds'll still want to get him but, with Matthew on his side, it won't be as bad as being alone. When his mother sees that he doesn't have the knife anymore she'll leave him alone. He gets to Matthew's house and runs up the stairs.

No one's home.

He's no sooner back on the street than he has that familiar creepy feeling of being watched. Sure enough, behind a No Parking sign on the shady side of the street, the black man waits. He wears Daddy's brown pants that have buttons instead of a zipper. Justin's eyes blur; the walk up and down the stairs has left him dizzy.

Get the matches.

I can't find them.

Hurry.

"Don't run away this time," the black man says, waving to him. "I just want to have a word with you."

Justin's too surprised and confused to move. He sees the man walking toward him, his mustache, his narrow eyes, his flat hat. It's him, all right, the one that didn't have any clothes on, the one at the house. He's halfway across the street.

Whatcha do with the matches, Bimbo?

I thought they were in my pocket.

You better have them by the time I get the oil opened. Okay, get ready.

Justin trembles as the man approaches. He runs, taking a crazy-quilt course through the streets to get away, falls, dizzy and breathless, against a car several blocks away. The metal burns his skin, the heat feels like a weight on his shoulders.

Now light it.

I dropped the matches.

Shine your flashlight here.

Kevin looked for them. Justin tried to run, Kevin pulled him down into the oil-soaked garbage. The flashlight fell.

Let me go, let me go!

Somebody in the house was moving around.

Kevin went to light a match. I'm going to fry you and the nigger together.

The door opened.

The next moment, a blur of oil fumes. Kevin lit a match, a bed of flame went up around them. A hand swooped down, pulled Justin out of it and flung him away. He ran out onto the street. He looked back, a claw of fire was tearing into the house.

Justin rubs his eyes. He's tired of running and hiding. He yearns for the black man to corner him and punch him out once and for all. Then he remembers: the black man said he wanted to talk to him. Or had Justin imagined it? No. But why would he want to? It made no sense, just as it made no sense that he let Justin get away each time. Something's going on. Justin begins walking, afraid to stay in one place for too long. There isn't a breeze. The dizziness slows to a pounding in his head. He walks faster, as though trying to get away from it.

Near Times Square he stops under a marquee, grateful for shade. One of the posters in the display windows shows a man without a shirt wrestling a woman to the ground. The man is huge; muscles bulge from his arms. The veins in his neck make it look like a tree trunk. He's tearing off her clothes. Her face is twisted with fear. Her titties spill out of what's left of her dress. Justin stares at them, feels the knife in his pocket, yearns to tear out the man's heart with it, the woman's too. He sees his mother's pearl dangling before his eyes.

A whistle shears through the street. It's Tony, he thinks, not bothering to look, shooting down a side street, expecting ant-eyed Eugene to cut him off somewhere or else Walt. The slaps of his sneakers echo down the street. He's almost at the pier before he realizes that no one's chasing him. Jesus, he must be going crazy. It's too hot. He's gotta sit down somewhere and rest. The pier is empty except for a few people sitting along the edge. His eyes hurt when he looks down at the planking and further out the water is a band of blinding glare. He remembered Uncle Frank had promised to take him for a drive soon to get out of the hot city for a day; maybe they could've gone somewhere that day even, to Freedomland, maybe up to Bear Mountain again. But now . . .

Way out at the end of the pier, sitting on the edge, he sees Matthew. Justin wants to run the other way, but he tells himself that he can't, not if he wants to clear things up. He feels the knife in his pocket, remembers what he's promised himself to do. He swallows and keeps going, trying to think of what he'll say.

Matthew turns, fixes him with an icy stare, daring him to approach.

"You still mad?" Justin says, walking slower.

"Yeah."

Justin swallows hard. "Sorry," he says.

"Sorry," Matthew sneers.

"It wasn't my fault the Bloodhounds jumped us."

"What about Mr. Sloane's house?"

"It's still there. It didn't burn all the way down."

"You wanted it to, didn't you?"

"Kevin did."

"So did you! He gave you his knife so you'd do it with him, didn't he? You didn't even know Mr. Sloane. Why'd you want to burn his house down?"

"He made fun of me that time, remember?" Justin's dazed and helpless. It's not going the way he thought it would. He figured they could just make up. His thoughts fall on top of each other. "Wait!" he says, holding up his hands.

Matthew looks at him.

Justin reaches into his pocket. Matthew springs back. "It's okay," he says, pulling out the knife. He holds it out. "I want to give it to you. Take it, Matty. You can have it."

"Why?"

"B-because, because . . . You want it, don't you?"

"I don't know." He looks at the knife, still missing its casing, cushioned in Justin's chubby palm.

Justin remembers Kevin giving him the knife. It had been a kind of trick, so that Justin would stay his friend. No wonder Matthew's suspicious. "It ain't a trap, Matty," says Justin. "Honest."

"How do I know? Maybe you're doing it just so that Kevin'll find it on me?"

"Kevin's a jerk. I'm out of the Bloodhounds. They're after me too because I gave you the knife that other time to fix."

"Yeah?"

Justin nods his head.

Matthew smiles, takes the knife, throws it over his shoulder into the water. Justin runs to the edge, stares at the little ripple the knife's left behind.

"Huh?" he says. "Why'd you do that?"

"Felt like it."

"Why'd you throw my knife in the river?" says Justin, beginning to yell.

"You said I could have it."

"I didn't say you could throw it in the river."

"Too late." He grins.

"You creep."

"I didn't want your stupid knife. You shoulda kept it. You're going to need it soon if—" He stops. The warning he is supposed to give to Justin sticks in Matthew's throat. He looks at Justin's squinting eyes, narrow and piglike above the pads of his cheeks. He thinks of Asa, the corner of one eye crusted in a scar.

"If what?" says Justin.

Matthew shakes his head. "Get lost, Fat Face."

Justin's mouth opens, he aims a punch at Matthew, who sidesteps it. A moment later they're grappling at each other in a lopsided waltz across the planks. Justin slugs at Matthew blindly, imagining he's Frank or his mother or the nigger or Kevin. They near the edge, their skin gleaming with sweat and grime. Justin's foot catches in a crack, and he stumbles.

"Watch out!"

Justin falls. His back hits the broad wooden tip of the pier. He lets out a sharp cry and lurches up to grab hold of Matthew's arm. His fingers slide off the sweat-slicked skin, he claws at Matthew's T-shirt. It rips under Justin's weight and pulls off Matthew like wet newspaper, letting Justin fall backward into the river. His body snaps against the water. His own T-shirt billows around his neck to sabotage the clumsy flutter of his arms.

Matthew looks over, terrified. A man shoots past him as if he had landed from the sky.

"Skip!"

Skip kicks off his shoes. "Get help," he shouts, and dives in where Justin has just gone under. A moment later he emerges with Justin's head crooked under his arm.

Other people are coming over. Matthew's mouth opens, a call for help on his lips. But he says nothing. He can't think of Justin; he can't think of anything except getting away from there as fast as he can.

★

"Asa, what are you doing here?" Matthew says, still running as they converge on the street near the viaduct.

"Can't talk now," he says, barely able to stand still. He's wearing the black pants and white shirt he had on when Matthew first met him. His eyes sparkle rebellion. One eye looks smaller than the other, and shadowed with a faint blue. "How come you aren't wearing any shirt?"

"Something happened. Is your dad chasing you again?"

"No, my mother!"

"Yeah?"

"She'll be here any minute. Can we go to your house?"

Matthew thinks about what's just happened to Justin, about his mother getting ready for singing tonight. "Better not. Let's go to Birdland."

"Here," Asa says, unbuttoning his shirt as they run. He pulls off his undershirt, gives it to Matthew, slips the other shirt back on. Once they're on the train they explode with talk.

"My father's really upset. Today's Yom Kippur, a big Jewish holiday when you go to shul and ask God to forgive you for all the bad things you've done. He was getting ready to go when he found the book where I write up what he does to me. Then he said he wasn't going to the shul because it would only be a mockery to ask for forgiveness after what he'd done."

"Did your parents really make you go back to that Jewish school again?"

"How do you know about that?"

"From your mom. I went up to your house."

Asa smiles. "How come you didn't want to go home?"

"I did something bad. I didn't mean to, it wasn't my fault but it happened anyway."

"Don't worry. Today is the day you can tell God you're sorry for all the bad stuff you did all year and he'll forgive you. Well, I don't know if it'd work for you, since you're not Jewish, but you could try."

"I was in a fight."

"That's not so bad. You don't even have to bother mentioning that to God."

"I think I made the guy drown."

Asa grows serious. "Yeah? Who?"

Matthew tells him.

"Good!" Asa shouts. "I hope he dies." The other people in the car look up. "God punished him for what he did to me."

"He used to be my friend, Asa. It happened so fast. He tried to hold onto my shirt but it ripped off."

"So, it's not your fault."

"If I didn't throw his knife in the river it wouldn't have happened."

"He could just swim to shore."

"Justin doesn't know how to swim."

"Tough luck."

"You can't swim, either. What if it happened to you?" Matthew's angry at Asa's callousness. It reminds him of the way Asa was when they first met.

"The kid deserved it," says Asa smugly.

"No, Asa! That's not right."

"Why not? Look what he did to me."

Matthew shakes his head, seeing the eye, unable to find an answer, but sure that there is one. They ride in silence.

"I have some money," Asa says after a while. "Let's have a picnic." They get out. Asa buys them candy and crackers and Yoo-Hoos to drink, then they get back on. Matthew follows in a daze.

Later, they lie on the beach, stripped down to their underwear, their bellies full of chocolate. Matthew can't stop thinking about what happened on the pier. What was Skip doing there? Had he been watching them the whole time? Matthew keeps hearing Justin's cry as he fell. Matthew was supposed to warn Justin. His thoughts coil tightly in his head. He looks at the water and imagines his insides storming and crashing.

"Asa," he says. "I'm scared." Asa reaches over and puts his arms around Matthew. He feels tiny and hard; his skin is warm and very smooth.

"What are you afraid of, Matthew?"

"What if something happens to Justin? What if the cops are looking for me when we go back to the city?" The coil in Matthew's head snaps. He begins to cry.

"We should just stay here," Asa says. "It's better than in the city."

"We can't."

"Why not?"

"Sal's coming back tonight."

"Who's that?"

"My mother's boyfriend. You remember?"

"We should still stay here." Asa pulls him closer. "I love you," he says. He looks at Matthew. A smile crowds his face. He leans over and kisses Matthew's cheek. "Do you want to kiss me now?" Asa says.

Matthew cranks himself up on his elbows. His eyes fall on the misshapen corner of Asa's eye. He kisses it. He glances at Asa's leg bruises. "They look a little better," he says.

"My father stopped beating me after what happened in school. When my father first told me I wasn't going to your school anymore I said I wasn't going to any school. I didn't care what he did to me. But he didn't even yell at me. He just walked out of the room." He looks at Matthew. "Let's kiss at the same time." He puts his arms around Matthew. Their lips touch.

Matthew pushes closer. His hands stroke Asa's shoulders. The hardness between Asa's legs surprises him; he presses against it. Asa's breath comes against Matthew's face in short hot puffs; his legs scissor back and forth in between Matthew's. They peel off their underwear.

"Look at your thingy," says Matthew, pointing.

"Look at yours."

They fall over each other.

"I don't think boys are supposed to kiss each other," Matthew says afterward.

"They can if they're friends," says Asa.

2

Frank hears an ambulance siren, looks up from the '56 DeSoto he's working on. After the fire at that house near the park he's seen more cops combing the streets than he has in a long time. He waits to hear where the siren's going but doesn't bother to walk out to see what's going on. These days he doesn't let much of anything get to him. He goes back to work. The car's a beauty, dark blue with grey interiors, a V-8 engine, hydromatic transmission, even a goddam shortwave radio built into the dash.

The night of Carlotta's birthday party, after Justin left, Frank had passed out. He came to in Carlotta's arms, aching and weak, the blood soaked through the towel.

"It would be better if someone at the Roosevelt ER had a look at the cut," Carlotta had said to him.

"It doesn't look so bad. I want to go home."

"You really should have it looked at," she said. "It could be infected. Who knows what was on that knife." She paused. "I'll go with you."

He looked at her. "I can make it by myself." He got up. "If I happen to see the kid I'll send him home," he said. He kissed her on the cheek, then left. The next day, right in the middle of the afternoon, he found himself staring at the white bandage the nurse in the ER had wrapped around his hand. He told the guys they could have the rest of the day off with pay. He rolled down the garage door, shut himself up in the office, and took out a fresh bottle of J & B from the bottom desk drawer. He began drinking and didn't stop until the bottle was empty. He went home, fell into bed with his clothes on, slept into the next morning, and then woke up in a sweat. He found a hammer, went to Carlotta's apartment, let himself in with his key—he hadn't bothered to think of what he would've done if someone had been home—and smashed the wardrobe. The sight of the clothing made him laugh; all those years he'd watched his brother getting ready for his dates, all the times he'd gagged walking into the bathroom after Ralph had stunk it up with his cologne. Frank pulled out fistfuls of the clothing, heaped it onto the floor, and trampled it like a peasant pressing grapes. He threw an armful out of the window, grabbed the rest, and headed out into the street with it. At the viaduct he heaved it over the railing and watched it rain down on the tracks.

He stayed in bed for a week. The guys from the garage called up to ask what was going on. He told them he was letting them go. Then he took on a lot of work to keep occupied. The wound on his hand was small but deep. It took a long time to heal; every time he had to turn a wrench the cut opened up. He'd returned to the clinic to have them look at it. He'd thought of going up to Carlotta's floor but he hadn't.

The siren sounds as though it's headed for the river. He looks up from the DeSoto, glances at his watch: a little after twelve.

Time for a break. That's the nice thing about working by yourself, he thinks: coming and going as you please, never worrying
about who's messing up while you're not there. He closes the
garage and starts down the block. He hasn't been down to the
river since he was a kid. Those days you could throw in a line
with some bait and pull out something. Mornings in summer
he'd go with a bunch of his cronies to the Seventy-ninth Street
Pier and fish off the dock. They swam there too, until Iggy
Fletcher cut his toe going in and died from tetanus a few days
later. Fishing was better than swimming anyway. Fishing meant
sitting on your duff for hours looking at the Palisades. He loved
those cliffs. As soon as he got his first car he drove it across the
George Washington Bridge, which they'd just finished, and
spent the afternoon wandering through the woods.

He'd gone there with Carlotta once too.

Just before reaching Twelfth Avenue he spots the ambulance
beacon and picks up his pace. There's a crowd. A paramedic's
kneeling over someone spread out on the pier. A cop's holding
people back. "Let the kid breathe," he tells them.

"What the hell was the kid doing swimming in the river?"
Frank hears someone say.

Frank peers through the crowd, then pushes to the front. He
sees Justin. "Champ!" he shouts. A cop holds him back.

"That's the kid's uncle," says a black man.

"Who are you?" Frank says to him.

"I'm the one who pulled him out."

"This kid's yours?" the cop asks Frank.

Frank doesn't answer, staring at the black man's wet clothes.

"Hey!" the cop says. "This kid yours?"

Frank nods, sinks down to his knees beside Justin. The kid's
face is white and heavy looking. A medic's giving mouth-to-
mouth. A second medic readies a tank with an oxygen mask.
Justin lies still beneath the push of the medic's hands on his
chest, his eyes half open.

"Oh God," Frank says.

Skip puts his arm around Frank's shoulder. "We'll get him
through," he says.

Justin's eyes begin to flutter. The medic pauses, begins again. Justin begins to cough.

"Get the mask on him," the medic shouts. When it's on, they then lift him onto a stretcher.

"We're taking him to Roosevelt," the cop says to Frank. "You can come with me and answer some questions."

He waits outside the ICU for hours. CarIotta sits by Justin's bed. She sees him through the door but won't come out to speak with him. It's almost seven by the time he leaves. He's about to head home but goes to the garage instead. He needs to mull things over, he tells himself. The garage is the only place he really feels at home in, safe in. He rolls the door shut behind him. The Goodyear Tires clock glows in the dark.

He begins a slow walk around the edge of the room. His footsteps leave a damp echo. It's strange how things turn out, he thinks. He's never believed in fate or good luck or bad luck or that if you did enough good deeds your soul would live on easy street for an eternity. But he did believe that most things were good, most people were good. Anything bad that happened meant something had gone wrong, but as soon as it got cleared up, the good would return. It might take a while, it might be hard to find out what went wrong, it might not stay good for long, but that was the general direction things went, he believed. What he and Carlotta had done wasn't good, but it wasn't bad, either; it just came at the wrong time. He figured he'd just have to wait until things settled down again so the good could return. He thought that time had come.

She made like I wasn't there, he thinks.

He stops. The clock at the other side glows like a distant moon. Frank shudders. He's always been afraid of the dark. He peeks into the back room. The other morning he'd come into the garage earlier than usual and found a kid sleeping there. Frank had been too choked to speak. The kid looked like a mangy little squirrel; his skin was almost the same color as the cinderblock walls. What was a kid his age doing sleeping on the cold floor of a garage? Was there a good reason for it? Frank couldn't believe the kid was there sleeping in the dirt because it had to be that way, because of fate. He went over to him. The kid awoke with a start and scampered back to the window like an ant discovered under a rock. He wishes the kid were there now so he could talk to him.

I just wanted to ask Carlotta if I could do anything, he thinks.

Carlotta was good. He'd felt it. But with her the good always kept slipping away. She pushed it away, she was afraid of it. His confusion sharpens to bitterness. He goes to the sink, splashes water on his face, goes to the desk. Since his binge after Carlotta's birthday, he's kept a bottle there to take a swig from every so often, never enough to do more than lighten things up a little. The bottle's half full. He lifts it to his mouth, deciding that he doesn't want to get drunk. He's angry, he's sad, but in the last month he's been both of these a hundred times so that's no reason to get drunk.

I want my boy, he thinks.

As they were driving to the hospital the cop told Frank that Justin had been seen fighting with a boy of roughly his age just before falling into the river. Did Frank know who that kid might have been? A friend of Justin's, someone he went to school with? How the hell should he know, Frank answered. Then he remembered Matthew. He asked the cop if he knew whether Justin fell or was pushed. No way of knowing, the cop said. Skip hadn't got there until Justin was already in. How come Skip was there just then? Frank wanted to know. Your kid's good luck, the cop answered.

Frank takes another sip. Justin's good luck, he thinks.

Why had Justin come at him with a knife like that? Carlotta deserved it more then he did, keeping Justin in that dream world of hers. He'd always been a strange kid, a little lonely, scared of his own shadow. No wonder Frank had taken a shine to him. They were cut from the same cloth, the way Frank saw it. Justin must have felt it, too. With Ralph away, they'd been like father and son, like brothers. Then Carlotta took him away when they moved. In the past couple of months, Justin had begun to return. Frank hadn't forced Justin; the boy had worked at the garage of his own free will. Week by week Justin had warmed up to him, begun liking him again. Then something happened. Justin started acting smart to him, just like all the jerks who ever worked for him. Justin was turning into the same kind of creep his father had been. Carlotta had something to do with it. Her hands had pulled the strings to make Justin aim that knife. She'd taken Justin away from him. Frank wanted him back.

Justin, he thinks, his sips becoming swallows. Only Justin matters now. In the hospital Carlotta'd acted as though Frank might break into the ICU and steal Justin away. She was a stupid, frightened woman, he tells himself. He'll never understand Carlotta, he no longer wants to. But Justin, yes. Justin was worth fighting for. He was still a kid, he could turn out okay. Frank loves Justin. He's sure that Justin's the closest he'll ever come to having a son; he'll stop anyone who tries to hurt him. Had it really been Matthew? Frank wonders. He pulls out the small pistol from the bottom desk drawer.

It doesn't matter.

3

Asa's father reads another page of the notebook. He sits at the edge of Asa's bed, still unmade from this morning. The blinds are drawn; a single shaft of brilliant sunlight slips through in a ripple over the crumpled sheet. He's alone. The house is very quiet. He turns over a page. He looks up for a moment when he hears the noonday siren, then returns to his reading.

The book had been under Asa's pillow, as if left from a bad dream, a simple spiral memo pad with a yellow cover. It had slipped out from under Asa's pillow this morning. He'd wanted to usher in the new year with his son. Since Asa understood Hebrew so well Nathan Schandau had decided to take him to the regular services this year instead of sending him to the Junior Congregation. Mr. Schandau had looked forward to the High Holidays so he might start things anew not only with his son but with his wife as well. He wanted them to live like married people again, to sleep in the same bed, to learn to love each other, at least to try. He'd gone to wake Asa instead of leaving that to his wife. Asa'd looked up, startled to see him there. When he went to stroke Asa's forehead, Asa had run from his bed, clutching his pillow. The notebook had fallen out. His father picked it up. His eyes fell on a sentence: "But no matter what he did to me, I wouldn't cry." He felt a pain in his side as though jabbed.

He thought of what day it was. It was no accident that he'd come across the book on such a day. It was a sign of a reckoning. He'd set the notebook on trembling knees and forced himself to read further. Asa and his mother squabbled in the kitchen as she tried to convince Asa to go with his father to the synagogue. Nathan Schandau kept on reading. He didn't stop when he heard the door slam once, then once more. He realized that the book was only the most recent in a whole series of such books; he searched through Asa's drawers until he found the others. He flipped to the very first entry, recording Asa's fateful outburst during the seder, written in a tangled scrawl, bearing a stamp of grease. Later on, as Asa's punishments grew more frequent, the handwriting lost its urgent messiness and assumed a chilling, clinical calm. If only Asa had shouted back at him, accused him, insulted him, instead of compiling this horrible record. Words crammed every inch of space, the blue lines seemed to bend under the weight. What a memory his Asa had! He searched for the description of Asa's beating at school. There was none. Asa seemed to be saying that an ignorant bully like Justin couldn't be held responsible for his actions. But he, Nathan Schandau, would not receive such pardon.

It's almost dark by the time he pauses. He rises from the bed, weak from not having eaten, selects one of the books, replaces the others, then puts a slice of bread into his pocket, and leaves the house. He doesn't go to the synagogue but heads toward the river. There, for the second time that year, he will perform the ritual of throwing bread into the water, a piece for each of the sins he dares to remember, for each bruise his crazy hand has inflicted on Asa, one for each time he's made his son, the light of his life, suffer.

4

Matthew and Asa are barely across Ninth Avenue before they hear a fussy voice lashing at them from behind.

"Where have you been? We been looking for you all day," Ancil says, doing a jittery dance. "You don't have to tell me, it's hardly important. Just come along." He glances at Asa. "Guess you better come along, too."

"What happened?" Matthew says.

"There isn't time for details," Ancil says, giving Matthew a little push from behind.

"Where are we going?" says Asa.

"You'll find out soon. Just don't stop."

Asa smiles, glad not to have to go home.

The others are waiting for them in the camp. Ovid rushes over, gives Matthew a clumsy hug. "We was so worried," he says.

Mr. Sloane pats Matthew on the shoulder. "It's good to see you're safe and sound."

It's the first time he's done that instead of shaking his hand, Matthew thinks. "What's going on?"

Asa looks around, open-mouthed.

"You hungry?" says Ephesus. "Ovid made some — "

"There isn't time for that," Mr. Sloane interrupts. "Matthew and I have to talk. Now tell me, Matthew. Exactly what happened on the pier this afternoon?"

"He started it!"

"Take it easy. I'm just asking you a question."

Matthew tells him the story of the fight.

"Why did you run away afterward?"

"I was scared."

"People saw you running. The police think Justin was thrown in by a kid who fits your description."

"You mean Skip told them?"

"Of course not. But there were other people on the pier."

"Is he dead?"

"He's in the hospital," Ancil says.

"I want you to stay here for the time being, Matthew. Your friend can stay as well. If a cop sees you on the street he might decide to take you in."

"I want to go home," Matthew says. "Sal is supposed to come over this evening. My mom's expecting me."

"That's not what you said the other day," says Ancil. "You said she was singing in some nightclub tonight."

"I want to go home," Matthew insists.

"You can," Mr. Sloane answers, "but not yet."

"Why not?"

"I already told you," he says, a little impatiently. "Ancil, give them something to eat and take them into the cave."

Ovid fills two bowls for them.

"What's in it?" Asa asks.

"Religion," says Ancil. "Come on, you two."

When they're in the cave Mr. Sloane turns to Ephesus. "Skip said he saw Justin's uncle a little while ago. He was drunk and had a gun on him. Make sure the two of them don't leave."

"Where are you going?"

"I have to check up on some things."

"You be careful, Mr. Sloane." He goes into the cave.

"How come you never told me about this place?" Asa asks Matthew.

"Cause Matthias know how to keep a secret," Ephesus answers, sitting down beside them with a bowl of soup. "I hope you can, too." He looks at Asa. "Are you a son of Israel?"

"Yes."

"I am one as well." He extends his hand for Asa to shake. *"Shalem alaykem."*

"Shalom aleichem," says Asa, bewildered.

"Why are those bones up there?" Asa says.

Ephesus starts to explain but Matthew cuts him short. He's not in the mood to hear Ephesus talk about spirits. "It's like a church."

"Really? I've never been in a church." He turns to Ephesus. "How can you be Jewish?"

"I am of the Ten Lost Tribes, a Falasha."

They begin to talk. Matthew eats a little more of the soup, then feels drowsy and dozes off on the carpet. He wakes up a little later with a start. Asa's curled beside him. Ephesus is gone.

"This is a neat place," Asa says. "Ephesus told me all about the bone chapel. I never knew chickens had such large vertebrae. You and I could live here, too."

"Did he tell you what's going on?"

"No."

"We gotta go."

"Why?"

"Because of Sal. My mom's not home, and if he comes and no one's there he might just go away again." Matthew goes to the door and peeks out. "They're sitting around the fire. There's a path we can take down to the railroad tracks. Let's go."

They leave the cave and crawl toward the far edge of the clearing. The ground is still warm from the day's sun. "It's too dark. I can't find the path," Matthew says. "But the tracks aren't far. Let's just head in here."

They push through the undergrowth. The leaves rustle loudly, alerting the others.

"Get back, you stinkers," Ancil shouts.

He and Ephesus set out after them. Asa sifts through the brush nimbly. A root trips Matthew, and he lands on his stomach. He hears Ephesus's big feet tamping down the weeds close behind, pulls himself up, and pushes through the branches snapping in his face. Finally the weeds thin; he reaches the track bed where Asa waits. "This way," he cries.

"Come back!" Ephesus's voice howls after them.

"You still don't want to go home?" Matthew asks as they run.

"No."

"Come to my house. You can meet Sal."

They climb up to the street at West Fifty-sixth Street. A block away from Matthew's house, a figure springs out of a doorway.

"B-B-Bonzai!" Walt shouts, a two-by-four in his hand. Eugene's with him.

Matthew and Asa veer in the opposite direction. Walt and Eugene follow. At least there's only two of them, Matthew thinks. Asa seems to be enjoying all the excitement. He takes the lead, his white shirt flapping merrily around him. They turn a corner, and the spindly figure of Ephesus looms up.

"The other way!" Asa cries. They run toward the river. They rest at the next corner. "Who were those kids?" Asa asks, catching his breath.

"Bloodhounds. Justin's friends with them." He hears Walt and Eugene approaching. "Wait, I know a place we can hide. This way," he says, leading them toward the pier building.

5

Sal stands before the front door, checking up and down the block, hoping to see either Marjorie or Matthew turn the corner. His hand has sweated through the paper wrapped around the bouquet he carries. The strong smell of the flowers has him feeling a little sick. He's been there an hour already. He's uncomfortable in his jacket but he doesn't take it off, expecting either one of them to arrive. A cop car cruises by, slows as it passes him as if checking him out, then drives on.

At first he'd been angry at Marjorie when he rang the bell and no one answered. Hadn't he written her, telling her he'd come? Was she standing on the other side of the door, waiting for him to go away? For all he knew she might have torn the letters up, the same way she'd hung up on him. Now he prays she will come. It worries him that no lights are on in the apartment.

"And where the hell is Matito at this hour," he mutters. He looks at his watch. Nine, a little after. Walking from the subway to the house, he passed people sitting on stoops and on parked cars, drinking beer and eating out of paper cartons from the deli— neighbors, families, old people that reminded him of his parents. The city is so calm tonight, he thinks. He doesn't remember it being like this for a long time.

He'd stayed up in the cottage after Marjorie and Matthew left, alone most of the time. It had done him good. He'd done some thinking. He'd gone to a small church up there, Protestant, but he didn't care. He'd spoken with the minister afterward. They'd gone over to the minister's house for coffee. The man had a small orchard, a vegetable garden. He got his eggs from a chicken in the back. He and Marjorie and Matthew could live like that too, Sal thought. He'd move the hell out of the city and get himself a small place. Then he'd remembered asking Marjorie if she'd like to live in the country. "You can, but I don't want to get stuck weeding the flowers," she'd told him. But if they were away from the craziness of the city, Sal had persisted, it might be better for them. Marjorie had said there wasn't anything crazy about the city. After leaving the minister's house Sal decided to return to New York, see Marjorie again, talk to her, and try to put things back together again.

The first few days back had been like a bad dream. He'd gotten off the bus and stared around him as though he didn't know where he was. A sickly vapor hung over the city. The streets seemed like rivers that had dried up. People scurried around as if daylight frightened them. He stumbled down into the subway feeling like he was falling into a pit. He knew he had to leave as soon as he could.

But not alone, he thought. With Marjorie, with Matthew.

He sits down on the front stoop. Plans, he thinks. He was always good at making them. His head was full of them before coming to New York. And what had happened? After so many years, he was still making plans, then doing his best to mess them up. The cop car cruises by again. Just to kill time he decides to see where it's heading. He slips the bouquet inside the hallway behind the door, follows the car.

Sal couldn't blame Matthew or Marjorie for getting scared of him. And it was crazy to tell a ten-year-old what Sal had told Matthew, he thinks, walking down the street. Did he really think a kid could keep a secret like that from his mother? But Sal'd had to tell someone. Who else was there to tell? His own father hadn't wanted to hear about it anymore. "You were always hot-headed,"

Sal's father said. "I was almost afraid to let you come down to the bone chapel with us in case you got angry at the priest and started swinging."

As he nears the river a pack of kids streak through a pool of light, then plunge out, invisible. Was one of them Matthew? He breaks into a run to follow. They move along the river, then slip into an abandoned pier building.

Sal hears his father say, "You are about to enter the Kingdom of the Dead once again, so watch your ass."

6

"I want my boy," Frank says, stumbling past the warehouses along the river. The gun chafes against his belly. He falls against the stanchions of the highway, knocks into lamp poles, missing by inches the odd car that rumbles down the cobblestones of Twelfth Avenue. His thoughts slop through the alcohol softness of his brain, the uneven sidewalk tricks him.

He walks toward a single street light that works. It blinds him like a sun. Something breaks across it. He squints and stares ahead as he might stare at the alarm clock that's just rung him out of a dream. Then he sees nothing. He feels like someone's playing tricks on him in the dark, like Ralph used to do, knowing how terrified Frank was of the dark and leaving a broom for him to trip over when he went to the bathroom at night.

"Goddam city," he says. "One fucking light on the whole street that works." The next moment he stumbles over the curb and lands in a puddle of cold water that's fed by a leaking johnny pump. He hoists himself up, wipes the water from his face with his arm, starts to cry. "Look at me," he says, "I'm a goddam Bowery bum." The water revives him, the alcohol begins to wear off, and leaves a clanging headache behind. A breeze from the river makes him shiver in his wet clothing. He hears voices. His eyes are clearer now and he sees some kids heading along the river to Pier 90.

A police siren reminds him of the gun he has. Get away, he thinks, starting to run along the broken asphalt. He comes to a ragged hole in the side of the building and goes in. The darkness swallows him whole. The police siren sounds like it's right outside. Get the hell outta here, he thinks, but the darkness paralyzes him. Sometimes Ralph would be waiting, and when Frank tripped over the broom, Ralph would make horrible sounds.

Frank reaches out, looking for something to lean on. All around him he hears whispers, the scuffle of feet. He imagines that he's surrounded by hundreds of people he can't see, but who can see him. What's going on here, where is he? He clings to the fragile metal wall, praying it won't collapse and bury him alive.

"I want my boy," he says, like a prayer repeated by heart. His voice is bloated up by echo, frightening him. Someone pulls past. Startled, he draws his gun. "I want my boy, gimme my boy!"

The police siren drowns him out. His gun hangs from his hand, almost too heavy to carry. He lurches forward into the darkness. Another figure frightens him. The door at the front of the building screeches and thunders as police force it open. Frank takes aim at the next thing that moves, and fires. Someone falls, he can't see who. A second blast, but not from his gun. He falls.

A thick white searchlight beam is trained into the darkness and begins sweeping back and forth through the building. Figures scatter, press against walls. Police enter, converge around Frank, around the other victim.

"Holy," whispers Matthew to Asa. They hide behind an oil drum, watching the commotion. "Do you know who that is?" He points to Kevin, lying still on the ground, a bloody furrow across his chest.

"Let's get a better look."

They start walking.

"Madre del Dios!" someone shouts.

Matthew turns to the man running toward him.

7

Carlotta tiptoes into Justin's room. He's still asleep. Good. She sits down, exhausted after her shift, unpins her nursing cap. Justin sleeps peacefully, his arms free of the tubes he'd had in the ICU. His face is still pale but at least it's lost that horrible white of the day before. She listens to his breathing, clocking it against her second hand. Slow but steady. Yesterday, just after he'd been transferred off the ICU, he'd started gasping for breath again; the doctors said it might be secondary drowning, a delayed after-effect, which could be fatal. Then his breathing became regular again. He was supposed to go home in a day or two.

"Excuse me, Nurse."

Carlotta turns around, startled. A slender black man in a porkpie hat stands in the doorway. She stares at the suit he has on. "Yes?"

"You the boy's mother, right?"

"Yes."

"You mind if I come in? I'm the one who pulled your little one out of the water. I wanted to see how he was doing." He offers his hand. He removes his hat. "My name is Samuel, but you'll make me happy if you call me Skip."

"God bless you," Carlotta says. "Please sit down."

"How's he doing?"

"Holding his own."

"Good, good. You know, I'm not used to such strenuous activity like rescuing people. My back's been killing me." He describes the symptoms.

"Sounds like a slipped disc," she says. "You should have it looked at."

"Well, maybe I will. Right about now I don't have too much time." He looks at her. "I'm busy fixing me up a house."

"You mean a real house and not an apartment?"

"That's right."

"It certainly would be nice to live in a house again. I did when

I was a little girl. We lived in a small town upstate. Justin and I live in a studio."

"One room? For the two of you?" His finger arcs back and forth between them.

"I'm going to find a bigger place as soon as he's better. Where's that house you're fixing up?"

"Oh, it's not very far from here. Across the street from Clinton Park. Nothin fancy, and not too big, but it's old. Goes back to the Civil War."

"Really? I like old buildings more than the modern ones. They have more character."

"You know, you might have heard about it. It was just in the news." He pauses. "Some kids tried to burn it down a week or so ago."

"What a shame."

"Yeah, specially after we just finished puttin a whole lot of work into it. New plumbing, new windows."

"Is that so."

"You know what's even more of a shame?" He taps the rim of his hat. "That one of them that did it has to have a mother as nice as you."

Carlotta looks at him. "What do you mean?"

Skips nods at Justin. "Your boy's been playing with some sorry individuals. And matches."

Carlotta turns to Justin. She recalls the evening a week or so ago that Justin stumbled home filthy and sweating, looking like he'd just seen a ghost. He'd had a funny smell, something like naphtha or gasoline. He wouldn't tell her where he'd been, just washed and went to bed. She figured he'd been at the garage again. "That can't be, it can't be . . ." She lowers her face into her hands and begins to cry.

Skip puts his arms around her. "I'm sorry I had to tell you this, but folks got to know what it is they do."

Carlotta nods.

"This has certainly been a summer," she says. "You know, my brother in-law is in this hospital too. They brought him in with a gunshot wound yesterday."

"I hope he be all right."

She looks at Justin, then turns back quickly. "Does anybody else know —"

"Nobody know what I just told you except me and you and my . . . my . . . the folks I'm fixing up my house with."

"You haven't told the police about it?"

"That's right."

"Are they going to tell them?"

"No."

"Will you?"

"Not hardly."

She looks a little scared. "Is there something you . . . want from me?"

He shakes his head. "No, Ma'am. But your son still has to answer for what he done." Carlotta looks puzzled. "With your permission I'd like to come back here when he's awake and have a little talk with him. May I?"

"Of course."

He goes to leave.

"Skip, I have to ask you something. How did you feel when you pulled my son out of the water and realized who he was?"

Skip smiles. "I knew that before I jumped in."

"Thank you," she says.

A moment after Skip leaves Justin's eyes open. Carlotta pulls her chair close to the bed.

"Mom?" he says. "That you?"

"Yes." She smiles, full of things to tell him. As if having heard her cue, she begins.